KINGS OF EARTH

JOE PONDER

ISBN-10: 0692540202
ISBN-13: 978-0692540206

Edited & Formatted by Michelle Josette:
Mjbookeditor.com

DEDICATION

I dedicate this book to you, the reader.
Thank you.

PART I: WAR

PROLOGUE

Three decades have passed since the Nuclear World War began. Giant piloted humanoid robots, called Mechs, engage in constant battle between U.N. forces and the Axis of Asia. The U.N. forces are comprised of the united nations of North America and Europe. The Axis of Asia is led by Paramount Leader Chao.

Thirty years ago, just after rising to the head of the Chinese government, Chao demanded immediate full payment of the multi-trillion dollar debt owed to China by the United States. When the U.S. refused, the new Paramount Leader threatened war. The United States attempted to negotiate payment but Chao would not engage in any kind of diplomacy.

After fellow communist nation North Korea allied itself with China, First Deputy Prime Minister of Russia Anna Petrov, suspected of communist ties, was approached by Paramount Leader Chao. Shortly after,

Russia's president and prime minister were assassinated, making Petrov the new president. Russia joined China after she took office.

Nuclear missiles were first launched from North Korea onto the unsuspecting islands of Hawaii, killing almost every man, woman, and child there. After the Paramount Leader seized control of Hawaii, the United States retaliated by launching nukes back on North Korea, and the country was wiped off the face of the earth. This event, along with the terrorist attack on Hawaii, gained Chao the support of fellow anti-American radicals, simply known as the Jihadi. The Jihadi mostly work in shadow and are led by Arab extremist Jin al-Azra. Not much else is known of them but with overwhelming support and resources, the Jihadi had secretly become a political superpower in the Middle East. The Paramount Leader called the alliance between China, Russia, and the Jihadi the Axis of Asia. With their combined power, they quickly conquered the entire continent of Asia. Owning half of the world's oil, the Axis cut off the supply of oil to everyone outside of its control. Fearing further spread of the terrorist empire, King Alistair Cooper of the United Kingdom, along with the most powerful European nations, allied themselves with the United States.

The Mechs were first used by U.N. forces. After Hawaii fell to nuclear attack, Dr. Cyrus King designed the sixty-foot-tall M-1 Trapper Mech, a piloted robot large enough to trap and redirect intercontinental nuclear missiles back at the enemy. His wife, U.S.

Secretary of the Navy Michelle King, commissioned the design into construction. One year after the nuclear attack on Hawaii, the Axis struck again. Nukes were launched from conquered Japan at California. It was in this attack that U.S. Navy pilots mobilized the Mechs for the first time. Soldiers from both sides were in awe at the sight of the metal goliaths as they zoomed across the sky at Mach speeds. Within minutes, the supersonic M-1 Trapper Mechs trapped the nuclear missiles, catching them in midair, and slung them back at the Axis. Unfortunately, the counterattack that saved millions of Americans also killed millions of innocent Japanese living in enemy-occupied Japan.

To defend the North American west coast against further possible attacks, Canada and Mexico joined the U.N. forces. Once Mexico joined, shipments of U.S. military weapons to Mexico created favorable opportunities for the Mexican Cartel of Tijuana. Led by El Capo Santana Guerrero, the Tijuana Cartel began to infrequently hijack military shipments. They kept what weapons they needed and sold what they didn't. In the midst of a nuclear war, the U.S. and Mexican governments focused their manpower on the Axis threat, leaving the cartel unchecked for decades to come, and Tijuana quickly became the crime capital of the world.

CHAPTER ONE

Five years into the war, on a cloudy night, atop the secluded rocky coastal cliffs of Tijuana, a sporty little roadster motors along a stretch of dark road when its Mexican teenage driver suddenly sees something in the distance. A bright light descending from the starless sky. Leaning over his steering wheel, the teenager squints his eyes to get a closer look.

"*Ay dios mio!*" he says under his breath. "A Mech!"

The Trapper Mech's boosters blaze as it lands on the narrow strip of beach at the foot of the rocky cliffs and kneels beneath a natural bridge. With twinjet engines on its back and a jet-like canopy over its two-seater cockpit, the grey Trapper's design is reminiscent of the F-14 Tomcat. With the cockpit built into its upper torso, the Trapper looks headless. The canopy slides open and an Asian man in his mid-twenties stands from the pilot's seat. With soot stains covering his shirt and cargo capri pants, the young Asian looks over the beach to make sure he has not been spotted.

Curled up in the rear seat of the cockpit is a scrawny Caucasian boy appearing three years of age. Passed out with his face in the seat, the boy is wearing clothes similar to that of a hospital patient and is also covered in soot. Implanted in the back of the boy's shaved head, scars surround a silver dollar-sized metal aperture. Inside the closed aperture resembles the spiral of a camera shutter.

The Asian man leaves the boy in the safety of the armored Trapper hidden within the cliffs. He walks down the narrow beach until he finds an even narrower road that leads up the cliffside. Just as the man reaches the topside of the cliffs, the sporty little roadster motors up and makes an abrupt stop right in front of him.

"Need a ride, *amigo*?" the friendly teenage driver asks through the open passenger-side window. The pale Mexican is thin with a thick, curly head of hair, and looks almost too young to drive.

"Do you know where a private airport is?" the Asian man asks.

"Yeah, but it's a little bit of a drive," the teenager responds. "Hop in. I'll give you a ride."

With few options, the Asian man enters the vehicle.

"I'm Flaco Guerrero," the teenager introduces. "What's your name, *amigo*?"

"Hiro," the young Asian responds as the sporty little roadster motors off.

Half an hour later, the two pull up to the barbed

wire front gate of a dark, rundown, and seemingly abandoned little airport. Stepping out of the roadster, Hiro notices a young mechanic sleeping in the guard shack.

"I can wait here until you get in," Flaco offers.

"I'm okay but thank you," Hiro says with a wave.

"Are you sure?"

Hiro frowns. "No thanks."

"Alright." Flaco smiles before slowly pulling off. He looks back at Hiro in his rearview mirror.

Once the little roadster is out of sight, Hiro darts around to the backside of the airport. He walks the length of the barbed wire fence until he finds two uneven, side-by-side fence posts. Climbing the posts, he easily gets over the fence. Once inside the airport, Hiro spots two tanker trucks marked 'Jet Fuel' tucked behind a large aircraft hangar. He hotwires the truck and reads the gauges. Both tanks are full. Hiro stomps on the gas and crashes straight through the front gate, waking the young mechanic. The mechanic runs out to the road and watches as the stolen truck drives off into the night.

"Dammit!" the mechanic says as he rushes back to his guard shack to grab a phone.

An hour and a half after leaving, Hiro returns to the cliffs on the beach. As he exits the fuel tanker at the bottom of the narrow road, he notices big tire tracks in the sand. Panicked, Hiro races down the beach to discover his Trapper stolen with the boy inside. He pauses in the sand.

"Flaco," Hiro says angrily under his breath before

dashing back to the fuel tanker. He backs the truck up the side of the cliff and races back toward Tijuana.

Hiro combs the dark streets of Tijuana for hours before spotting the sporty little roadster parked in front of a bar in the worst part of town. 'El Sanchez Sucio' is painted on the front of the bar. Hiro parks right behind the roadster and barges into the crowded and rowdy building. The decrepit tavern smells of sweat and cigarette smoke. Making his way through the crowd, Hiro spots Flaco drinking at the bar and charges him, snatching Flaco by the collar.

"Where is it?" Hiro demands.

Flaco's voice trembles. *"Amigo, que pasa?* Where's what?!"

Hiro smacks him in the mouth and Flaco screams in pain. "Return what you stole!" Hiro yells. "I won't ask again!"

"Puto!" Flaco screams, holding his bloody lip before suddenly blaring out a short series of high-pitched whistles.

"What was that?"

"The call of the mountain lion," Flaco answers with a more sinister demeanor. After the signaling whistle, Hiro notices the crowd is quiet as all the tattooed patrons in the bar start to surround him.

"You don't know who you're fucking with!" Flaco says. "We are the Cartel de Tijuana!" The pale teenager smiles as he pulls away from Hiro's grip and joins the tattooed *cholo* gangsters.

"You need to return my Mech," Hiro demands. The

cholos laugh as they pull out machetes.

Flaco grins. "Looks like we'll be keeping it."

"You guys even know how to use those things?" Hiro asks with a confident smile.

Flaco's grin fades. "Juan! José!" he yells. "Kill this cocky *puto chino!*"

Armed with machetes, the top two cartel enforcers charge Hiro. He quickly disarms them and knocks them out. Wielding their dual machetes, Hiro asks, "Who's next?"

All the cholos in the bar attack Hiro and with skillful precision he proceeds to mow them down one by one. In the midst of the bloody massacre, a burly, tattooed Mexican with a mustache and goatee steps into the bar from a back room. The middle-aged man is wearing a tailored three-piece linen suit with a red shirt and matching red handkerchief in his front jacket pocket. Pulling a pearl-handled, gold pistol engraved with Aztec art from his back, the man fires a shot at Hiro. Hiro ricochets the bullet off his machete and into the wall right next to the man's head. Impressed, the man in the linen suit smirks.

"Enough, *cabróns!*" he orders. The cholos immediately stop attacking and back away from Hiro as all look to the man in the linen suit. "Why are you attacking my men?" the man asks Hiro.

Hiro pauses. "If they are your men, then you know why. Your men stole from me."

"Ah yes," the man in the linen suit says, "the robot."

"So you do have it," Hiro says, stepping toward him.

The man in the linen suit cracks a gold-toothed grin. "Stop right there, *amigo*," he says, reaching back behind the doorway and pulling the scrawny, blue-eyed Caucasian boy in front of himself. Hiro stops in his tracks as the man firmly holds the boy by the shoulder.

"Well you know, señor…" The man gestures to Hiro for his name.

"The *chino's* name is Hiro, Papa!" Flaco answers, still tending to his bloody lip.

"Gracias." The man grabs the red handkerchief from his pocket and throws it to his son. "Wipe your lip, *mijo*," he says before turning back to Hiro. "Señor Hiro, it seems you have stolen from me as well. I couldn't help but notice my fuel tanker sitting outside."

"The tanker is yours?" Hiro asks, unconvinced.

"I am El Capo Santana Guerrero, Boss of the Tijuana Cartel!" the man boasts wildly. "This city and everything in it belongs to me! Now drop your weapons!"

Hiro grips his machetes tighter.

"Don't test me, Señor Hiro. I'd hate to put another hole in the boy's head," El Capo threatens, tapping his gold pistol against the metal aperture implanted in the back of the boy's skull. Hiro immediately drops his machetes, and Santana smiles. "This boy is obviously not your blood," he says. "What is your relation to him?"

Hiro remains silent.

9

Santana puts his hand on top of the boy's shaved head and leans it forward to get a better look at the metal aperture. "This is some pretty nasty surgery on the back of the *niño's* head here," Santana says. "You're not some sort of sick pedophile, are you Señor Hiro? You Asians are some sexual deviants."

"I would never harm a child!"

Santana laughs. "Calm down. I believe you." The Capo subtly nods to his enforcers Juan and José and they immediately strike Hiro in the back of the head, knocking him unconscious.

"Flaco, watch the boy until I get back," Santana orders. "And don't kill him."

"Don't worry, Papa," Flaco responds. "I'll watch the little *gringo*."

"Nice job finding that Mech, *mijo*," the Capo tells his son.

Flaco smiles with pride. "*Gracias*, Papa."

"Juan. José," Santana directs. "Tie Señor Hiro's hands and feet and bring him this way."

The Capo walks through the back door of the bar into a dark alley where a sand-covered semi sits with a flatbed trailer hooked up to it. On the flatbed, a tan tarp fastened down with brown ratcheting straps covers something massive. As Santana climbs into the driver's seat, his two enforcers tie up Hiro and carry him to the back of the flatbed trailer. The tan tarp is marked 'CAUTION: OVERSIZE LOAD' and beneath it lies

Hiro's Trapper Mech. The enforcers toss Hiro under the tarp, between the legs of the Mech.

CHAPTER TWO

Sometime later, Hiro is awakened by a gold pistol-whip to his head. He yells in pain. Realizing he is tied up, Hiro struggles trying to break free.

"Don't move!" El Capo Santana says, shoving the gold pistol into Hiro's face. Hiro lies still as Santana begins patting him down for weapons. "I'm only going to ask you this once, Señor Hiro," El Capo asserts, "and if you want to keep your life, I suggest you answer truthfully because I have no patience for liars."

Hiro nods in agreement.

"Why are you in my city?"

"Because of the boy," Hiro says.

"The boy?" Santana asks, pausing his pat-down.

"Yes. I saved him from the same people I stole the Mech from," Hiro tells him. "During my flight here, I cross-searched the boy's image with reported missing children and found nothing. I believe he is an orphan.

Given the place I found him in, it is in the child's best interest that he be placed where there is no government involvement."

"This war has got the government all tied up, much like yourself." Santana laughs. "They are too busy to pay Tijuana any mind. *Es bueno* for me. Good for business."

"That is why I escaped here," Hiro says.

"An escape goes better unnoticed. And stealing a Mech is about the worst way to do that."

"I know, but I need it to get to Japan. I just stopped here to refuel."

"Japan?" Santana asks. "Are you with the Axis?"

"No, I'm Japanese."

"But I hear the Axis are killing the Japanese in Japan," Santana says with a confused expression before continuing to pat Hiro down.

"I know," Hiro says. "That's why I must go. To save my people."

"You saved the boy and now you have to save your people. You really are a hero, Señor Hiro. Admirable," Santana says as he pulls a switchblade with a cherry-wood handle from Hiro's pocket. Hiro looks at the switchblade apprehensively. "So let me get this straight, Señor Hiro. Your plan was to fly an armed Mech marked with American flags into enemy Axis territory and somehow save your people, all while simultaneously protecting the boy?"

"Yeah, pretty much."

Santana laughs. "I like you, *cabrón*! You got *cojones* and that is why I will help you." Santana cuts Hiro's binds with the switchblade.

Hiro crawls off of the flatbed and looks around. The semi is parked inside the large hangar at the same dark, rundown little airport that Hiro just stole the tanker from. He quickly realizes that the hangar is a chop shop stocked full of custom cars, planes, and choppers just as the young mechanic from before runs from behind a jet to Santana.

"Here you are, Capo," the mechanic says, nervously handing Santana some keys.

"Güey, is it fueled?" Santana asks sternly as he plays with the switchblade in his hand.

"Yes, Capo. Topped off."

"Grab the low-rider and wait for me at the front gate. When I get done with this *cabrón*, we can discuss your incompetence," the Capo says.

"Yes, Capo," Güey responds, visibly intimidated. He climbs into a custom, white pearlescent 1964 Chevrolet Impala with gold rims and drives out of the hangar.

Santana tosses Hiro the keys. "I will make you a trade, *amigo*. I keep the Mech and you may take one of my long-range private jets. Should make it a little easier for you to get into Japan without getting shot down by the Axis. If you can pilot a Mech, I assume you can pilot a jet?"

"I can," Hiro says, "but what about the boy?"

"The boy will be cared for," Santana assures him. "I too was an abandoned orphan so I can sympathize. He will be safe. Or as safe as one can be in Tijuana, anyway."

Hiro looks at Santana, his brows furrowed. "Why are you helping me?" he asks.

Santana smiles. "You're an honorable man, Hiro. I admire that you are willing to risk yourself to protect your people and a helpless child. We are the same in that aspect. I would do anything for my men. And even more to protect an innocent child. Perhaps if I'd had someone decent like you looking out for me when I was a boy." Santana pauses. "Perhaps life would have turned out different for me. Now go, *amigo*."

"Thank you, Santana," Hiro says before running to the jet.

The Capo watches the long-range jet roll out of the hangar and take off into the night sky. He walks through the scrap of what used to be his front gate to the waiting pearlescent Impala. Sitting in the back seat of the low-rider, Santana puts a cigar in his mouth.

"Where to, Capo?" Güey asks, leaning back to light Santana's cigar.

The white low-rider cruises through the black night back to El Sanchez Sucio bar.

"Take the tanker back to the airport," Santana orders pointing at the jet-fuel truck parked in front of him.

"Yes Capo," Güey responds before hopping out of the low-rider and into the truck.

As the tanker truck drives by, Santana enters El Sanchez Sucio and hears roaring laughter from the back room.

"Sanchez, what's all that ruckus about?" Santana asks the husky bartender.

"That gringo kid has been cutting up all night," Sanchez responds. "He's messing with Flaco and got the boys falling out of their seats."

"Is that right?" Santana says. The Capo enters the back room of the bar and finds the boy talking and joking amongst all of the cartel cholos. Santana smiles.

"So I hear you are picking on Flaco!" Santana yells jovially as the boy looks up at him. "Who the hell do you think you are messing with my son?"

"I don't know. Who the hell are you?" the boy asks genuinely.

Santana laughs. "I am El Capo Santana Guerrero, Boss of the Cartel de Tijuana."

"That's a long name," the boy responds.

"Yes, but it's a good name." Santana smiles. "So what is your name, *niño*?"

"I already said I don't know," the boy repeats.

El Capo lets out a long breath. *Is the boy testing my patience?* "How do you not remember your own damn name?" he asks.

"I don't know," the boy says. "I can't remember anything before waking up here."

Santana notices a tattoo written sideways on the inside of the boy's right forearm.

"Nice tattoo," he says, crouching down and holding the boy's forearm to get a closer look. "Is this your name?" Santana asks, reading the tattoo. "LEO? Does that ring a bell?"

The boy thinks for a moment before shaking his head.

"You must have been in a coma," Santana says. He removes his linen suit jacket and rolls up his red shirtsleeve. On his burly forearm, Santana reveals a tattoo of an Aztec warrior with the head of a mountain lion.

"Leo is also a good name. It means lion and lions are strong. That is what you have to be to survive in this world. Do you like that name, Leo?" Santana asks.

The boy smiles and nods. "Yes, I like that name. I like it better than the name Gringo," Leo says.

Santana raises an eyebrow. "Who called you Gringo?"

"Him," Leo says, pointing at Flaco. "I asked him why he called me Gringo. I'm not green!"

Santana laughs and asks, "So what did Flaco say?"

"Flaco said he called me Gringo because my skin is white. I don't get it. Flaco's paler than me so I called him White-go."

Santana and the cartel cholos all burst into roaring laughter. All except Flaco who sits scowling in the corner. Santana wipes a tear of laughter from his eye.

"I like you, *hijo*," Santana says. "You and your Asian friend are some characters."

"Asian friend?" Leo asks.

"The man who brought you here. The one who just tore up my bar. You don't remember flying in with him either?"

Leo stares at Santana, confused.

"You get rid of that Asian *chino*?" Flaco asks, still holding his lip.

"I hope you used a blade on him, Capo, like he did on us," another cut-up cholo adds.

Santana pulls Hiro's switchblade from his inner suit pocket. "I did in fact."

The cholos laugh in approval as Santana looks down at the boy who is still struggling to recollect. "Don't worry about remembering the Asian man, Leo. The chances of you seeing him alive again are highly unlikely," Santana says, tossing the switchblade to the boy. Leo catches it and sees the letters 'HT' carved into its cherry-wood handle.

Still pouting, Flaco gets up from the corner and approaches his father. "So what are we going to do with the little gring – " He pauses before finishing the word, " – with the little *niño*?" he asks impatiently.

Santana looks at Leo and smiles. "He stays with us."

"Why?" Flaco raises his voice grabbing the attention of the other cartel members.

Santana narrows his eyes at his son. "You questioning me?"

"No, Papa," Flaco tells him, backing down. "Never."

"Listen!" Santana announces to his men. "Leo, the boy, stays with us. We can use him to push product to other gringos. It will be easier for him to go unnoticed. Any opposed?"

The room is quiet for a moment before one of the

cholos yells, "The *niño's* cool with us, Capo!"

The cholos cheer in agreement as they crowd around Leo, and the boy smiles as they welcome him. Santana walks to Leo and puts his hand on his shoulder.

"Its official, *hijo*. You are one of us now. Welcome to the Tijuana Cartel."

CHAPTER THREE

A blinding light shines in Leo's face as he sits reclined in a cold, dark room.

"Don't worry," a man in shadow says, looking down at Leo, "this will be quick." The man suddenly stabs Leo in the back of the skull.

Leo screams in horror and grabs the aperture in the back of his head as he wakes up in his room. Morning light shines through the bedroom window and Santana stands over Leo.

"You're okay, *mijo*," Santana says in a soothing voice. "You were just having a bad dream."

Weeks have passed since El Capo Santana welcomed Leo to live in his lavish home. The cartel treat Leo like family and each day he grows closer with them, learning the ways of their business from Santana. The cartel profits off drugs, guns, girls, gambling, and grand theft auto, and Santana ensures that both his boys, Flaco and Leo, are exposed to every aspect.

"Get dressed and come downstairs. We're heading out this morning. *Ándale!*" Santana tells Leo before walking out of the room.

Leo throws on some clothes and pulls open the large and ornately-carved wooden double doors to his room. He runs down one of the winding staircases with its forged-iron railing and jumps over the last step onto the colorful mosaic-tiled floor. Smelling the aroma of food cooking, Leo raises his nose. Above, walnut beams span across the high white ceilings they support. Following his nose, Leo runs down a white stucco hall lined with palatial wood-trimmed windows and archways. He arrives in the dining room where Santana and Flaco sit at a grand banquet table with three scantily-clad young women serving them breakfast. Lustrous beneath a regal iron chandelier, the table is abound with delicious dishes of chorizo sausage, salsa, fried potatoes, scrambled eggs seasoned with chili pepper, refried beans, corn tortillas, and ice-cold glasses of Coca-Cola.

"What are you waiting for?" Santana says. "Have a seat."

Leo sits down and one of the women walks over to him. "Good morning, sweetie," she says, putting a plate of food down in front of him. As she bends over to place a napkin across his lap, her huge breasts stick right in Leo's face. Embarrassed, Leo quickly turns away.

"Look! The whitey is turning red!" Flaco laughs.

"Don't be shy, *mijo*," Santana tells Leo. "Those are some nice *chi-chis*. Look at them! She'd be offended if you didn't want to."

Leo slowly turns his head back and looks at the *chi-chis* in his face. The girl smiles and shakes them a little.

"There you go!" Santana laughs wildly, clapping his hands.

Leo smiles back at the girl. "You're really pretty."

"Well thank you, sweetie. You're pretty cute yourself," the girl says before kissing Leo on the cheek and walking back into the kitchen.

"Leo, my boy, we should have named you Don Juan! You've got smooth moves!" Santana laughs.

"I'm done eating," Flaco interrupts. "Can we go to the Cinco de Mayo fiesta now, Papa?"

"What's a fiesta?" Leo asks.

"It's a festival for Mexicanos," Flaco responds curtly.

"It's a festival for everyone to have a good time — as long as they have money to pay for a good time, that is," Santana says. "Fiestas bring many business opportunities for us to take advantage of, *mijos*. So eat up! We have a busy day in front of us."

After breakfast, Santana walks the three girls to the front door. "Señoritas! Thank you for this morning and last night." El Capo grins as he hands each of them a knot of cash. "There will be an even bigger bonus later if you all make me some real money today."

"Thank you, *papi*," the girls reply flirtatiously.

"See you later, Leo," the girl with the *chi-chis* says.

Leo waves and smiles.

Outside, Güey the mechanic leans on a Maybach luxury sedan parked in the circular cobblestone driveway. He gets up and opens the doors for the girls as they get in.

"Get the girls back to the cathouse quick," Santana tells Güey. "Today's a holiday. There will be a lot of lonely johns willing to pay for some company to celebrate with."

"Right away, Capo," Güey says before hopping in the driver's seat and speeding off.

"Alright boys, let's go!" Santana says, walking out to his custom Impala low-rider parked on the side of the driveway.

"Papa, why don't you ever take one of the sports cars?" Flaco asks, disappointed.

"Because this is my favorite car, Flaco," Santana responds, sliding into the low-rider.

"Why is this your favorite?" Leo asks.

Santana shines his gold-toothed grin. He hits the hydraulic switches and the front of the car starts hopping up and down. With each hop the car goes higher and higher.

Leo bursts out laughing as he looks up at the car's front tires hang in the air. "This is my favorite too!" he yells.

Cruising through the festive, crowded streets of Tijuana, Santana and his sons pass the cartel bar El Sanchez Sucio.

"Why the fuck is the bar closed?" Santana curses as

he comes to a screeching stop in front of the bar. "Come on, boys." He gets out and unlocks the front door of the bar. Once inside, Santana and his sons see Sanchez the bartender stepping out of the back room.

"Sanchez!" the Capo barks. "You better have a good excuse for not opening my bar on one of the most profitable days of the year!"

"Apologies, Capo, but we have a problem," Sanchez says as José the enforcer drags in a bloody policeman from the back room and throws him to the floor at Santana's feet. The Capo takes a close look at the officer's face.

"This *chota* cop is on my payroll," Santana says.

"Yes, Capo," Sanchez responds. "Apparently he didn't feel his pay was generous enough. This morning, our enforcer, Juan, drove out on the weekly rounds to collect the cash pickups from the stash houses. This *chota* must have been tailing him. One of our guys saw him pull Juan over and shoot him in the head before making off with the cash. After I got the call about what happened, I closed the bar and we ran straight out and caught the *chota* red-handed. We brought him back just before you walked in." Sanchez shows the Capo a large bloodstained laundry bag stuffed with money. "It's still wet with Juan's blood," he tells him.

The cop begins to sob uncontrollably and shamelessly. "El Capo, *señor*, I beg for your mercy!" the policeman pleads. "I will do anything you ask. Please, just give me a second chance!"

Grave and silent, the Capo strokes his mustache

and goatee. "I am a man that believes in second chances," he finally says. "José, let him up."

The enforcer pulls the cop to his feet and steps back.

Santana rolls his sleeve cuffs up on his burly arms. "I'll make you a deal, officer," he proposes. "You came up behind my enforcer and shot him without giving him a chance. Let's see how you fare in a fight face-to-face. You beat me, you go free. No repercussions."

The sweating cop trembles in fear.

"This is your second chance, officer, and your only chance to walk out of here alive. I suggest you take it," El Capo adds.

The cop timidly swings at Santana. Disgusted, El Capo wrenches the *chota's* arm behind his back and shoves him into the barstools before proceeding to smash the cop's teeth into the edge of the bar. In a violent rage, he continues slamming the cop's face against the bar top long after the lifeless skull is cracked to pieces. The man's head bouncing off the bar reminds Leo of the low-rider bouncing off the cobblestone. Breathing heavily, Santana steps back and lets the body splash to the floor in its own blood.

"Do you see what this is?" Santana asks Flaco and Leo.

"A dead *chota*," Flaco answers as Leo quietly stares at the cop's corpse.

"Yes," Santana says. "This is what happens to cowards with no *cojones*. If you're not strong, you're already dead." Sanchez hands the Capo a rag to wipe the blood from his hands. "Good job," Santana commends Sanchez and José. "Now clean this up and open the bar for business."

"Yes, Capo," the cholos respond as Santana exits with Flaco and Leo.

The low-rider continues through the crowd of people down to the fiesta at the beach. Boozed-up men and bikini-clad women celebrate and dance as *mariachi* music blares throughout the city of Tijuana. Santana parks and exits the low-rider. Everyone instantly recognizes El Capo and respectfully gets out of his way. Santana, Flaco, and Leo make their way to the center of the seaside jubilee. In the middle of the beach, a wrestling ring has been set up for a *lucha libre* exhibition. Giant, shirtless men wearing colorful masks and tights hype up the crowd before a match.

"Are they superheroes?" Leo asks.

"To some people," Santana responds as he sits down in reserved ringside seats. Leo and Flaco sit on either side of him as he lays his arms across the backs of their chairs. "They are wrestlers called *luchadores*," Santana explains, "The ones in blue are *técnicos* and the ones in red are *rudos*. The *rudos* are viewed as bad guys and the *técnicos* are supposed to be the good guys."

"Supposed to be?" Leo asks.

"There are no good guys or bad guys, *mijo*. The truth is everyone does good and bad. The ones labeled bad guys are usually just the most honest."

"Capo!" a cartel cholo calls as he walks to Santana. "All bets are in, Capo, favoring *técnicos* to win." The cholo unzips a Louis Vuitton duffle bag stuffed with thousands of dollars of cash. "This is the last bag. Cartel's counting the other bags now."

"*Bueno*," El Capo says, zipping the bag closed. Santana walks to the side of the ring and calls over one of the *técnicos*. The blue masked 'good guy' jogs to the side of the ring and kneels next to Santana. As Santana whispers in his ear, the *técnico* nods in agreement. The blue *luchador* returns to his ring corner and Santana lounges back in his seat between Leo and Flaco.

"The *técnico* is undefeated and twice the size of that *rudo*! No way he can lose!" Flaco says.

The bell rings and the match starts. The blue *técnico* puts on an amazing display of acrobatic moves and wrestling skill. He beats the red *rudo* into near submission before trapping him in the corner. Just before he gets ready to finish the *rudo*, the *técnico* suspiciously trips and hits his head on the corner post. The blue luchador tumbles to the canvas mat, and the *rudo* quickly seizes the opportunity. He pins the *técnico* to win the match. The crowd boos and hisses, many hysterical because they just lost a lot of money. Their loss on the fixed fight equals Santana and the cartel's gain.

"Remember, Leo, strength has nothing to do with size. It's all about being fearless and seizing opportunities," Santana enlightens.

"Unless you're a little gringo kid in the middle of Tijuana. Then you should pray to get big quick!" Flaco laughs.

"You think you're pretty tough, Flaco?" Santana asks his son. "Why don't you get in the ring with Leo?"

"Papa, I don't want to get in the ring with Leo."

Santana laughs. "Are you scared of little Leo?"

"No! I just don't want to look like an *idiota* fighting a little kid," Flaco reasons.

"So you are scared! Scared of being embarrassed." Santana stands from his seat. "Come on, tough guy. Just take Leo in the ring and show him some moves. It'll be fun." Santana walks Flaco and Leo to the side of the ring, where the blue luchador jogs back over and kneels.

"Good job making that trip look real, *amigo*," Santana whispers to the luchador, "Hey, my boys Flaco and Leo want to give it a try."

"Sure thing, Capo," the luchador says as he pulls an excited Leo up into the ring. Flaco reluctantly crawls under the ropes behind them.

"In this corner, we have Capo Junior!" the luchador announces to the crowd. "And in this corner, we have the Lion Kid! *El Niño León*!" The luchador laughs.

"This is so stupid," Flaco whines. "I'm not going to fight a little kid."

"Come on, White-go Junior!" Leo laughs as he hops around Flaco, punching him in the legs.

"Come on, Flaco! Just have fun with it!" Santana yells from the side ropes.

"Papa, can we please just get out of here!" Flaco says, turning his back to Leo as he continues to get punched in the legs. Bouncing around, Leo accidentally hits Flaco right in between his legs. With a painful scream, Flaco's eyes get big as he grabs his sore *cojones*.

"You stupid little gringo!" Flaco snatches Leo by the collar of his shirt and lifts him in the air. Leo looks down at Flaco's furious wide eyes.

"Alright Flaco, it was an accident." Santana laughs. "Take it easy before you hurt him."

Infuriated, Flaco tightens the collar around Leo's neck until Leo is gasping for air.

"Flaco! That's enough!" Santana yells as he enters the ring. Looking into Flaco's wide eyes, Leo thinks to himself, *Seize opportunity*. With his little finger, Leo quickly pokes Flaco in the eye just before Santana can get to them.

Flaco drops Leo to the canvas mat. "Fucking gringo!" he cries. With one hand on his eye and the other on his *cojones*, Flaco runs past his father and out of the ring.

"And the winner is..." the luchador announces, raising Leo's arm in the air, "...*El Niño León*!"

Entertained by Leo's antics, the crowd cheers wildly as the blue luchador puts Leo on his shoulder and parades him around the ring. Unable to contain his excitement, Leo shouts at the top of his lungs, "Yeeeeaah!"

PART II: BREACHED

CHAPTER FOUR

Now, three decades into the Nuclear World War, an M-2 Stalker Mech soars over the sunny Pacific. A blue band with white letters reading 'U.N.' is painted on one of the Mech's arms and the number '332' on the other. The M-2 Stalker is similar to its predecessor, the M-1 Trapper, but has increased armor and weaponry. It has missile launchers in its back and carries a standard-issue assault rifle with mounted rocket launcher. The M-2 Stalker also features two back-to-back pilot's seats. Copiloting from Stalker 332's rear-facing seat is Navy Lieutenant Iris "Deadeye" King. She wears the same blue U.N. band on one sleeve of her olive drab flight suit and a U.S. patch on the other. On the side of her flight helmet is an emblem of an eyeball inside crosshairs.

In the pilot's seat in front of Iris sits Chuck "Canuck" Devereux. With a Maple Leaf emblazoned on the side of his helmet and on his arm, the dark-skinned

Canadian is in his mid-twenties and could pass for a male model. Beside Iris and Canuck's Stalker, a second Stalker struggles to fly in formation.

"Hey, Deadeye," Canuck radios Iris. "I think Triple Three might need some training wheels."

"Shut up, Canuck!" Stalker 333's pilot, Mason "Stonewall" Jackson, yells out in a thick southern accent over the mic inside his stone-patterned flight helmet. The Texan is in his late twenties with fire-red hair and a hot temper to match. Sitting behind the ornery redhead is his copilot, Felix "El Gato" Rojas. The same age as Canuck, El Gato has a black cat painted on the side of his helmet and a Mexican flag on his arm.

"How you doing back there, Deadeye?" Canuck asks Iris.

"Bored. You?" Iris responds.

"I'd be better if these back-to-back seats were side-by-side," Canuck suggests.

Iris rolls her eye.

"Actually, I meant, how are you since your brother went M.I.A.? It's been, what, six months now?"

"One hundred ninety-one days since anyone has heard from Michael," Iris says before staring off into the distance, a mournful expression on her face.

"I always respected your brother. He was a good man and an even better pilot. You two made a hell of a team." Canuck pauses and looks back at Iris. "I guess what I'm trying to say is that even though I'm sitting in his seat now, no one can ever take your brother's place. And if you ever need someone to talk to, I'm here."

Iris turns around in her seat. "Thanks, Canuck," she says with a subtle smile.

"Anytime," Canuck responds, still looking back at her. Iris' smile quickly disappears as she notices something flying in the distance. The red triangle markings on the black aircraft make it obvious.

"Canuck, we got an Axis Tora Mech up ahead!" she tells him.

The stealthily-designed Totaro Type 2 Tora with its sharp edges and flat surfaces is reminiscent of the F-117 Nighthawk. The fifty-five-foot Tora is inferior to the Stalker in durability but superior in maneuverability. It has a single seat cockpit built into its upper torso, an automatic gun mounted on its right arm, and a rocket launcher mounted to its left.

Iris turns back in her seat. "I'm not picking it up on radar. It must have an advanced radar jammer," she says. "Stalker 333, we got an enemy Mech up ahead. Follow our lead and prepare to engage. Over."

"Roger that, Stalker 332," Stonewall radios back.

The two Stalkers zoom across the ocean toward the enemy Axis Tora in the distance, when out of nowhere, bullets rain as two more Toras dive straight down from cloud cover directly in front of them. Canuck manages to dodge them but Stalker 333 is not so lucky.

"Stalker 333, come in. Are you okay, 333?" Iris asks.

"We're hit!" Stonewall yells over the radio as smoke pours from his stalling engines. "Gato's bleeding heavy!" As Stalker 333 begins to fall out of the sky, the two Toras loop and line up behind Stalker 332. Iris gets face-to-face with the enemy Mechs.

"Canuck, look out!" she yells as the enemy Mechs open fire. Canuck struggles to dodge and fight off the attacking Toras.

"Canuck, catch Stalker 333!" Iris commands.

"I can't hold Stalker 333 and fight off the bogeys!" Canuck responds.

"Just focus on catching Stalker 333!" Iris orders. She hits a switch and a Gatling gun immediately rises from between Stalker 332's back-mounted jet engines. "I'll fight off the bogeys!"

"Yes, ma'am," Canuck says with a grin. Forcing his two triggered joysticks forward, Canuck dives for Stonewall and El Gato with the bogeys hot on his tail.

"Canuck, drop our rifle! Stonewall, catch it!" Iris orders.

Canuck drops the rifle and Stonewall catches it. Just before Stonewall and El Gato hit the water, Stalker 332 catches Stalker 333 beneath the arms and zooms across the Pacific.

"Got 'em!" Canuck yells. "Up to you now, Deadeye!"

Stalker 332's rear-facing Gatling gun roars as Iris uses her precision aim to shoot down the first pursuing Tora.

"One more!" Iris yells as she targets the last bogey and fires. The second Tora bursts into flames but just before it drops from the sky, the enemy Mech manages to fire off a rocket from its arm-mounted launcher. Alert sirens sound inside of Stalker 332's cockpit.

"Incoming rocket!" Canuck yells.

"I got it," Iris responds. With a single pull of her joystick trigger, Iris shoots the rocket and it explodes directly behind the Stalkers.

"What about the third one?" Canuck asks.

"Drop me!" Stonewall yells over the radio. "Y'all can still take it down!"

Iris watches the distant Tora as it speeds off to the west.

"It's too far out of range, Stonewall," she responds. "Let's get back to base and get El Gato a medic."

Stalker 332 aids Stalker 333 in flying back to Naval Base San Diego where medics are already standing by. Stonewall and the medics get El Gato out of the still-smoking Stalker 333. Iris exits Stalker 332 and runs to El Gato as he is laid on a stretcher.

"Is he going to be okay?" she asks the medics.

"He's stabilized but we need to get him to the E.R., stat!" a medic responds.

As Stonewall and the medics rush the wounded pilot away, El Gato raises his hand and gives a thumbs-up. Iris smiles.

"El Gato's tough. He'll pull through," Canuck says to Iris, brushing his hair with one hand and holding his helmet with the other. "Speaking of which, way to pull us through that ambush. You're a hell of a marksman, Deadeye, and a natural leader. Your brother would be proud."

"Thanks," Iris says, removing her flight helmet. The gorgeous 26-year-old light-skinned African-American wears an eye-patch over her left eye.

"Hey," Canuck says, recomposing his dropped jaw, "I'm going to grab a drink. You want to come with?"

"Actually, I need to go and report what happened to the Secnav," Iris responds.

"Alright, have fun with that," Canuck says sarcastically as Iris heads to the office building on base.

As she walks down the hall toward the Secnav's office, Iris can hear her yelling at somebody. Not an uncommon occurrence. Iris knocks on the office door.

"Who is it?!" the Secnav yells angrily.

"Iris."

The Secnav's voice instantly calms. "Come in."

Iris opens the door as a shaken old captain scuttles out. With his bushy white eyebrows and mustache, the short and portly man reminds her of Cap'n Crunch. Standing behind the desk is Secnav Michelle King in a navy blue skirt suit. The tall African-American woman wears glasses. She's in her sixties but looks younger. Many of the sailors say her lack of wrinkles is because she has never smiled.

Splayed across the wall behind the Secnav are numerous degrees and plaques of accolades. Amongst them is an old framed photo of the Secnav with her late husband and their colleagues. They were in their mid-thirties then. Her husband was bald with a thick beard and also wore glasses.

"Hey, Mom," Iris says.

The Secnav peers over her glasses in disapproval.

"I mean, ma'am," Iris corrects, saluting her mother.

"I'm glad you're here, Iris," the Secnav finally says. "I have a special assignment for you."

CHAPTER FIVE

That warm summer night, a large cargo ship calmly pushes west through the Pacific. The USNS Cyrus King is en route to the U.N. naval frontline between America and Hawaii. A small skiff carrying two men dressed in black long-sleeved jumpsuits quietly motors toward the tall cargo ship.

Towering in the back of the skiff, the Tijuana Cartel's newest member, Ángel, carries a suppressed pistol in one hand as he steers the rear-mounted motor with the other. The six-foot-six-inch Spanish-speaking savant is slender but muscular and has a thin mustache with a rough goatee. At 29 years old, he is the cartel's number one wheelman.

"*Amigo*, you're so white you're glowing in the dark," Ángel jokes to his friend at the front of the skiff. "Put your mask on before you give away our position."

Leo laughs as he looks back at Ángel. "You're the

last one to be telling me about being inconspicuous, Jolly Bean Giant."

"Low blow, *amigo*." Ángel laughs.

Leo holds a suppressed shotgun in his left hand, rope and grappling hook in his right. The same age as Ángel, Leo has proven himself the cartel's roughest fighter and is their top enforcer. He pulls a black ski mask down over his stubbled face. His long wavy dark hair sticking out from below the mask hides the metal aperture in the back of his head. Leo signals Ángel to cut off the motor. Ángel pulls his own mask down over his curly head and quietly steers the skiff alongside the unsuspecting cargo ship. Throwing the grappling hook over the port side, Leo quickly but bunglingly climbs up and boards the ship.

"Come on up—" Before Leo can get the words out, Ángel shimmies up the rope and quietly leaps to his feet beside Leo. Leo frowns. "You know, it's unnatural for an *hombre* as big as you to move so gracefully."

"It's my culture, *amigo*. Smooth moves and suaveness is in my blood." Ángel smiles.

"Whatever you say, ballerina," Leo jokes, bumping Ángel's arm with his elbow. "Let's go."

Leo and Ángel crouch down around the corner from the entrance to the cargo bay, where an armed sailor stands by the entrance. Without hesitation, Leo tackles the sailor to the ground. Dropping their guns, the two wrestle until the sailor manages to pin Leo on his back.

"Is that all you got?" Leo laughs as he blocks the

sailor's punches. Ángel knocks the sailor out cold with the butt of Leo's shotgun.

"Stealth, *amigo*. Stealth," Ángel says as he extends the shotgun butt toward Leo.

"It's called a decoy," Leo slyly remarks, grabbing the butt of the gun. Ángel pulls Leo to his feet and Leo reclaims his shotgun.

"Right," Ángel replies sarcastically.

The two walk down the stairwell into the cargo bay. Inside, there are one hundred brand-new, fully-armed M-2 Stalker Mechs.

"Jackpot," Leo says.

Leo and Ángel raise their masks and lower their guns as they approach a Stalker Mech closest to the port side hull. Ángel climbs into the front pilot's seat of the open cockpit and powers it on.

"You sure you can fly this thing?" Leo asks, climbing into the rear-facing seat behind Ángel.

"My name's Ángel. I can fly anything." He grins.

"Let's go then, Maverick—" Leo is cut short by the sound of alerted sailors.

"Man down! Over here!" a voice calls from the cargo bay door. Several armed sailors enter the cargo bay and start shooting at Leo and Ángel. Ángel hits a switch, causing the canopy to close over the cockpit as bullets bounce off the canopy glass.

"What are you waiting for?" Leo shouts. "Let's punch it!"

"I need to disconnect the GPS tracker," Ángel tells him. "Hand me your knife."

Leo hesitantly pulls the cherry-handled switchblade from his pocket. He rubs his thumb across the 'HT' carved into its handle.

"Leo?" Ángel asks.

"Here!" Leo says, reluctantly handing the switchblade to Ángel. "Just be careful with it, alright?"

"I'm always careful," Ángel says, using the switchblade to cut a wire beneath his seat.

"Weapons online," the Stalker Mech says in a robotic voice.

"Oops," Ángel says.

"You sure you know what you're doing...?" Leo tries to ask before a Gatling gun quickly rises in front of him from the Stalker's back. "Never mind." He grabs the triggered joystick and starts shooting wildly as sailors scramble for cover.

Ángel finally cuts the GPS tracker wire before grabbing the two-triggered joysticks in front of him. Pointing the Stalker's giant rifle-mounted rocket launcher directly at the hull, Ángel blasts a huge opening in the side of the ship.

"They've breached the hull! Stop them, now!" one sailor yells as more sailors pour into the cargo bay.

"We've...got...more...company!" Leo yells with wild bursts from his Gatling gun between each word.

Ángel flicks the ignition switch and the Mech's jet engines fire up.

From the command bridge in the ship's control tower, Lieutenant Iris "Deadeye" King sees the stolen Stalker launch out the side of the ship. Wielding rocket launchers, two sailors run to the new opening in the hull and fire at the airborne Mech as it soars out over the Pacific.

"Oh shit!" Leo yells as he watches two RPGs racing directly at him.

In one quick and fluid motion, Ángel drops his Stalker's rifle, maneuvers the Mech into a sideways somersault, grasps an RPG in each of the Mech's hands, and gracefully throws them down into the ocean before catching the rifle.

"Michael?" Iris murmurs, amazed by the feat she just witnessed. She reaches for her gun bag and pulls out a sniper rifle nearly as tall as her. The lightweight carbon fiber rifle is bolt-action with an extended stainless steel barrel, oversized scope, and collapsible stock. Loading an unusually high-tech box magazine into the rifle, Iris runs outside to the windy catwalk on the side of the control tower. From three thousand yards out, she holds her breath as she aims at the stolen Stalker and fires.

CHAPTER SIX

"Home, sweet home!" Leo says excitedly as he and Ángel fly over the Tijuana coast.

"We're stashing it there!" Leo says, pointing to a dark, rundown, and seemingly abandoned little airport. The Mech lands on the unmarked runway knocking dust into the air. Leo exits the cockpit and jogs toward the hangar as he unzips his black jumpsuit. With the top of his jumpsuit hanging from his waist, Leo wears a sleeveless shirt revealing a sleeve of tattoos covering his brawny right arm. Leo holds down a button to slide open the fifty-foot-tall hangar door and Ángel crouches the stolen Stalker inside.

With wide eyes, Ángel exits the Mech as he gazes on the collection of custom cars, planes, and choppers.

"Are these El Capo's?" Ángel asks.

"Yup, this is the chop shop," Leo says, opening a key box hanging on the hangar wall. "So which one you want to take for a spin?"

"How about that one?" Ángel asks, pointing.

Leo tosses Ángel the keys.

"You're going to let me drive?" Ángel asks, surprised.

"Yeah, I trust you," Leo tells him. "Besides, I can't drive stick shift."

With its convertible top down, a navy blue Lamborghini sits on the street in front of El Sanchez Sucio. The familiar scent of sweat and cigarette smoke lingers in the air as Leo and Ángel sit at the bar over bottles of Corona watching a bull fight on TV.

The bull-fighting matador stands with a red cape draped down his back and his back to the bull. The bull charges. The matador tosses his cape over the bull's face and steps out of the way before killing the bull with a single strike of his sword to its heart.

"I bet you could handle a bull the way you handled those rockets. That was some crazy shit you did back there!" an intoxicated Leo exclaims. "We're legendary now, *hermano!*"

A balding cartel member overhears Leo and Ángel and approaches them. "I presume the job went well?" he asks.

"White-go!" Leo exclaims, patting the now balding Flaco on the back a little too hard. "Job went great thanks to this guy!" Leo says, pointing at Ángel. "Flaco, meet our new recruit, Ángel. Ángel, this is Flaco."

"*Hola, amigo,*" Ángel greets Flaco.

"So you're the one who piloted the Mech. Where did you learn to fly?" Flaco asks.

"From my years as a mercenary," Ángel answers.

"Why give up being a mercenary to join us?"

"Got fired after charging into a dogfight and nearly getting my partner killed. So when I heard you all were hunting for recruits, couldn't think of a better way for a guy with my particular set of skills to make some fast *dinero*."

Flaco stares suspiciously at Ángel. "Your accent sounds funny."

"And your face looks funny!" Leo interrupts. "Stop interrogating the guy! Ángel just pulled off the biggest heist this gang has ever seen!"

"You forget I was the first in this gang to steal a Mech!" Flaco says offensively.

"Technically, the whole gang stole that Trapper Mech. You just found it."

"Yeah, and I wish I never had! That way I would have never had to deal with you, cholo gringo!" Flaco screams.

"Calm down, Flaco." Leo laughs, turning to the husky bartender. "Sanchez, get this guy a drink, on me."

Sanchez slides Flaco a Corona.

"I'm watching you," Flaco says to Ángel.

"You need to watch your hairline. It's escaping!" Leo jokes.

"Fuck you, Leo!" Flaco says as he snatches the beer from the bar and walks away.

Leo turns to Ángel and smiles. "Don't worry about

him, *hermano*. He's like that with everyone." Laughing, he raises his arm to down another Corona.

Ángel takes a swig as well. "You got some badass tats, mane," he says, looking at Leo's raised right arm.

"They're a timeline of my life. This represents the guy El Capo Santana found me with when I was a kid." Leo points at a tattoo of a samurai on his right shoulder. "This luchador mask is for my first fight, and this one I got when Santana made me his top enforcer." Leo points at a tattoo of a vicious lion's head on the inside of his right forearm. Between the Lion's roaring teeth is Leo's very first tattoo—the tattoo of his own name.

"So when are we delivering the Mech to El Capo Santana anyways?" Ángel asks.

"No can do. I'm delivering solo tomorrow, *hermano*," Leo responds.

"How? You can't drive a semi?" Ángel says jokingly.

"Hey, I can drive a semi. Just not a stick shift."

"So you don't trust me? It's cool," Ángel jokes.

"Nah mane, I trust you," Leo says genuinely. "But Santana don't trust nobody."

"He trusts you."

"The guy raised me," Leo tells him. "We're like family."

"He's like a father to you?"

"More like a crazy uncle who taught me everything I know." Leo laughs, raising his bottle.

"I see." Ángel raises his Corona and taps the bottle to Leo's.

As Leo downs the Corona, his eyes peer over his glass at a stunning young woman at the other end of the bar. In awe, Leo coughs as he suddenly chokes on his beer.

"You see what I see?" Leo asks, clearing his throat. Still drinking, Ángel turns to see what has got his friend all choked up. Holding her purple cellphone in front of her face, a sexy caramel-skinned girl with short, dark hair seductively swooped over one eye sits at the bar wearing no more than a white bikini and cutoff jean shorts hugging her perfectly-shaped body. Making eye contact with the girl, Ángel coughs as he chokes on his Corona, too.

"You see?" Leo laughs before Ángel stands and walks over to the girl.

"What are you doing here?" Ángel whispers angrily at her.

"I could ask you the same thing," she responds.

"You need to leave, now," Ángel whispers impatiently.

"I am not leaving until we talk."

"This isn't a game, Iris," Ángel pleads under his breath. "All these guys in here are cartel. They're killers."

"Including your cute friend over there that keeps gawking at me?" Iris asks, waving at Leo. Leo smiles and awkwardly waves back. "Maybe I should go over and say hello."

"Okay, let's talk. Outside."

Iris smiles. "Let's go."

Ángel snatches her by the arm and the two exit the bar.

"What are you doing here, Iris?" Ángel demands again. "You know I'm undercover!"

"I don't know anything that's going on with you, Michael!" Iris yells at Ángel. "You haven't called in with me, Mom, U.N. forces, anybody! I didn't know if you were dead or alive! Do you know what these past six months have been like for me? Why did you abandon me?!"

"I felt guilty after the accident. When I saw that shrapnel lodged into your face, I felt my heart rip from my chest. When I was piloting our Mech that day, I was cocky and I was careless. We were outnumbered but I flew right into that dogfight with total disregard for your safety. It's my fault you lost your eye and almost lost your life. I didn't abandon you, Iris. I was trying to protect you. I chose to work solo to protect you...from me. I could never deal with my little sister or anybody ever again getting hurt because of me."

"Michael, I may be your little sister but I am a soldier first. I knew the risks when I signed up for war," Iris says firmly. "It's not your job to protect me. It's our job to protect others."

"I know you're strong, Iris, just like Mom. But I'm not strong enough to lose. When Dad died, I promised myself that I would protect the family I have left. You being a soldier will never change the fact that I will always be responsible for protecting you."

"Stop trying to protect me and just start being there for me!" Iris demands as she hails a nearby taxi. "Come back with me now," she pleads, looking back at Michael with sincerity.

Michael takes a deep breath as the taxi pulls up to the curb. "Alright, I'll go."

The taxi drops Michael and Iris off near the coast. Michael follows his sister down a narrow strip of beach at the foot of the rocky coastal cliffs where Iris' Mech, Stalker 332, is hidden beneath a natural bridge. Iris climbs into the cockpit behind her brother and the Stalker takes off.

"By the way," Michael says, glancing back at his sister, "what the hell are you wearing?"

Iris laughs. "I knew if I went into town wearing this, you'd be more likely to chaperone me back."

"Well, cover up before I vomit."

"Jerk!" Iris laughs. "Your cartel friend at the bar seemed like it."

"Leo was just being polite."

"Leo, huh?" Iris pauses. "So you're not denying that cute cartel guy is your friend?" Michael remains silent. "By the way," Iris tells him, "you stink like sweat and cigarettes. Crack a window before I vomit for real!"

Michael breaks his silence with laughter.

CHAPTER SEVEN

Flying miles over the Pacific, Michael and Iris eventually return to the USNS Cyrus King. Mechanics work on patching the big hole in the ship's hull as Stalker 332 lands on its upper deck. The two siblings exit the Mech laughing.

"Hey, Archangel!" Canuck yells from across the deck.

The name grabs the attention of Stonewall, El Gato, and the rest of the sailors on deck. Seeing Michael, they quickly surround him with smiles and warm greetings.

"Welcome back, Archangel!" some say, shaking Michael's hand.

"We thought you were dead! Where you been?" others ask.

"Good to see you, Archangel!" more cheer.

"I can't see what can possibly be cause for celebration." The cheering comes to an abrupt stop as

Secnav Michelle King approaches her children wearing a navy blue pantsuit.

"Ma'am," Michael says as he and Iris salute their mother.

"When did you get here?" Iris asks.

"As soon as I heard that you allowed a hole to get blasted in the side of this ship. But I suppose you made up for your blunder by returning the prodigal son. This was indeed a *special* assignment for you after all, Iris," the Secnav says before turning to her son. "I hope you have a good explanation for your going AWOL for six months, Michael. I should have you court-martialed."

"I was undercover as you ordered, ma'am," Michael responds.

"Don't be a smartass. I know you were undercover. You were also ordered to report back weekly. It's been months since anyone heard from you. I assigned another officer to investigate the missing military shipments case and now I find out that you're alive which means I just wasted resources," the Secnav scolds.

"Sorry to disappoint you, ma'am," Michael says.

"It's your father who would be disappointed!" the Secnav barks.

Michael pauses. "I can give you a full report now on what I've discovered in my investigation."

"Iris," the Secnav says, looking over her glasses at her daughter with contempt, "what are you wearing?"

"I was undercover." Iris says.

"You need to cover!" the Secnav quickly scoffs.

Michael begins to laugh but is immediately

rendered silent by the Secnav's sharp, debilitating scowl.

"Debrief," the Secnav commands as she about-faces. "Now." The siblings look at each other and snicker as they follow their mother inside the ship's control tower. Michael and Iris follow the Secnav through the command bridge and into the occupied captain's cabin.

"Get out," the Secnav orders Captain Crunch. The short and portly captain grudgingly scuttles out as the Secnav sits in his seat behind the desk. She pushes her glasses back on her nose and gestures Michael to speak.

"With many of the military shipments to Mexico disappearing, I started my investigation in Mexico's most centralized area of illegal activity: Tijuana," Michael begins, "One month in, I got a tipoff that weapons were being smuggled through a bar called El Sanchez Sucio."

"*El Sanchez Sucio*? That is vile," the Secnav says in disgust. "Continue."

"I staked the place out and witnessed a U.S. military shipment being smuggled in the bar from a back alley. I found out El Sanchez Sucio is the watering hole for the Tijuana Cartel and that the cartel was looking for some hired help. I was able to convince their top enforcer that I was a former mercenary named Ángel. From him, I've learned that the Tijuana Cartel is headed by one man they call El Capo Santana Guerrero. I've been doing odd jobs with the enforcer in order to get close enough to the Capo to bring him in."

"Who is this enforcer?" the Secnav asks.

"Just another cartel cholo," Michael says

dismissively. "The Capo is the target. He's the one who orchestrates everything. If we take down Santana, we take down the cartel and stop the military shipment thefts."

"He can't be just another cholo if he is a top enforcer who is able to get close to the Capo," the Secnav says impatiently.

"The enforcer's name is Leo," Iris says. Pulling out her purple cellphone, she shows a picture to her mother of Michael and Leo laughing together at the bar.

The Secnav is suddenly stunned with an expression of overwhelming shock on her face.

"Mom? Are you okay?" Iris asks.

"Where is this Leo now?" the Secnav asks, grabbing the cellphone to get a closer look at the picture.

"I'm not sure but he's planning on delivering the Mech we stole to the Capo tomorrow," Michael responds.

"We?" the Secnav asks.

"It was Leo and I who stole the Stalker from this ship earlier tonight."

"You?!" The Secnav scowls. "You're responsible for blowing a hole in your father's ship? Michael, how could you?!"

"I was undercover. I'm so close to stopping the cartel, it would blow my cover if I had turned down a job now. All I have to do is tail Leo's delivery to Santana and bring the Capo in."

"No more solo missions, Michael," the Secnav orders. "We'll send in a team. I want Santana and Leo brought back to this ship alive!"

"It will be easier and less noticeable if I tail him alone."

"We don't have to tail him," Iris says. "I have a tracker on the stolen Stalker."

"You do?" Michael asks his sister.

"I attached a tracker bullet to it when you first flew out the ship." Iris points to her sniper rifle loaded with the unusually high-tech ammo magazine still sitting in the command bridge. "That's how I tracked you down at that bar."

"Why bring in Leo if the Capo is the objective?" Michael asks his mother, disgruntled.

"Why do you care?" the Secnav asks, looking up from the picture of Michael and Leo laughing together. She hands the cellphone back to Iris.

"I don't," Michael tells her. "I just don't see the reason to waste manpower on capturing a pawn when you can easily get to the king."

"This isn't chess, Michael, nor is it your concern!" the Secnav says sternly as she stands. "The objective is whatever I say it is whether or not you see the reason in it! Do I make myself clear, Lieutenant Commander?"

"Yes, ma'am," Michael responds submissively.

"Good." Standing tall and square-shouldered, the Secnav pushes her glasses back on her nose. "Be ready to move out first thing in the morning. I want your team on Leo the second he moves. You are both dismissed."

Without another word, Michael and his sister exit the cabin.

CHRPTER EIGHT

Leo stares up at the ceiling light as he sits reclined in a cold, dark room. His breath forms a cloud in the cold above him.

"M-Zero Subject prepped," a man wearing spectacles and a surgical mask says in an Australian accent as he hovers over Leo. Light reflects off the spectacles as they push through the cold breath cloud toward Leo's face. "Don't worry, mate," the man says. "This will be quick." The man suddenly stabs Leo in the back of the skull.

Leo yells in horror and grabs the back of his head as he wakes up at the bar inside El Sanchez Sucio.

"Another nightmare?" Sanchez the bartender asks.

"Yeah," Leo responds, still rubbing the metal aperture in the back of his head as he raises his face from the bar top.

"You good?" Sanchez asks.

"Yeah," Leo says, pulling a sticky bar nut from his

beard stubble, "just *magnífico*." His head aches as he recalls his dream. "M-Zero?" Leo says to himself. He props himself up in the barstool to grab a black leather journal from the back pocket of his black jumpsuit and begins writing down the bad dream. He has been recording his nightmares for as long as he can remember.

Leo's cellphone rings. He answers the phone, clenching it between his ear and shoulder as he slides the journal back into his pocket.

"Hey, *Tío*. I'm on my way," Leo says, getting up from the bar. Leo steps outside where the navy blue Lamborghini remains undisturbed. Santana's custom cars are well known in Tijuana. Even with the convertible top down, no one in the crime capital would ever risk messing with anything belonging to El Capo.

Leo hops into the Lamborghini. Looking up at the overcast morning sky, he puts up the convertible top before starting the car and grinding the stick shift gears all the way back to the airport.

As Leo pulls into the open hangar, a mechanic walks up to him covered in matte gold paint and wearing a respirator.

"Leo! *Que pasa, amigo*?!" the mechanic says.

"How you doing, Güey?" Leo responds as he bumps knuckles with the now middle-aged mechanic. "What you working on?" he asks, pointing to Güey's respirator.

"Doing a new paint job on the Hummer. When you

going to let me do another tattoo on you?" Güey asks.

"We can do one when I get back from delivering the Mech to Santana." Leo stares for a moment at the tarp-covered Mech on the back of a semi truck's flatbed. "Looks like you already got it loaded?"

"Yeah, mane. She's locked down and good to go," Güey responds.

"*Bueno*," Leo says climbing behind the wheel of the truck.

"*Hasta luego*!" Güey says as Leo hangs out of the truck's window.

"Catch you later, Güey." Leo waves, then drives the Mech-loaded semi out of the hangar. He cruises far out to the southern edge of Tijuana. A familiar Spanish mansion with white stucco walls, red-tiled roof, and arched verandas sits tucked away in seclusion beneath the shade of green palm trees. Leo pulls the semi into the mansion's circular cobblestone driveway. As he parks behind the white pearlescent, gold-rimmed '64 Impala lowrider, a white-haired, gold-toothed 64-year-old Capo steps out of the mansion to greet him.

"Leo my boy, how nice of you to visit!" Santana yells.

"Only nice because I brought your old ass a gift, *Tío*," Leo jokes to Santana.

"Old? I'll show you old," Santana says, playfully throwing punches at Leo. Leo laughs as he blocks the punches. Santana bear-hugs Leo and the two laugh loud and wild.

Santana suddenly pauses. "*Mijo*, did you hear

something?"

Leo looks up at the overcast sky. Hidden within cloud cover, Stalker 332 quietly hovers. Looking back at Leo through the oversized scope of her sniper rifle, Iris stands with one foot propped up on the edge of the open cockpit.

"Targets identified," Iris says to her brother who sits in the front seat. "It's Leo and Santana."

"You heard her, fellas. Remember, this is a quick extraction. Grab the targets and go," Lieutenant Commander Michael "Archangel" King says into his flight helmet mic.

"Copy that, Archangel," Stonewall responds from Stalker 333.

"Try not to get shot down this time," Canuck says to Stonewall from the copilot's seat behind him.

"Try shutting up sometime!" Stonewall snaps before diving behind Stalker 332 out of cloud cover.

"*Hombres*! The military is here!" Santana hollers. A horde of cartel cholos armed with AK rifles pour out of the mansion. "*Mijo*, move! *Ándale!*" Santana tells Leo as he runs against the crowd of cartel. AK bullets deflect off the speeding Stalkers as Leo follows Santana into the mansion. Michael fires a flashbang grenade into the horde. The flashbang's blinding light disorients the cholos before the Mechs smash into the cobblestone driveway, sending the cholos flying back. More cartel point rocket launchers at the Stalkers from the mansion's second-story windows. Stonewall fires a grenade at them, causing the mansion to cave in.

"Easy, Stonewall!" Michael orders. "We have to bring Leo and Santana in alive!"

Stalker 333 steps near the decimated mansion and is suddenly pulled underground by an old M-1 Trapper Mech hidden within the basement. The Trapper raises its fist above Stalker 333 and just before it smashes in the cockpit, Stonewall and Canuck eject. Stepping on the destroyed Stalker, the Trapper climbs out from the rubble of the mansion and charges at Stalker 332. With his Mech's right hand, Michael grabs the Trapper by the back of the neck and slams it on its butt. With his other hand, he proceeds to rip off the Trapper's canopy and pull Santana from the pilot's seat.

Crawling from the mansion basement, Leo sees Santana in the Mech's grip. He picks up one of the rocket launchers from the rubble and aims it directly at Michael. Just as Leo squeezes the trigger, Canuck shoots a bullet that grazes Leo's right shoulder. Losing his aim, Leo's rocket fires and severs Stalker 332's left arm off with Santana still in its hand. The arm drops to the ground and Santana escapes its grip.

Santana runs until a bullet shoots through his calf. He drops to the dirt and looks back to see Iris pointing a smoking sniper rifle at him.

"Don't move, Santana!" Iris orders.

Infuriated, Leo drops the rocket launcher and tackles Canuck to the ground, knocking the Canadian's pistol loose. He rams his fist into Canuck's helmet until the visor cracks. With bloody knuckles, Leo breaks through the visor and bashes Canuck's brow before suddenly getting pistol-whipped in the back of the head by Stonewall. The steel pistol dings against the metal aperture in the back of Leo's head as he falls face-first to the ground.

Leo looks across the crushed cobblestone driveway sprawled with wounded cartel. He sees a short pilot pointing a sniper rifle at Santana's head as a tall pilot zip-ties the Capo's hands behind his back. As the tall six-foot-six-inch pilot turns and walks toward him, Leo looks at the front of the pilot's closed helmet and sees an emblem of the letter 'A' with wings.

"Ángel?" Leo murmurs.

"Shut up!" Stonewall yells, shoving Leo's face into the cobblestone with his boot.

"That's enough!" Michael says, approaching his fellow soldiers.

Stonewall hands the pistol back to Canuck before zip-tying Leo's hands behind his back. With cracked helmet in hand and a bleeding brow, Canuck looks at the back of Leo's head as Stonewall raises his boot off of it.

"What the hell is that?" Canuck asks with wide eyes.

"Looks like a camera shutter," Stonewall tells him.

Surprised, Michael looks at the silver dollar-sized metal aperture in the back of Leo's scarred head and responds, "Never noticed it before."

"What?" Stonewall asks.

"I mean, never seen anything like this before," Michael says before changing the subject. "Stonewall, you escort Santana back to the ship in the stolen Stalker. Canuck, help him unload the stolen Stalker and fly Stalker 332 back with Iris. I'm flying Leo."

"In what?" Stonewall asks Michael.

"In that," Michael says, pointing at Santana's M-1 Trapper.

"You can pilot that ancient thing?" Canuck asks.

"I can fly anything," Michael responds, much to Leo's suspicion.

With Leo restrained in the familiar back seat, Michael takes off in the old M-1 Trapper. Stonewall and Santana follow behind him in the stolen Stalker with Canuck and Iris behind them in the one-armed Stalker 332. Iris deploys and aims the back-mounted Gatling gun at the wrecked Stalker 333 still lying within the mansion. She fires at 333's fuel tank and it explodes, completely destroying the mansion and all within it.

CHAPTER NINE

After returning to the USNS Cyrus King, Stonewall escorts Santana to the med bay to get his gunshot wound treated while Michael escorts Leo down into the empty brig area. With his hands still zip-tied behind his back, Leo stops and turns to face his captor.

"How long you plan on hiding behind that mask, Ángel?"

Michael removes his helmet. Clean-shaven with a crew cut, he faces Leo.

"Who are you?" Leo asks, disgusted.

"I'm your friend," Michael responds genuinely.

"Is everything alright, Michael?" Iris suddenly interrupts as she enters the brig.

"Michael? You mean Ángel's not even your real name?" Leo asks angrily.

"Yes. Well, kind of," Michael responds. "Archangel is my Navy call sign. I'm a pilot with the U.N. forces. I was never a mercenary."

Leo squints his eyes at Michael. "Your accent's gone, *amigo*," Leo points out. "What the fuck, mane? You're not even Mexican!"

"Now, I never said I was Mexican," Michael explains. "I'm mixed."

"You said you grew up near Tijuana!"

"I did…" Michael hesitates. "In San Diego."

"Give me a break, *hermano*!" Leo exclaims before turning to Iris. "And you!"

"Me?" she responds.

"I know you," Leo says. "You're that sexy *bonita* from the bar. You were spying on me too?"

Iris smiles and bats her right eye. "Actually, I was spying on him," she says, pointing at Michael.

"So this is your girlfriend, Michael? You two some sort of spy couple?"

Michael and Iris cringe at the thought.

"Dude, no! Don't make me vomit!" Michael exclaims.

"He's my big brother!" Iris explains.

"Oh," Leo responds, smirking at Iris.

Just then, Canuck runs downstairs into the brig. "Archangel, the Secnav needs you for debrief."

"We need to process the prisoner first," Michael tells him.

"I can help, Deadeye," Canuck suggests with a smirk.

"Hey, pretty boy!" Leo barks at Canuck. "What the fuck's wrong with you calling her Deadeye? Show some respect before I crack your head again, *cabrón!*"

Intimidated, Canuck's smirk vanishes as he touches the bandaged cut on his brow.

"Thanks, but I don't need any help processing this guy," Iris responds.

"You sure?" Michael asks.

"I got it. You can both go," she adds firmly.

"Alright," Michael hesitantly agrees before he and Canuck exit the brig.

Iris laughs subtly as she struts behind Leo.

"Why you so giggly?" Leo asks.

"That guy wasn't being disrespectful," she responds. "Deadeye is my call sign."

"Either way, it's disrespectful calling a chick with an eye-patch Deadeye."

"A lot of call signs are a little offensive. That guy is French-Canadian and his call sign is Canuck. But if it really bugs you, just call me Iris," she explains as she begins patting Leo down from behind.

"You know, Iris," Leo says with a cocky smile, "this almost makes getting captured worth it. You must be excited too, to pat down Tijuana Cartel's top enforcer."

Iris rolls her eye. "I can see you're a real humble guy," she responds sarcastically.

"If that's what you're looking for, then I'm the best at being humble."

Iris pulls the little black leather book from the back pocket of Leo's black jumpsuit. "What is this, Don Juan?" she asks with a smile before cutting loose Leo's zip-tied wrists.

"You're just as disrespectful as your pretty boy friend back there," Leo jokes as he faces Iris. "It's personal. Don't you got any respect for people's private things?"

"Not yours," Iris responds, handing him a bar of soap. "Now strip down, pretty boy."

Iris stands watch as Leo takes his clothes off in the prison shower.

Naked and cocky, Leo faces Iris with the bar of soap in his hand. The brawny cholo gringo is covered with tats.

Looking below Leo's chiseled abs, Iris nods her head in approval. "Mine's bigger," she says, holding a large water hose.

"Isn't there a law against sexual harassment?" Leo flirts.

"This is just regular harassment," Iris clarifies, pointing the hose at Leo. "Don't drop the soap," she says before cutting the water hose on full-throttle.

"COLD!" Leo cries as Iris shoots him with the freezing jet burst of water.

After spraying him down, Iris hands Leo a towel. "Nice ink," she compliments, slapping a bandage on his bullet-grazed right shoulder.

"Thanks," Leo says sorely through gritting teeth. "You got any?"

"Just one."

"I showed you mine, you show me yours," Leo flirts.

"Maybe later," Iris says, handing him clean clothes.

Leo puts on the boxers, blue pants and shirt marked 'PRISONER,' and socks with sandals.

"So what happened to your eye?" he asks bluntly as Iris walks him to the back of the brig.

"I was copiloting with Michael in a thick dogfight when an Axis Tora Mech exploded above us," Iris tells him. "A piece of shrapnel broke through the cockpit and lodged in my eye."

"So you got screwed over by him too," Leo says. "At least that's one story your brother didn't lie about."

"Shit happens in war. I don't blame Michael. He does enough of that for the both of us. And you shouldn't blame my brother either! He really does consider you his friend, you know? I could tell by the way he fought to convince the Secnav not to bring you in. He just wanted to stop you all from stealing military shipments from U.N. forces. But we were ordered to capture you. We followed the Secnav's orders just like you follow El Capo's."

"I guess," Leo says in consideration. "Who is the Secnav?"

"Secretary Michelle King runs the United States Navy," Iris replies as they stand by an open cell, "and she also happens to be our mother."

"You're an open book, *bonita*." Leo says turning to face Iris. "You really don't care about keeping private things?"

Iris leans close to Leo. "Sure I do," she says with a seductive smile as she roughly grabs his crotch. Leo winces as she pushes him by the balls back into the cell and slams the barred door shut on him. Leo leans his head against the bars to admire Iris' backside as she walks away.

"Conjugal visit next time!" Leo yells with a grin.

"Bye, Leo," Iris says flirtatiously before exiting. She passes Stonewall as he escorts a handcuffed Santana to the back of the brig. Wearing matching blue 'PRISONER' uniforms, the Capo and Leo are locked in the cell together.

"Hands," Stonewall orders. Santana puts his hands through an opening in the bars and Stonewall removes the handcuffs before exiting.

"You okay, *Tío*?" Leo asks as Santana rubs his wrists.

"I'm alive, aren't I?" Santana replies, climbing into the top bunk.

"Sorry about this, *Tío. Lo siento*. One of our guys was crooked. He betrayed me," Leo says.

"We're gangsters, *mijo*. We're all crooked. There's no loyalty among thieves." Santana laughs. "Don't be sorry, *mijo*. I always figured the law would eventually catch up to me. I've only been doing this for half a century. Took them long enough," the Capo says nonchalantly as he lies down in the top bunk.

"You're *loco*, *Tío*." Leo laughs. Waiting for a response, Leo hears only the sound of Santana snoring in the bunk above him.

CHAPTER TEN

Leo stands in the ocean and looks at the California Gold Coast shining under the sun. Iris stands on the beach in her white bikini smiling at Leo. Leo smiles back when suddenly the sun blazes in a blinding flash. Leo raises his hand to cover his eyes. When he lowers it, he finds the entire coast engulfed in flames and Iris crying out to him.

"Leo! Leo! Leo!"

"Iris!" Leo yells as he wakes up in the bottom bunk aboard the USNS Cyrus King.

"Leo! Leo! Get control of yourself! I am not Iris. I am U.S. Secretary of the Navy Michelle King." Light reflects off the Secnav's glasses as she stands over him in a black pantsuit. Leo reaches for his black leather journal. Patting his empty back pocket, he is reminded that Iris took it.

"Dammit!" he yells, waking Santana in the top

bunk.

"Ooh *bonita mamacita*," Santana says, sitting up and looking at the Secnav. "Let the boy alone, I'm the man you want." He winks.

"In your dreams, Guerrero," the Secnav scoffs as she cuffs Leo's hands behind his back.

"More likely my nightmares," Santana replies.

The Secnav rolls her eyes before exiting the cell with Leo.

"Hey, wait!" Santana yells, climbing out of the bunk as the Secnav locks the cell. "Where are you taking him?!"

"To visit an old friend," the Secnav says before escorting Leo off the ship.

Outside, Leo squints his eyes at the morning dawn. "Where are we?" he asks.

"Naval Base San Diego, in America's finest city," the Secnav responds, walking him to a black military police car. She opens the door to the back seat. "Get in."

"Who is this old friend?" Leo asks, turning to the Secnav. She pulls out a pistol and puts it to Leo's head.

"You'll find out soon enough." She taps the pistol against the metal aperture in the back of Leo's head. "Just like Stonewall reported and still intact," the Secnav says. "Now, get in."

The Secnav drives the black car through the base with Leo caged in the back seat. "Thirty years ago, I led a team of SEALs on an intel-gathering mission en route to Hawaii just after it had been nuked by the Axis," the Secnav starts. "It was storming that night. Our ship crashed hard against the waves. We were about a thousand nautical miles off the coast of this naval base when the ship was suddenly struck by an airborne projectile. But it only swiped the side of the ship's hull. There was no explosion. We figured it was a dud missile. I ordered divers to investigate but what we found wasn't a missile. It was an aircraft-sized mechanical humanoid. The first Mech.

"We got it out of the ocean and had it secretly airlifted to a subterranean facility in Roswell. I codenamed it the Mech Type Zero, later shortened to M-Zero, and decided to duplicate it for anti-nuclear weapon defense. Other than the SEALs initially involved, only a small team of scientists and engineers led by my husband, the late Dr. Cyrus King, knew about the M-Zero Project. After they managed to pry open the M-Zero's head, we found the pilot's seat with an odd egg-shaped headpiece linked to it and foreign writing engraved all over the inside of the cockpit. Initially, I thought the writing was Chinese and the Mech an Axis weapon but quickly realized not only was it not from China, it wasn't even from Earth."

"Why are you telling me all this?" Leo asks as the black car parks at a small, old warehouse tucked in a forgotten corner of the naval base. Exiting the car, the Secnav grabs a long rope from the trunk of the car and hangs it over her shoulder before pulling Leo from the back seat.

"You're not as smart as I thought you'd be," she responds, escorting Leo at gunpoint to the warehouse door. She presses her thumbprint to a sensor hidden by the door. It unlocks and the two enter the dark warehouse.

"Even though we had gained access to the M-Zero's cockpit, we still couldn't get it to activate," the Secnav continues as she walks Leo down a long, steep, dark corridor. "Even stranger, we couldn't get through its armor. Every time the engineers would cut into it, the M-Zero would instantly mend itself. We had to rely on X-ray scans to study the extraterrestrial Mech's inner-workings and duplicated them as best we could. What we created were the first man-made Mechs, the M-1 Trappers.

"Shortly after the Trappers were assembled, I ordered them in the counterattack against the Axis' second nuclear strike. The M-1 Trappers proved their worth but my husband and I wanted to know more about the M-Zero. We still didn't know how to activate it or how it healed itself so we continued work on the project in Roswell. My husband determined that the egg-shaped headpiece linked to the pilot's seat was the M-Zero's sole controller and that it could only be operated using the mind."

The Secnav stops at the end of the corridor. "Here we are," she says, switching on a generator. The loud generator powers up and the lights turn on, revealing the large extraterrestrial Mech reclined in a steel cradle. With its head open to the cockpit, the fifty-foot-tall and slender Mech shines like polished ivory and is plated in armor that resembles muscular anatomy. Heavy steel restraints lock down its long skeletal-like hands and digitigrade feet. The Mech almost appears more human than machine.

"This is the M-Zero," the Secnav announces as she walks Leo to the pilot's seat inside the diagonally-reclined Mech's head. "Have a seat," she says removing Leo's handcuffs.

Rubbing his wrists, Leo turns to face her. "Think I'll pass."

The Secnav wrenches her gun into Leo's bullet wound in his right shoulder as he yells out in pain. "That wasn't a request."

With teeth gritting and blood seeping through his right sleeve, Leo grudgingly sits back inside the M-Zero's cockpit. The Secnav keeps her pistol pointed at Leo as she uses the long rope to bind his arms and legs to the inverted seat.

"After we determined that the M-Zero could only be mentally operated, the scientists tried using its egg-shaped headpiece themselves but to no avail," the Secnav explains. "My husband developed a neuro-adapter for the M-Zero's headpiece that inserted directly into the brain. We needed subjects to test the neuro-adapter on so I authorized human experimentation. That's where you came in. Thirty-six young subjects died in testing before we had our first breakthrough. You, Leo. Lucky Subject Number 037."

The Secnav grabs Leo's right forearm and looks at his '⊏⊒⊓' tattoo framed within lion's teeth. "Wait a minute," she says, looking from the tattoo to Leo, "did you think this read LEO?" she asks condescendingly. Leo frowns and turns his face away as she bursts into laughter. "Is this how you got your name, by reading your identification number upside down? That is too cute!" The Secnav laughs as she continues tying the other end of the long rope around her waist.

"Anyways, the first time we plugged you in, it was quite a sight. All of the M-Zero's lights lit up like Christmas. But before we could even get a chance to analyze anything, you went completely berserk! As you were screaming and flailing in this same seat, the M-Zero was flailing exactly the same. We finally had a subject that could mentally control the Mech. I'll never forget the expression of excitement on my husband's face. Five long years working on the project, it was the first time he saw the M-Zero come to life and the last time I saw my beloved husband alive. In that moment, the Mech's chest plate opened and emitted a bright blue beam that created a suction so powerful it sent personnel and everything else not bolted down flying across the room and crashing into the electrical equipment. Sparks flew and the facility caught on fire. In all the chaos, I attempted to restrain you but you knocked me unconscious with the M-Zero's flailing leg."

The Secnav brushes back her hair to reveal a scar on the side of her forehead. "When I came to in the military hospital, the doctor told me that the SEALs had pulled me from the burning facility. Then he tells me I'm a month pregnant. I asked the doctor where my husband was and if he was okay. He told me that everything in the subterranean facility in Roswell was incinerated in the fire and no other survivors were found. I was devastated." The Secnav pauses before recomposing herself and pushing her glasses back on her nose. "I had the M-Zero secretly relocated here in San Diego, close to home. It was the only property that survived the fire. Or so I thought, until my son coincidently found you in Tijuana."

CHAPTER ELEVEN

Back on the USNS Cyrus King, Michael walks through the ship in his olive drab flight suit. Entering the women's quarters, the female sailors turn and smile as he walks by in his pilot's uniform. Michael finds Iris sleeping in a small cabin wearing grey shorts and a purple Los Angeles Sparks basketball jersey with the black leather journal opened on her face.

"Iris. Iris," Michael says as he nudges his sister.

"Leo?" Iris says, rising from the lower bunk. The journal falls from her face to the floor.

"Nope, just me," Michael responds.

"Michael?" Iris says, yawning and stretching. "Where have you been?"

"Yesterday, I spent the rest of the day debriefing with Mom. She only asked questions about Leo. She didn't even seem interested in us retrieving the stolen Stalker, capturing Santana, or finally putting an end to the cartel's military shipment thefts." Michael picks the black leather journal up from the floor. "What's this?"

"Your friend's journal," Iris responds as Michael hands it back to her. "It's full of disturbing, repeated detailed accounts. I'm not sure if they're nightmares, memories, or visions. Maybe all three."

"Any issues processing Leo yesterday?" Michael asks.

"Nope," Iris responds with a smile. "But I can see why you're friends with him. Leo's rough around the edges but you and he share the same rudimentary good qualities." Iris opens the journal and reads Leo's last entry. "Ever heard of M-Zero?" she asks her brother.

"Sounds familiar," Michael says, taking a moment to reflect. "Seems like I remember Dad mentioning it when I was a kid."

"That's it!" Iris says excitedly as she remembers for herself. "Dad was holding a black book marked 'M-Zero' in that old framed photo hanging in Mom's office." Iris' excitement fades as she thinks about her father. "You know, that's the only picture I've ever seen of Dad."

"It's the only one Mom's got. She's not exactly the sentimental type." Michael smirks.

"I wish I could have met him just once," Iris says sadly. "What else do you remember about Dad?"

"Nothing, really," Michael says. "I just remember Mom being happier when he was around."

"I can't even picture Mom happy." Iris says before walking across the small cabin and looking out a circular window in the ship's hull. "I thought we were still delivering the Stalkers to the naval frontline?" she says, confused, before looking back at her brother. "What are we doing back in San Diego?"

Back at the warehouse, the Secnav pulls the long rope tight as she knots it around her waist, tethering herself to the pilot's seat in which Leo is restrained. Stepping behind him, she grabs the metal neuro-adapter rod linked to the egg-shaped headpiece on the back of Leo's seat.

"I was careless before," the Secnav says, blowing dust from the neuro-adapter. "I won't make that mistake this time."

"This time?" Leo asks.

"That's right," the Secnav responds. "The M-Zero is still an asset to our war effort. Look at all we've built from the limited study of its technology. Imagine what more we can accomplish after fully dissecting it and its abilities. With you, we can harness the destructive power of the M-Zero's beam against our enemies. Or make armor for our soldiers that regenerates itself. But these possibilities are impossible without you, 037. My husband and all of his work were destroyed in the fire you caused. No one has been able to duplicate his work since. You are the last remnant of that work and an asset of the U.S. government." The Secnav steps from behind Leo's seat to face him. "In war, we all have to make sacrifices for the greater good. It's about time you fulfill your honorable duty to protect your country. You can understand why I'm doing this, can't you?"

"Yeah," Leo responds, "because you're psycho!"

The Secnav laughs. "Well, don't worry," she says, positioning the metal neuro-adapter rod behind Leo as it automatically opens the aperture in the back of his head. "You'll get the point."

The Secnav jabs the neuro-adapter rod into the opened aperture and Leo screams in agony. His brain feels like it's frying inside his skull as memories of his past come flooding back. Immediately, M-Zero begins to power up, and blue lights illuminate throughout its shining ivory structure as they did twenty-six years ago. The Mech's chest plate opens and a raging blue beam erupts from it. Leo's eyes roll back in his head as he screams in excruciating pain. The more he screams, the larger and more ferocious the beam grows. The Secnav's glasses fall off her face as she is snatched into the air by the beam's powerful suction, but the rope around her waist jerks her like a ragdoll, barely saving her from getting sucked in. The blue beam bursts through the ceiling of the warehouse and quickly grows so large and wide it can be seen from miles away.

Looking directly into the beam, the Secnav's eyes grow wide. "Oh my god," she says in a whisper.

A gargantuan mountain-sized four-legged ivory Mech suddenly tears through the blue beam. Larger than an aircraft carrier and as tall as a skyscraper, the mechanical mammoth monstrosity steps over M-Zero like a bug.

Still dangling, the Secnav grabs the rope at her

waist and strains to pull herself down toward Leo.

The USNS Cyrus King rocks in the water from the gravitational pull of M-Zero's beam. Bright blue light shines on Iris' face as she stares out the circular cabin window.

"Michael," Iris says wide-eyed, "you might want to take a look at this."

Michael approaches the window and sees the ivory Mammoth fully emerged from the blue beam. He notices a similar blue light emanating from within its bowels. A huge opening reveals itself at the front of the Mammoth and in a blinding flash of light, hundreds of extraterrestrial Mechs burst through. They somewhat resemble M-Zero but are twice as large and made of dark corroded metal. With terrifying speed, the invading Mechs begin demolishing San Diego, slashing through buildings, cars, and people with their long skeletal-like fingers. Civilians scramble in fear, skyscrapers crumble, and flames erupt as America's finest city quickly breaks out into complete pandemonium.

"The city's under attack! We have to stop this!" Michael yells as he looks back at his sister.

Already zipping her flight suit over her purple Sparks jersey, Iris responds, "What should we do with Leo and Santana?"

"They should be safe here on the ship," Michael responds. "Now, let's move." He sounds the alarm before sprinting through the ship alongside his sister.

Iris runs into El Gato. With his arm in a sling, El

Gato grabs the side of his chest in pain. "El Gato, I'm sorry. Are you alright?" she asks.

"I'm good," the injured soldier responds sorely. "What's going on?"

"City's under attack," Iris says.

"Axis made it through our frontlines?" El Gato asks in disbelief.

"I don't think it's Axis," Michael responds.

"We're headed to the cargo bay now to fly out. Can you open the upper deck main bay doors?" Iris asks El Gato.

"I'm on it," El Gato says, racing to the command bridge.

Hundreds of Navy pilots flood into the cargo bay and load into the new M-2 Stalkers. A female mechanic crawls out of Stalker 332's cockpit as Michael and Iris run up.

"Archangel!" the mechanic says with a smile. "Just finished ops-checking the new arm. He's good to go." The mechanic hands Michael his angel-winged helmet.

"Thanks," Michael responds. "You're a miracle-worker."

From the control tower, El Gato sees the ivory Mammoth and its unnaturally quick extraterrestrial Mechs ripping San Diego to pieces. Angrily, he hits the switch to open the huge bay doors above the awaiting M-2 Stalkers.

"You ready, sis?" Michael asks, throwing on his helmet.

"Hell yeah!" Iris yells, locking into the rear seat behind her brother.

"Let's fly!" Michael hits the ignition switch, and instantly, 332's jet engines fire up. Along with a hundred other Stalkers, Michael and Iris zoom in to battle the alien Mechs.

CHAPTER TWELVE

Back at the warehouse, the Secnav pulls herself along the rope closer and closer toward Leo, intent on taking control of him and the M-Zero. Amidst his screaming in agony, Leo suddenly hears a deep voice.

Leo, the calming voice calls. *Leo, relax*. The voice seems to be coming from M-Zero but Leo struggles to pay attention through his immense pain. *Leo*, the voice calls again, *you must control your emotions. Clear your mind and focus. Visualize breaking loose from your restraints. You must gain control.*

Fighting through the pain, Leo convulses and grunts violently as he struggles to focus.

"I...can't," Leo groans.

Clear your mind, Leo, the voice says again. *Relax. Focus. You can do it.*

Leo closes his eyes as he visualizes his arm breaking loose, and as he does, M-Zero's arm breaks free from its heavy steel restraint. The Secnav, still anchored by the rope to M-Zero, is astonished by the sight.

"Well, I'll be," she says, grinning. Pulling on the rope, the Secnav doubles her pace to commandeer Leo and the M-Zero.

The wise voice continues to speak to Leo. *Good, Leo. You have control. Now, close the portal.*

Leo takes a slow, deep breath. As he relaxes and focuses, the beaming blue portal steadily stabilizes and shrinks. As the portal shrinks, a large curved windshield gently slides closed over M-Zero's cockpit. The portal vanishes into the ivory Mech's closing chest and its suction with it, dropping Secnav Michelle King hard onto the windshield of M-Zero's now sealed cockpit. She looks at Leo through the glass as he slowly opens his eyes and calmly stares back at her. The Secnav picks up the end of the rope that has been cut off by the windshield. Infuriated, she bangs on the glass.

"Open this cockpit right now, 037!" the Secnav demands. "You are in possession of U.S. government property!"

Unable to hear the Secnav screaming through the windshield, Leo focuses on the voice calling to him once more.

Rise, Leo.

Calm and focused, Leo raises M-Zero from its steel cradle, breaking its restraints. The Secnav slides off the Mech and falls to the ground as Leo slowly ascends through the breached roof of the warehouse. The Secnav looks up as blue flames softly roar from jet nozzles in M-

Zero's calves and on either side of its exterior spine. Sunlight shines down on M-Zero as its panoramic windshield transitions to dark tint. Hovering high in the sky, Leo beholds the other alien Mechs mercilessly killing soldiers and civilians. Without hesitation, he engages the extraterrestrial enemy.

Leo rips through a dark cluster of corroded Mechs with M-Zero's long skeletal fingers. Spotting two Stalkers getting torn to shreds by a pack of alien Mechs, Leo charges them. The pack pounces and claws into M-Zero, covering it in scratches and leaving deep gouges in its chest plate. Leo yells in pain as he grabs his own chest inside the cockpit. He looks down at M-Zero's chest plate and the gouges suddenly begin to heal. Within seconds, not a single trace of damage is left on M-Zero's ivory exterior.

Leo tears the heads up off the giant corroded Mechs. Several aliens fall out of each huge, corroded Mech body and a few fall from each corroded head's cockpit. Leo notices similar egg-shaped mental controller headpieces inside the head cockpits before one of the alien pilots lands on M-Zero's tinted windshield. Looking up at the seven-foot-tall, muscular alien, Leo untints the windshield to get a better look at the savage beast. Grey-skinned and white-eyed with a short dorsal fin atop its noseless head, the alien looks like an anthropomorphic shark. Wearing no more than what looks like grey spandex shorts, the snarling creature struggles to keep from sliding off of M-Zero's windshield, pressing its four-fingered hands and four-toed digitigrade feet against the glass. The beast suddenly lunges its head at Leo and cracks the windshield. Leo notices its head slopes back to a point like an egg as the cracked glass mends itself. The creature finally slides off of the hovering ivory Mech and plummets from the sky.

Looking down at the dead red stain, Leo sees the two shredded Stalkers and grabs their guns. Wielding dual assault rifles, Leo tears through countless attacking alien Mechs with blinding speed. Corroded metal and bloody alien bits fall from the sky as Leo rains bullets and rockets along with a barrage of explosive melee attacks.

Not too far away, Michael and Iris see the lightning-fast ivory Mech in action.

"What is that?" Iris asks Michael from the back seat of Stalker 332.

"It matches that ivory Mammoth but looks like it's fighting on our side," Michael responds. "Let's lend it some backup."

Michael radios his fellow Stalkers as he flies toward the ivory Mech, "Calling all Stalkers, this is Archangel. We have an unusual ally taking down the enemy, an unidentified ivory Mech positioned over downtown San Diego near the harbor. All available troops, let's lend it a hand."

Michael and the Stalkers rally around M-Zero and together they begin to squash the alien invaders.

Secnav Michelle King races up the long corridor of the warehouse and exits back out onto Naval Base San Diego. U.N. ground forces attack the extraterrestrial enemy from the base as the Secnav spots M-Zero fighting alongside the Stalkers in the sky. Ducking gunfire, she runs back to the black military police car and grabs a radio from the dashboard.

"Calling all Stalkers! This is U.S Secretary of the Navy Michelle King!" she announces.

"Reading you loud and clear, ma'am. This is Archangel," Michael radios in.

"Michael, I need all Stalkers to close in on M-Zero's position and capture it!"

"M-Zero, ma'am?" Michael asks.

"The ivory Mech!" the Secnav yells.

"Oh my god! That's the M-Zero Project!" Iris exclaims to her brother.

"But, ma'am, the ivory Mech is aiding us and we are already fully engaged with the enemy," Michael responds.

"I'm giving you a direct order, Michael! This is priority! I want you and the Stalkers to bring me that Mech, now!"

Reluctantly, Michael and the Stalkers fighting alongside M-Zero turn their weapons on the ivory Mech. Surrounded by U.N. forces, M-Zero cooperatively lands with the Stalkers on base next to Secnav Michelle King.

I really don't want to have to kill you guys, Leo thinks to himself.

"Kill us? Leo?" Michael responds. "Is that you?"

"*Hermano*?" Leo says. "Yeah, it's me. Where are you?"

"We're piloting Stalker 332," Iris responds. "Are you alright? Where are you?"

"Iris?" Leo says as M-Zero turns to face Stalker 332. "I'm fine. I'm piloting M-Zero."

"You're the one piloting M-Zero?!" Iris asks, surprised. *Where did he steal this one from?* she thinks.

"I didn't steal it! You're psycho mama stuck me in this thing! She wants you all to bring me in so the government can experiment on me again!" Leo responds. "And how can you guys hear me?"

"What do you mean? We're wearing radio headsets," Michael tells him.

"I'm not…" Leo says.

"Archangel, Deadeye, who are you two talking to?" Canuck asks, sitting behind Stonewall in a nearby Stalker.

A perplexed expression crosses Iris' face. "Does anyone else have radio contact with the ivory Mech, M-Zero?" she asks.

"Negative."

"Negative."

"Negative," a wave of Stalker pilots radio in response.

Michael and Iris look back at each other, puzzled. Iris unplugs her radio headset and thinks quietly to herself, *Leo, can you hear me?*

"Yeah, Iris. I can still hear you."

"We can communicate telepathically!" Iris exclaims to Michael and Leo.

"Really?" Leo responds.

Can you hear my thoughts? Michael thinks.

I can hear both of your thoughts, hermano, Leo telepathizes. *I wonder what color panties Iris got on?*

Ivory-colored, Iris thinks.

Get my sister's drawers out of your head, bruh! Michael responds defensively.

Nice, Leo responds, laughing.

Stalker 332 flies between M-Zero and the Stalkers' aimed assault rifles. "Stalkers, this is Archangel piloting 332," Michael radios as Iris plugs her headset back in. "Stand down. Repeat, Stand down. M-Zero is a friendly."

"The Secnav just gave a direct order to bring M-Zero in," Stonewall asserts.

"Listen, Stonewall, we know this pilot and M-Zero is not a threat. Let Michael and I handle this one," Iris orders. "I saved you before, Stonewall. Let me do the same for the M-Zero pilot."

"Negative!" the Secnav barks. "Iris, fall in line or step aside!"

"We can't do that, ma'am," Michael responds.

There's a long radio silence. "Ma'am, Archangel and Deadeye aren't backing down," Canuck says. "How do you want us to proceed?"

The Secnav hesitates before putting the radio to her mouth. "In war, we all have to make sacrifices for the greater good. We do not compromise in the face of treason," Secnav Michelle King says. "I ordered you all to bring me M-Zero. Gun down anything that obstructs that order."

"Archangel, Deadeye, you heard your ma," Stonewall says as he puts his finger on the trigger. "So, what's it going to be?"

Devastated by his mother's words, Michael sinks back in his seat.

Stonewall points his gun at Stalker 332 as the rest of the Stalkers steady their aim on M-Zero.

"Alright, that's enough drama," Leo says. Before Stonewall can squeeze the trigger, Leo disarms the Texan with lightning speed and Stalker 332 fires a flashbang grenade, blinding the other Stalkers. Michael quickly takes off and Leo immediately follows behind.

"Fire! Fire! Shoot them down, goddammit!" the Secnav screams as Leo and Michael easily dodge the hailstorm of bullets.

The Stalkers fly after M-Zero and 332.

"They're gaining on us!" Iris yells, facing the pursuers.

"I don't know how much longer we can keep this up!" Michael says.

M-Zero drops its dual rifles, flies up behind 332, and grabs it under the arms.

"Hold on," Leo says and in a flash of blue light, M-Zero tears off at hypersonic speed over the Pacific. The pursuing Stalkers stop dead in their tracks with no possible chance of catching up to the ivory mech.

Once clear of the U.N. forces, Leo releases Stalker 332.

"Michael, Leo," Iris communicates, "we'll continue west, over the Pacific. Now that the Secnav's got it out for us, we won't be safe in any areas under U.S. control."

Still somewhat devastated, Michael sits quiet in the cockpit as Leo pulls alongside him flying M-Zero backwards.

Michael smiles. "You still can't drive stick shift, *cabrón*!" he jokes.

Leo laughs. "You're the wheelman, *hermano*. I'm just a scrapper."

CHAPTER THIRTEEN

As the sun sets on the Pacific horizon, Leo, Michael, and Iris approach Hawaii. They land in a large clearing in a thick tropical forest near the northeast shore of the island. Michael is surprised at how easy they're able to infiltrate the Axis-controlled island. He grabs his suppressed pistol as Iris gazes at a volcano in the distance. The two exit Stalker 332 and run toward M-Zero. The ivory Mech kneels on one knee, planting its opposite fist in the dirt as the windshield on its head slides open. Michael and Iris climb M-Zero and enter the open cockpit. Inside, a long cut-off rope leads across the floor to Leo who is still tied down to the seat.

"Nice of you guys to show up," Leo says with a smile.

Michael pulls out Leo's switchblade with cherrywood handle and cuts the long rope binding Leo's arms and legs before returning the blade back to him. As

Leo rubs his brawny arms, Iris looks at the metal neuro-adapter plugged into the back of his head.

"Our mother did this?" she asks wide-eyed.

"Along with some help from your *padre*," Leo adds.

"Our father?" Michael asks, also looking at the neuro-adapter.

"That's what your mama said," Leo responds. "Get this thing out of my head and I'll tell you the whole story."

"Does it hurt?" Iris asks.

"Not now, only when your mama jammed it in my head."

"I'm sorry about this, Leo," Michael says with great guilt. "For all of this."

Leo looks up at Michael. "I understand you were just doing your job. Iris already told me the Secnav forced you to bring me in. If El Capo had ordered me to do the same to you—" Leo pauses. "At that time, I'd probably have made the same mistake. Let's bury it and push forward, *hermano*."

Iris smiles as her brother and Leo bump fists.

"So how do we disconnect this thing?" Michael asks.

"Just yank it out," Leo tells him.

Walking to the edge of M-Zero's cockpit, Iris leans toward a branch of a tree and breaks a small stick off. Peeling off the bark as she walks back to Leo, she puts the smooth stick to his mouth and says, "Bite down on this. It'll help with the pain."

Leo puts the stick between his teeth as Michael

grasps the neuro-adapter.

"You ready?" Michael asks.

Leo nods and Michael counts.

"One. Two. Three!"

Leo hollers in pain as all of M-Zero's lights go dim.

That night, Leo throws the smooth stick on the campfire that Michael is tending to.

"Got some MREs!" Iris announces as she climbs down from 332's cockpit and walks to Leo. "I got this too," she says, handing Leo his black leather journal. "There's some disturbing stuff in there. After today, it's making a little more sense but I'd still like to know the whole story."

Leo grins. "I'm not sure I know the whole story but if you cook up those MREs, I'll tell you what I do know."

As Leo and Iris join Michael around the campfire, Leo tells them what all took place earlier that day. He tells them what the Secnav told him and how she called him Subject 037. He talks about his reoccurring nightmares. For hours, the group bonds, sharing life stories and eating MREs as they sit between the two giant armored Mechs.

Thunder crashes and it begins to rain. Iris flips her and Michael's flight helmets upside-down to gather drinking water. As Michael drinks from his angel-winged helmet, rainwater quenches thirst and the campfire.

"I'm going to rest up. We can figure out our next move in the morning," Michael says.

"Goodnight," Iris and Leo say.

"Goodnight," Michael responds before climbing into Stalker 332's cockpit and closing the glass canopy.

"You two seem alright for just getting betrayed by your own mama," Leo says bluntly to Iris.

"I'm only putting on a tough face for Michael. It's affecting him a lot more than he puts on. But I'm having difficulty as well, coming to terms with what our mother did. I've always known she was a little harsh but even I didn't think she was capable of all this."

"Makes me kind of glad I never knew my family," Leo jokes before noticing Iris' somber expression. "Hey, it's going to be alright," Leo says in a comforting tone as he hands Iris her helmet of water. "You still got your brother and me."

Iris drinks from the helmet. "It's funny," she says, "when those alien Mechs started attacking, for some reason, the first person I thought of was you."

"You were late then, *bonita*," Leo says, "because you were on my mind when I woke up first thing this morning."

Iris smiles as she looks into Leo's blue eyes. "We should get out of this rain," she says, handing Leo her helmet of water.

"Yeah. You headed up with your brother?" Leo asks before drinking from the helmet.

"I'd rather sleep with you," she says.

Leo coughs as he chokes on the helmet water.

"I mean, we can both sleep in M-Zero's cockpit. If

that's okay?" Iris clarifies.

"Sure," Leo says, dumbfounded.

Leo assists Iris into the ivory Mech and sits in the pilot's seat to take off his shoes. With her backside to Leo, Iris slides out of her flight suit revealing her purple jersey and little, grey spandex shorts. She turns to find Leo gawking at her the same way he had when he first saw her in the bar back in Tijuana.

"What?" Iris asks with a smile.

"It's just that I saw someone else wearing those exact same shorts earlier today," Leo responds. "They look a lot better on you."

"Do they now?" Iris asks as she flirtatiously walks toward Leo. She plays with his long wavy dark hair near the now closed aperture in the back of his head and stares at him intensely.

"What are you doing?" Leo asks.

"Trying to hear what you're thinking," she says, still staring.

"I haven't heard any thoughts since you guys unplugged me but you don't need telepathy to know what I'm thinking about right now."

Iris playfully smacks his chest.

"What?" Leo laughs.

"The telepathy must only work while you're plugged into M-Zero," Iris says as she curls up in Leo's lap, tucking her head under his chin.

"This I could get used to," he says as Iris suddenly begins to snore.

"Worse than Santana." Leo laughs again. His face

turns somber as he thinks about his friend. "I'll come back for you, *Tío*."

Leo yawns before joining Iris in falling asleep.

CHAPTER FOURTEEN

"Leo! Leo! Leo!" Wearing a white bikini top, the curvaceous Iris leans over Leo as sunrays kiss her supple brown skin.

"Another dream," Leo thinks out loud.

"I seem too good to be true?" Iris asks playfully.

Realizing he isn't dreaming, Leo stands from M-Zero's pilot's seat stretching and cracking his joints. "We are not sleeping like that again," he says, rubbing a crick in his neck.

"A little ocean therapy at the beach can help with that crick," Iris suggests. Other than her white bikini, she wears her flight suit with the top unzipped and hanging from her waist.

"Sounds good to me." Leo grins before noticing 332's empty cockpit. "Where's Michael?"

"He was using my cell phone to try and contact for help but couldn't get a signal. He said he was going to head for higher ground and see if he could get better reception," Iris explains.

"We'll catch him when we get back then."

Leo and Iris walk a ways through the lush tropical forest before finally arriving to the picturesque Hawaiian beach. Sunlight sparkles off the crystal blue ocean as tranquil waves caress the majestic white sands.

"Wow," Iris says in awe. Walking toward the water, she slides out of her flight suit before entering the tranquil sea. Leo beholds the beauty in her white bikini as she glides out into the water and gracefully dives in. Stripping down to his boxers, Leo swims after her. Iris splashes Leo and the two laugh as they playfully wrestle in the chest-high water. Holding her from behind, Leo notices the letters 'F.T.G.G.' tattooed on the back of her shoulder.

"What's this?" Leo asks, gently running his fingertips across the small tattoo. Iris bites her lip at his touch.

"F.T.G.G. Full throttle Gatling guns?" Leo jokes.

"No." Iris giggles and turns to face Leo. "For the greater good. It was my father's mantra."

Chests pressed, their breathing is heard over serenading seagulls and the soft rippling of the water. Iris and Leo look deeply into each other's eyes, immersed in desire. Yearning eyes close and lips linger before the two kiss passionately.

Two hours pass before Leo and Iris return to the campsite. They emerge from the thick forest laughing, but their laughter is cut short by the sight of a strange man inspecting M-Zero. The man is Asian and looks to be in his fifties. He wears cargo capri pants and a faded red t-shirt with Jimi Hendrix on it as well as an orange metallic wristwatch.

"Hello. I was just admiring this ivory Mech. It's been over twenty years since I've seen it. Did you fly it here?" the man asks, looking at Leo. The man has a genuine and friendly face.

"Yeah," Leo responds, puzzled, as Iris picks her shirt up off M-Zero's foot.

"You look familiar," she says, slipping the purple Sparks jersey over her head. "Who are you?"

"My name is Hiro Totaro," the man says, extending his hand to Leo.

"Hiro?" Leo says curiously as he shakes the man's hand. "I'm Leo."

"And you are?" Hiro asks Iris, extending his hand to her.

"Not friendly to Axis!" Michael answers, emerging from the dense forest with his suppressed pistol pointed at the back of Hiro's head.

"No need for weapons," Hiro says calmly as he raises his hands in the air. "I am unarmed."

"That's funny coming from you, Hiro Totaro. I've seen your name in intel reports. You're the Axis' weapons manufacturer," Michael says, patting down Hiro.

"I don't manufacture Axis weapons. That's the Russians. I manufacture Mechs," Hiro responds.

"And your Mechs have killed a lot of my fellow soldiers."

"My Mechs have not killed anyone. The soldiers

that fly them do."

"I know where I've seen you before," Iris says, recollecting. "In an old photo with my father...you were smiling and leaning on his shoulder with your elbow."

"Who is your father?" Hiro asks, unfazed, as Michael steps in front of him with the pistol still pointed at his head.

"Dr. Cyrus King," Iris responds.

"Yes, I knew your father," Hiro tells her. "I was born and raised in Oakland, California. I had just graduated from college and was working as a robotic prosthetics engineer at a hospital in San Diego when I first met Dr. King. Your father was impressed with my work and convinced the Secnav to offer me a higher-paying government job in Roswell."

"The Secnav is our mother," Iris tells Hiro as she gestures to her brother.

"You must be Michael then," Hiro says, looking at the 'King' nametag on Michael's flight suit. "Your father always bragged about you."

Curious, Michael lowers his pistol.

"Leo and Michael." Hiro chuckles before turning to the girl in the purple jersey. "And you must be Donatello? Where's the fourth ninja turtle?" Hiro laughs alone.

"My name is Iris," she says, not amused.

"Tough crowd." Hiro gives up the joke. "But it's still a pleasure to meet you all."

"You worked on the M-Zero Project then?" Leo asks.

"With this extraterrestrial Mech?" Hiro responds, gesturing up to the ivory Mech gallantly posed behind Leo. "I did, though not directly. I had to rely on X-ray scans of M-Zero's inner-workings and duplicated them as best I could to create the Trapper Mechs."

"Our father created the M-1 Trappers," Michael tells him.

"Dr. Cyrus King was a brilliant man, a talented neurosurgeon and engineer," Hiro responds. "But he did not create the Trapper Mechs. The Totaro Type 2 Tora is the successor of the Totaro Type 1 Trapper. Your mother changed the name to M-1 Trapper and credited its creation to her late husband."

"So what was our father's hand in the M-Zero Project?" Iris asks.

"The M-Zero Project was located in a subterranean U.S. government facility in Roswell. The facility was split into two departments. I headed the engineering department and Cyrus headed the science department. The scientists had full access to the engineering department but we engineers were not permitted to enter the science department, which contained the M-Zero," Hiro explains as he walks over to where the campfire was and sits down in the grass. Leo, Michael, and Iris follow Hiro and do the same.

"One night, twenty-six years ago," Hiro continues, "I was working late at the facility. All of the other engineers had already left for the day. As I completed the assembly on a new Trapper Mech, I heard screaming and crashing coming from the science department. As I moved toward the commotion, I smelled smoke and saw blue light coming from behind the locked doors of the science department. The doors suddenly flung open and a powerful suction swept me off my feet. I quickly pulled out my cherry-handled switchblade and plunged it into the wall. The entire department was engulfed in flames. Hanging horizontally, I looked back and saw the M-Zero Mech for the first time. The ivory Mech was flailing wildly with the blue beam of light emanating from its chest. The beam was sucking in scientists and disintegrating them like a bug zapper. Sitting in the open cockpit of the M-Zero's head, directly behind me, I saw a child violently convulsing and screaming in pain with a metal rod impaled in the back of his head. It was you, Leo."

Grasping, Leo pulls out the cherry-handled switchblade and rubs his thumb across the 'HT' carved into its handle. "Hiro Totaro," he says, "it was you that Santana first found me with when I was a kid. You're the samurai!" Leo says excitedly, rolling up his right sleeve and ripping the bandage from his shoulder. Leo's excitement is quickly shot down as he finds the bullet graze has scarred his prized samurai tattoo unrecognizable. "Fuck. Canuck," Leo says through gritting teeth.

"May I?" Hiro asks Leo, gesturing for his cherry-handled switchblade.

Leo looks at Michael who is still holding the suppressed pistol. "I guess you ain't winning no gunfight with a switchblade," he says.

"I wouldn't be too sure about that," Hiro replies.

"Whatever," Leo says before reluctantly returning the knife to Hiro. "I know it's yours but just be careful with it, alright?"

"So, like I said, young Leo was sitting in the M-Zero's open cockpit convulsing in pain with a metal rod impaled in the back of his head. Quickly figuring you were powering the M-Zero, I used this cherry-handled switchblade to climb back toward you. Repeatedly plunging the knife into the wall with one hand, I used my other hand to balance myself along the wall. The nearer I got, the stronger the blue beam pulled me. Once I got close enough to you, I strained to grip the switchblade as I reached for the metal rod and unplugged it from your head. The blue beam instantly cut off and everything dropped to the floor. I saw nothing but dead bodies cooking in the fire. I got up and ran to the cockpit where you were lying unconscious, and I saw the metal aperture in the back of your head spiral close like a camera shutter. Seeing you, an innocent child being experimented on by the U.S. government, reminded me of my people, the Japanese. They were also innocent victims, mercilessly killed by the U.S. government's counterattack against enemy-occupied Japan.

"Infuriated, I picked you up and raced back to the Trapper I was working on in the engineering department. I loaded you into the Trapper, used this switchblade to cut the GPS tracker wire beneath the seat, and flew it straight through the ceiling. Fed up and frustrated, I fled the country foolishly intent on flying straight to Japan to save my people with you still in the back seat. But the fuel light came on just before I made it to the Pacific. In my rage, I had forgotten that the Trapper had never been fully fueled. Wanting to avoid the U.S., I rerouted and landed in Tijuana, Mexico to refuel. I got into a swordfight with the Tijuana Cartel, which actually led to a fortuitous meeting with a man named Santana. Santana helped me get to Japan."

"Santana and the cartel raised me like family," Leo says.

"Santana said you would be cared for. I'm glad to hear he kept his word. I trusted that he would," Hiro says with a smile. "Where is he now?"

"Imprisoned under our mother," Michael says.

"I plan on freeing him," Leo says.

"After we rectify bigger issues," Iris adds.

"Interesting," Hiro says, rubbing his chin.

"So how did he help you get to Japan?" Leo asks.

"After I was captured by the cartel, Santana had the opportunity to kill me. But he didn't. Instead, he traded me his less-conspicuous and fully-fueled long-range jet for my empty Trapper Mech."

"That must have been the same Trapper I confiscated from his mansion two days ago," Michael adds.

"He still had it?" Hiro says with a smile.

"Yeah, and it was a smoother ride than the M-2 Stalker."

"Of course. The M-2 Stalker is a cheap, overweight,

gun-toting knockoff of my original design," Hiro declares. "But I digress. Santana's less conspicuous long-range jet allowed me to fly deep into Axis-controlled airspace. I was eventually shot down by the Axis over China's east coast. Luckily, I was able to belly-land the jet and walked away with only cuts and bruises before allowing myself to get captured and imprisoned by the Axis.

"During my imprisonment, I overheard rumors that Paramount Leader Chao was desperate to get Mechs for the Axis. Weeks passed before I finally convinced the Axis soldiers to let me meet with the Paramount Leader. After proving to Chao that I had built the Mechs, we struck a deal. I agreed to produce continuously-improved Mechs for the Axis as long as my people were protected and fully cared for. A reasonable man, Chao agreed to my terms with one condition. He said the Japanese had to assist me in manufacturing Mechs for the Axis. Chao had a state-of-the-art, fully-equipped factory constructed in Japan and in less than one year, we had produced a formidable fleet of Totaro Type 2 Toras. But the true achievement is that with Chao's and my opposing views, we have come to mutually respect each other, much like Santana and I did. Chao has kept his word, continuing to protect and fully care for my people as long as I have continuously produced improved Mechs for him.

"That's what brought me to Hawaii. I've been on this island making modifications to my improved Toras with new advanced radar jammers. The Axis test pilots were running field tests just three days ago."

"Were you running these field tests with three Toras off the coast of San Diego?" Iris asks.

"I was."

"You nearly got my wingman killed!" Iris yells angrily, standing to her feet.

"El Gato?" Michael asks his sister as he and Leo stand beside her.

"Yes! His Toras attacked us three days ago!"

"Not that it matters, but I understood that you went after them first," Hiro says.

"I'm tired of listening to this disloyalist," Michael says, pointing his suppressed pistol at Hiro again.

"Disloyalist?" Hiro says objectively. "I'm no disloyalist, Michael. I had to choose between loyalty to my country that had committed atrocities of mercilessly killing innocent Japanese and condoning cruel child experimentation, or loyalty to my people who were getting slaughtered from both sides by the Axis and U.N. forces! I chose to save my people! Nobody else cared to." Hiro looks down at the ground somberly. "America, with all its faults, is still the greatest country in the world. But when the greatest country in the world failed me, I had to make a hard decision. And I do not regret my decision. I create Mechs but I did not create this war. I don't believe in it. But I will survive it. And I will do everything in my power to help the helpless survive it as well. I know you all can understand that, with the helpless civilians of San Diego currently under alien attack."

"How do you know about that?" Leo asks.

"With U.N. forces fully engaged with the attack, my Toras equipped with the advanced radar jammers were able to get close enough to the coast of San Diego to record footage of the mountain-sized ivory Mammoth as well as the creatures and corroded Mechs that continue to exit from it. Since the corroded Mechs share similar features with M-Zero, I assume they share its extraterrestrial origins as well."

"You're right but you know what they say when you assume. You make an ass of yourself," Leo says.

"You make an ass out of you and me." Hiro corrects.

"Hey, you're the one who assumed coming here would be a good idea. Now you've given two pissed off U.N. soldiers every reason to kill you. Yeah, I'd say you've pretty much just made an ass out of yourself, *amigo*." Leo jokes.

"Glad to know I'm not the only one with a sense of humor." Hiro chuckles. "Here's something else funny. When I was studying the footage yesterday, two Mechs popped up on radar flying west from San Diego. I thought they were my two missing Toras from three days ago and that their jammers had failed. But it turned out to be you all. By the way, I assume you shot down the two Toras, Iris?"

"You're damn right I did," Iris says with an attitude.

"When we finally got a visual on your Mechs, the Axis soldiers wanted to shoot you down too but I ordered them not to because I suspected that this was M-Zero. Being a friend of the Paramount Leader comes with a bit of pull," Hiro says jokingly. "Now that I have confirmed that this is indeed M-Zero, we can adjourn this pow-wow."

Hiro lets out a familiar short series of high-pitched whistles and a dozen red Axis soldiers emerge from the dense forest with rifles pointed at Leo, Michael, and Iris.

"Drop the gun!" a red soldier barks at Michael. Michael grips the pistol tighter and the soldiers aim to kill.

"Hold your fire!" Hiro orders. "Everyone relax. Nobody is going to shoot anybody. Michael, please give me the gun," he pleads, approaching Michael. "I didn't let them shoot you down yesterday. I'm not going to let them shoot you now. You have my word."

With no viable options, Michael reluctantly hands Hiro the gun.

"Thank you. You have nothing to worry about. I promise," Hiro reassures him before speaking into his orange metallic wristwatch. "Yin, we're ready for pickup."

Just then, an incredibly large cargo jet appears overhead. Its six loud jet engine nozzles rotate downward, blowing heavy heat. Everyone but Leo guards their faces as the dark grey megaship lands vertically in between M-Zero and Stalker 332.

"It's the size of a football field," Iris says.

"It's a Russian-made Antonov cargo jet," Michael responds.

"Yes, but I modified it," Hiro replies. "It's a VTOL with armor-plating and overall better performance. A Totaro-customized Antonov."

"The Totanov," Leo adds.

"The Totanov. I like that." Hiro chuckles before ordering the Axis soldiers, "Carefully take our guests aboard and load up their two Mechs."

The Axis soldiers remove Leo, Michael, and Iris' communication devices and prepare to handcuff them before Hiro stops them. "That won't be necessary," he says.

Walking into the back of the Totanov, the three of them follow Hiro up the loading ramp and into the large cargo bay when, suddenly, a large robotic tiger jolts from a side stairway and heavily slams down right in front of them. Iris screams as Hiro walks up and pets the robot tiger.

"This is Yin, my droid," Hiro introduces. "I don't go anywhere without her. She's the yin to my yang. She can plug into the ship and pilot it."

With her tail straight up, Yin gently rubs against Iris and sniffs her. The tiger droid looks up at Iris with big, digital, anime eyes.

"*Anata wa umi no soyokaze no yōna nioi,*" Yin says in a perky Japanese female voice.

"Wow, she can speak," Iris says, pleasantly surprised. "What did she say?"

"She said you smell like ocean breeze," Hiro responds with a smile.

"Bad ass," Leo says, watching as the large tiger

droid walks up the wall and across the ceiling of the cargo bay with her magnetic paws. Yin's metal chassis is orange with black accessory components. Michael watches as the Axis soldiers finish loading M-Zero and Stalker 332 into the cargo bay. The red soldiers buckle into the fold-down seats that line the cargo bay walls.

"Come on up. I'll give you the grand tour." Hiro waves to Leo, Michael, and Iris as Yin runs up the stairs behind him. They ascend the stairway into the galley of the ship's upper deck. Aft of the galley is the lounge, which has a sectional couch, some chairs, table, and a television. Aft of the lounge are crew and guest quarters, all of which have bunk beds. Aft of that is laundry and a lavatory with the med bay in the back. Forward of the galley is Hiro's quarters. It has a bed, workbench, lavatory, and swords hanging on the wall. Forward of Hiro's quarters is the flight deck, which has a docking station for Yin as well as seating for a crew of six.

"Time to go, Yin," Hiro says as the tiger droid follows him into the flight deck.

"*Doko iku no*?" Yin asks.

"We're going home, Yin," Hiro answers, climbing into the captain's seat. Michael buckles into the other pilot's seat as Leo and Iris sit in the back with Yin.

As the cargo bay door closes in the back, the Totanov's engines fire up. The massive jet steadily ascends before shooting off like a rocket away from the tropical island.

CHAPTER FIFTEEN

Hours later and still aboard the Totanov, Iris snores loudly from the seat behind Hiro. Leo leans forward toward Michael.

"Has she always snored like this?" Leo asks his friend.

"No," Michael responds. "She used to be loud."

Deploying a small chainsaw from her droid frame, Yin revs it, mocking Iris, and the group bursts into laughter.

"What! Where are we?" Iris yells, awaken by the noise.

"Tokyo, Japan," Hiro answers through his chuckling.

The group looks out the window upon the populous metropolis as the Totanov descends onto the rooftop helipad of a rather ordinary building situated right next to Tokyo Bay.

"Is *this* where you build Mechs?" Leo asks unimpressed.

"Yes, this is where I do all my work," Hiro says proudly.

"Thought it would have been bigger, maybe a little nicer," Leo responds.

Hiro laughs. "You can't judge a book by its cover."

The Totanov trembles as the helipad begins to move. It descends into the building and several stories below ground as doors close over the rooftop opening above. High-tech equipment and hundreds of lively Japanese workers buzz about the expansive and brightly-lit factory as the helipad elevator settles in the midst of it all. The hundred-acre, state-of-the-art, subterranean factory is lined with large windows that look out at the aquatic life living within the depths of Tokyo Bay.

Leo, Michael, and Iris look in wonder as Hiro is distracted by a big, gaudy red helicopter parked next to the helipad elevator.

"He's here," Hiro says before darting out the cockpit. The rest of the group exchange puzzled glances.

Exiting out the back of the Totanov's already opened cargo bay, Hiro finds the dozen Axis soldiers standing at attention in two straight lines facing each other.

"Paramount Leader on deck!" one red soldier announces as the dozen all salute in flawless formation.

"Good to see you, my friend!" Paramount Leader Chao greets with open arms as he walks between the two lines of soldiers toward Hiro. The bald Chinese man is in his sixties and has a salt-and-pepper horseshoe mustache. He wears a black suit with a red Axis triangle pin in his lapel.

"Didn't we just have a surprise inspection?" Hiro asks, embracing Chao.

"I just flew in for a special visit. My men contacted me from Hawaii and informed me that you found something intriguing?" Chao alludes.

"Do you remember back when we first met?" Hiro asks. "I told you about the American government experimenting on a boy and how they surgically connected his brain to a technologically-advanced extraterrestrial Mech."

"Vaguely. I'm not a fan of science-fiction," Chao says, less than intrigued.

"It's not fiction. I brought them both back with me," Hiro says as Leo, Michael, and Iris exit the ship with Yin. "This is Leo. He is that boy," Hiro introduces to Chao, "and he is the only human that can pilot the extraterrestrial M-Zero Mech."

"And how is he supposed to help me?" Chao asks condescendingly.

"Who said I was going to help you?" Leo responds brazenly.

"You must," Hiro says.

"For what?" Leo asks.

"To save humanity," Hiro responds before turning to his pet tiger droid. "Yin, please play the footage of the San Diego invasion."

As Yin walks to Hiro, the top of her head flips open, revealing a video display.

"In this obtained footage, I noticed something interesting," Hiro says, addressing everyone. "One of the grey aliens faced a mild civilian and the civilian's aggressive pet dog. The Grey completely bypassed the clearly threatening, attacking dog to kill the fleeing, non-threatening civilian. I saw several examples of this same type of event reoccurring throughout the footage. I'm not sure what the Greys' motives are but their only objective seems to be killing humans."

"Good!" Chao interrupts. "Let the Americans suffer under these Greys like the rest of the world suffers under the Americans. The enemy of my enemy is my friend."

"I am your friend, Chao. And as your friend, I am asking you to put aside your animosity toward the Americans and do not leave the Greys unchecked," Hiro pleads. "If my assumption is correct and the Greys' objective is to kill humans, why would they differentiate between U.N. forces and Axis? I don't know exactly how many Greys there are but they haven't decreased their rate of entry from the ivory Mammoth since they got here. The Mammoth appears to be creating a portal from which the corroded Mechs are travelling through. If they continue migrating here and attacking at their current rate, all of humanity will be extinct in roughly seven years. But I believe Leo and the M-Zero may be the key to saving the world."

Chao bursts into laughter. "I'm all for using Leo

and the M-Zero to build improved Axis Mechs. But the stuff about space robots, alien invasions, magic portals, and saving the world is a bit much. You have got to lay off the comic books, my friend! The Greys are probably the result of another one of the Americans' sick experiments come back to bite them in the ass! Americans pretend to be so moralistic but they are unnecessarily aggressive and will do anything for greed. They chose war over paying their debts and even commit atrocities against their own people to build machines for war. Regardless of whatever is wreaking havoc on the Americans, it's about time they got a taste of their own medicine. For once, let America feel what it's like to be bullied by a superior power."

"That's the last time you slander my country!" Michael threatens as Iris stands beside him.

Chao peers at the American soldier with a sharp evil eye. "Who are these other two you've brought with you?" Chao asks Hiro.

"They're siblings, Michael and Iris," Hiro answers.

"They're U.N. forces. Are they part of this M-Zero Project?" Chao asks.

"Well, no."

"Men!" Chao orders the dozen Axis soldiers. "Bring these two U.N. soldiers with us. I'm going to publically execute them to send a message to the Americans."

"Like hell you are!" Leo yells, charging for Chao. Axis soldiers immediately jump on Leo. It takes three of them to finally pin him down. The rest of the Axis soldiers fight to handcuff Michael and Iris. The Japanese workers in the factory stop and stare at the rumpus as Yin growls at Chao.

"Did you program it to do that?" Chao asks, intimidated by the tiger.

"No, Yin is A.I. She has a mind of her own," Hiro answers.

"She should mind some manners!" Chao scoffs.

"I do hope you are not talking about me, darling!" Russian President Anna Petrov announces as she exits Chao's red helicopter. The fighting immediately stops as the blonde president approaches them. Wearing a red skirt suit, Anna is in her fifties and wears the same Axis pin in her lapel as Chao.

"As the king of Asia, I would never speak of Asia's queen in such a way," Chao says charmingly. "I was referring to Hiro's kooky contraption here."

"*Hitori wa hitori o shitte iru no ni kakaru*," Yin mocks Chao.

Hiro snickers.

"What did it say?" Chao demands.

"She said, 'Takes one, to know one' and I like Hiro's kooky contraptions," Anna interrupts as she pets Yin on the head. "Speaking of which, I love what you've done with the old Antonov," Anna compliments Hiro.

"Thank you for donating it to me, Miss President," Hiro responds.

"Don't mention it, darling. Russia is focused on manufacturing weapons for the Axis. We had no use for this old thing." Anna shrugs before looking at a restrained, angry, and exhausted Leo, Michael, and Iris.

"So what is going on here?" she asks.

"These two disrespectful Americans are U.N. forces," Chao explains, pointing at Michael and Iris. "I'm flying them back to China to have them publically executed!"

"And who is this one?" Anna asks, looking at Leo who is still struggling against the three red soldiers.

"Another disrespectful American. He's friends with these two!" Chao says.

"I'm not American. I'm from Mexico, dumbass!" Leo responds.

"You see what I'm talking about?" Chao says to Anna. "They're animals!"

"So why are you not killing him too?"

"Because Hiro needs him to build us improved Mechs," Chao explains.

"If this one is friends with these two, and Hiro needs this one to build us improved Mechs, wouldn't killing this one's friends demotivate him to help us?" Anna asks.

Chao stubbornly contemplates.

"And wouldn't killing these two publically only motivate U.N. forces against us?" she adds.

"So what would you have me do with them?" Chao asks adversely.

"Release them into my care," Hiro answers.

Chao contemplates further before coming to terms. "Alright," he says, "I will release them into your care. But if they cause any problems, Hiro, I will hold you personally responsible."

"Of course, I take full responsibility for them," Hiro says with a smile.

"I'm glad you boys can come to an agreement." Anna smiles. "Now let's leave Mister Hiro to his business so he can produce more of those kooky contraptions that are the only reason we are still in this war. Meanwhile, you and I can take care of some business of our own," Anna says to Chao seductively.

Chao chuckles. "That sounds good to me, my dear."

"Nice seeing you again, Hiro," Anna says, escorting Chao away.

"You as well, Miss President," Hiro responds.

"Men!" Anna says, ordering the Axis soldiers to follow as she walks Chao back onboard his helicopter.

"Quickly, clear the Totanov from the elevator!" Hiro orders the Japanese workers.

Scrambling, the workers tow the Totanov off of the helipad elevator as Chao's helicopter is towed on.

"She is something," Leo says to Hiro as the big, gaudy red helicopter exits the factory.

"I know," Hiro replies before addressing the crowd of Japanese workers. "Good work everyone! Now, I have two Mechs onboard! Please, carefully unload them and place them in Zone Eight. I'd like the whole R&D Team on the ivory Mech, right away. It's our top priority!"

Immediately, the lively Japanese workers scramble to unload M-Zero and Stalker 332 as Hiro guides Leo, Michael, and Iris to a golf cart.

"I apologize for Chao," Hiro says before sitting in the driver's seat of the cart. "He can be intense. But now that he's left, we can rest easy. Let me show you to the living quarters."

"Cut the friendly act, Hiro," Michael interrupts. "You only brought us here with intentions that we would help you build Mechs for Chao. No one has forgotten how your so-called reasonable buddy nuked Hawaii and tried to nuke California. The Axis is not concerned with helping against the Greys' invasion so we're not concerned with helping you with M-Zero. The fact is we're prisoners, so just go ahead and show us where you intend to keep us."

"I am building Mechs for Chao but my intentions have always only been to help people," Hiro explains. "I built Trappers for your mother to defend people against nuclear attack and I build Toras for Chao in order to protect my people. And you should know that Chao never launched any nuclear weapons. The media said he did but North Korea acted alone in nuking Hawaii, as did the Jihadi in launching nukes from Japan at California. Chao did demand full payment of the U.S. trillion-dollar debt owed to China but it was only so he could provide for his country. He's trying to protect his people like I am. I do not agree with his bad methods but in his good intentions, I find Chao admirable. Just as I find you all admirable. My friendliness is not an act and you are not prisoners. You're guests, free to come and go as you please. But if you choose to leave my factory, your safety is out of my hands. And if you choose not to help me with M-Zero, you won't have to concern yourselves with the Axis because the Greys will kill us all while we continue to bicker amongst ourselves."

Everyone stands quiet.

"We've all had a long day," Hiro adds calmly. "Let me show you to your rooms. Take some time to unwind and reconsider helping me. I believe you will agree that uniting favors us all."

Hiro drives Leo, Michael, and Iris in the golf cart to their three separate rooms which are simple yet fully accommodating with the exception of phone or Internet access. Each small room has light mats covering the floor and is decorated with cherrywood furnishings, bamboo plants, traditional Japanese art, and paper lamps. The softly-lit rooms are divided in half by sliding wood-framed paper doors. The front area has a short and square table with floor cushions set on each side as well as a refrigerator and cabinet against the wall. The elevated back area has a bed sitting low to the floor and a dresser. A bathroom and closet line one wall of the back area while a wide window looking into Tokyo Bay lines another.

"Feel free to explore as you please," Hiro says. "Wall intercoms are mounted in each of your rooms and throughout the factory. If you need anything, just press the attendant button on the intercom and someone will assist you."

"Thank you, Hiro," Iris says before entering her room to take a shower.

Leo and Michael also thank Hiro.

"Don't mention it." Hiro smiles as the tiger droid walks up beside him.

Leo and Michael enter their separate rooms as Hiro walks away with Yin.

CHAPTER SIXTEEN

Moonlight shines through Tokyo Bay and into the window of Leo's room. Steam pours into the room as a showered Leo steps out of the bathroom in a hooded bathrobe. Leo falls back on the wide bed and looks up at a painting of a samurai hanging on the wall. In the quiet, the soothing sound of water flows against his window. His eyes grow heavy as they stare at the samurai. Suddenly, Leo hears the faint sound of thwacking and yelling. Curious, he hops into his sandals and exits the room to follow the noise. Leo prowls the endless halls of the subterranean factory. The noise grows louder as he nears its source, leading him into a huge gymnasium. Leo stands in the doorway of the one-acre, cube-shaped gymnasium. In the center of the floor, Hiro yells as he combats two opponents with wooden swords. He and his opponents are dressed in padded uniforms that remind Leo of the samurai painting. Hiro is the only combatant not wearing a barred facemask helmet. Leo watches as Hiro swordfights. Dodging and striking, Hiro effortlessly takes down both opponents.

"Would you like to try?" Hiro yells across the room as he helps one of his downed opponents to their feet.

Just realizing that Hiro is speaking to him, Leo responds, "Who? Me?"

"Yes, you." Hiro laughs. "Don't worry. We'll take it easy first go-around. What do you say?"

"You're the one that should be worried." Leo grins.

"That's the spirit!" Hiro says before turning to the opponent he just helped up. "Can you please help Leo into some gear?"

"Of course, sir," the opponent responds before turning to Leo. "Come with me."

After putting on the padded uniform, Leo steps to the center of the gymnasium floor.

"Catch!" Hiro says, tossing Leo a wooden sword. "It's called a shinai, a bamboo sword used for Kendo. Kendo is the study of the way of the sword. It is a martial arts style that descended from the swordsmanship of the ancient Samurai."

"Looks like a stick to me," Leo responds as Hiro points his shinai at Leo.

"Shall I teach you the way of the sword?" Hiro asks.

Grinning, Leo crosses his shinai with Hiro's. "Let's go."

Hiro shows Leo some basic striking and blocking

techniques.

"I got it," Leo says.

Hiro smiles before suddenly swinging at Leo's head. Quickly, Leo blocks the shinai.

"Very good, Leo."

Without responding, Leo strikes back and is blocked by Hiro. The two engage in a swordfight that quickly grows intense.

"That's it, Leo," Hiro says with a smile in the midst of the fight. "Now what would you do if I struck at you like *this!*" Hiro spins and swings his shinai at Leo's feet. Without hesitation, Leo does a back flip, dodging the attack. Hiro's jaw drops as he watches Leo fly through the air. Leo lands on his feet and yells as he charges at Hiro. Somewhat caught off guard, Hiro pushes away the charging shinai with his hand while simultaneously tripping Leo with his foot. Leo tumbles forward to the ground. He quickly turns over to find the tip of Hiro's shinai greeting his face.

"You have some impressive moves." Hiro pulls back his shinai and extends his hand to Leo. "Where did you learn that?" he asks.

"Watching *lucha libre*," Leo answers as Hiro helps him to his feet. "You got some moves yourself for a guy who doesn't seem like a fighter."

"The purpose of Kendo isn't fighting. It is to learn discipline by practicing the principles of the katana," Hiro responds. "Through strict training, one shapes the mind, body, and soul while learning the principles of courtesy, honor, sincerity, and forever striving to improve oneself. Thus will one be able to promote love, peace, and prosperity among all people. Leo, I have something else I'd like to show you. Wait here." Hiro rushes out a side door of the gymnasium.

As Leo takes off his Kendo gear, a wall of the gymnasium begins to rumble. Leo steps back as the wall slides open, revealing a unique Tora Mech. It is the same color as Hiro's tiger and carries dual black katanas at its sides with no firearms. The lightly-armored Tora's agility is superior to all other man-made Mechs. It raises one of its twenty-foot katanas from its side. Leo looks up defensively as a suspended ceiling light reflects off the mirror-like black blade. Just then, the cockpit opens.

"This is my Totaro Type 2 Tora model 10.0, ToraX for short," Hiro announces from the cockpit. "It's one of a kind."

"I thought you said you didn't make weapons."

"No, I said I didn't make Axis weapons," Hiro responds. "The only weapons I make are swords and Chao finds them primitive. But when mastered, the sword can be superior to a gun."

Distracted by the swanky Mech, Leo comments, "You sure do like orange."

"Actually, my favorite color is green." Hiro kneels ToraX on one knee and lowers its giant hand to Leo. Leo steps into the hand before the Mech walks back behind the gymnasium wall. He sees a sign overhead that reads 'ZONE 8' as ToraX walks past M-Zero and Stalker 332 to Hiro's assortment of Mech-sized swords. Displayed on the wall, Hiro has a European rapier, an African sickle, one Middle Eastern scimitar, a North American cavalry saber, and a South American machete.

"What's that one?" Leo asks, pointing to a sword at the end of the display wall.

"This one?" Hiro asks, grabbing a thirty-foot titanium boomerang with a razor-sharp edge. "This is the returning boomerang blade. I came up with this concept while studying the aboriginal people of Australia. But it's a failed experiment."

"What's wrong with it?" Leo asks.

"There's nothing wrong with the sword. I just haven't built a Mech dexterous enough to effectively use it." Hiro pauses. "Wait a minute. Wait a minute!" he says excitedly. "M-Zero! It's the most agile Mech I've ever seen. Perhaps its dexterity is refined enough to wield the boomerang blade. Leo, care to pilot M-Zero and test my theory?"

"I'm not sure about that, Hiro," Leo responds.

"Why not?"

"Last time I hooked up to M-Zero, it opened the portal for the Greys."

"You opened the portal? I thought the ivory Mammoth had created its own entry portal," Hiro says. "If you opened it, how did you close it?"

"There was a voice. It helped me close the portal and control the Mech."

"A voice?" Hiro asks. "From M-Zero?"

"I think so," Leo replies.

"Interesting," Hiro says, rubbing his chin. "Well, if you controlled it then, I have faith you can control it now. If things go awry, I'll unplug you."

Leo groans. "If your place here gets tore up, don't blame me."

Hiro smiles before the two return to M-Zero and enter its cockpit. Leo grabs the metal neuro-adapter and sits in the pilot's seat.

"What did M-Zero tell you to do to close the portal?" Hiro asks, standing beside Leo.

"Relax," Leo answers.

"Sounds simple enough." Hiro shrugs. "Just do that."

"Thanks," Leo responds sarcastically. He takes a deep breath before holding the neuro-adapter behind his head to open his aperture. "Here goes nothing," Leo says, clenching his jaw and eyes shut before plugging the neuro-adapter into his head. M-Zero illuminates blue as it powers up. Focused and controlled, Leo pops open an eye and looks down at M-Zero's closed chest.

"How do you feel?" Hiro asks.

Leo grins. "Bad ass."

Moments later, M-Zero and ToraX reenter the gymnasium. Rock music blares from the orange Mech's whopping Sony speakers as Hiro wields the boomerang blade.

"What's this song?" Leo asks over the radio headset.

"'Astro Man' by Jimi Hendrix," Hiro says. "You like it?"

"Yeah, mane! I do," Leo responds.

"Good. Here's something else you'll like," Hiro says, raising the boomerang blade. "Now what you want to do, Leo, is fling it hard like this." Hiro hurls the blade. The whirling boomerang flies a distance but hits the ground, unable to fully return to ToraX.

"You see what I mean?" he says. "Outside of ToraX, I am skilled at throwing a regular boomerang, and this Mech-sized boomerang is built to perfect scale and balance. But even my most dexterous Mech cannot wield the boomerang blade."

M-Zero walks over to the far end of the gymnasium and picks up the boomerang blade. "So just fling it like this?" Leo asks as he effortlessly launches the blade. The spinning sword accidentally slices off one of the suspended lights above Hiro's Mech. ToraX jumps out of the way as the light crashes into the ground just in time to witness the boomerang blade loop around and whiz back into M-Zero's grip.

"My fault!" Leo calls to Hiro. "You okay over there?"

"Amazing," Hiro says with a smile before getting ToraX on its feet and walking to Leo. "Looks good on you." Hiro beholds M-Zero with the boomerang blade. "You can keep it as a reward for returning my cherrywood switchblade to me. With a little more training you may very well master the boomerang blade."

"Thought I already had," Leo says as he launches the boomerang blade again.

PART III: EXILE

CHAPTER SEVENTEEN

Summer burns out.

Autumn falls.

Winter takes over.

In half a year, fifty million Greys have invaded Earth and killed half a billion humans.

Moving east, the extraterrestrials have methodically murdered nearly every human from the American Pacific coast to the center of the Americas. They attack all day and retreat back into the Pacific Ocean with their corroded Mechs each night. U.N. forces launched a covert night-ops nuclear strike on the Greys but learned the extraterrestrials never fully sleep. The ever-alert Greys quickly diverted the nukes back on the humans and destroyed California. Every continent but Asia has joined the U.N. forces in the desperate fight to hold the frontline against the Greys along the 104 degree west longitude.

As mankind is falling, morning snow falls in Tokyo, Japan. Yin's metal tiger paws click on the hard floor as she prowls the halls of Hiro's subterranean factory. Turning a doorknob with her mouth, Yin nudges the door open and stealthily crawls across the floor toward a bed. Quietly and cautiously, she raises her head to the foot of the bed before suddenly letting out a loud and terrifying roar.

"Holy shit!" Leo and Iris scream in terror as they spring awake from the bed.

Yin immediately rolls back on the floor, giggling at the naked couple.

"*Bibiri*! *Bibiri*!" Yin laughs.

"Who you calling scaredy cats?" Iris asks, also laughing.

Leo rubs the back of his buzz-cut head as he stretches. Without his long wavy dark hair, the aperture in the back of his head is as exposed as Iris' breasts. "We'll see who the scaredy cat is when I push you in some water," Leo threatens.

With big, innocent, digital eyes, Yin folds down her ears and tucks her tail.

"Aw, you scared her, Leo," Iris says, sympathetically petting Yin's head. The video display on top of the tiger droid's head suddenly pops open.

"Good morning!" Hiro says from the display. Iris quickly snatches the sheet over her nude body.

"Oh! I'm so sorry, Iris. Pardon me," Hiro quickly apologizes, covering his eyes as Leo laughs.

"Morning, Hiro. You ready to run another test?" Leo asks.

"I am," Hiro responds with his hands still covering his eyes. "Can you meet me outside?"

"We'll be there," Leo says before closing the top of Yin's head. "Get out of here, troublemaker!" Leo tells Yin after petting her. The tiger bounces out of the room and Leo locks the door.

"Let's ask Michael if he wants to go too," Iris says as she bounces to the shower.

"You already know what he's going to say. He's barely left his room since we got here."

"He's deeply depressed," Iris says. "Which is why we shouldn't leave him alone."

"I'm about to get deep in something," Leo says, joining her in the shower.

"I'm being serious," Iris tells him. "I'm worried about my brother's mental stability."

"You don't give him enough credit. Michael's the most stable guy I know." Leo says. "But if you really want to help him, we can right after you help me."

"Help you with what?" Iris asks before feeling something hard on her backside. "Oh," she says with a big smile, "I might have something for that."

An hour passes. After getting dressed in their winter wear, Leo and Iris knock on Michael's door.

"It's Leo and your sister!" Leo calls through the door.

The door to the dimly-lit room opens and Leo and

Iris enter. With a long, grungy beard and dingy tank top, Michael stands in the center of the trashed room.

"*Hermano*! You look terrible," Leo says.

"Thanks," Michael sarcastically responds in a dull tone.

"We're going outside," Iris says to her brother. "You should come with us. Get some fresh air."

"I'm tired."

"From what? Sleeping?" Leo remarks. "Look, I'm doing some underwater test runs with M-Zero. I need you to watch my back in case things go south."

Michael takes his time before answering.

"Alright," he finally agrees.

Just outside the factory on the snowy shore, Leo walks M-Zero to the edge of the frozen-over Tokyo Bay as Michael and Iris watch from the foot of ToraX. A winch in the orange Mech's forearm has a long extending steel cable that is tethered around M-Zero's waist. Inside ToraX's cockpit, Hiro sits in the pilot's seat with Yin in the docking station behind him.

"Why is Leo trying to short circuit his Mech in the water?" Michael asks, putting his hands in his jacket pockets. Michael's brown leather flight jacket has a white wool collar and large wool-trimmed hood.

"Hiro thinks the Greys' Mechs constantly retreat to the ocean to refuel," Iris tells him. "He believes the Greys built M-Zero and, like the Greys' Mechs, M-Zero is a submersible that runs off water, or the hydrogen in the water. Hiro wants to test to see if M-Zero's power boosts in the water."

"Alright, Leo," Hiro says via telecom, "now just submerge into the water nice and slow. I'll pull you up in case—" Before Hiro can finish, M-Zero heedlessly jumps through the ice into the bay.

The ivory Mech's blue lights glow as it descends into the watery depths. The longer it's in the water, the brighter M-Zero's lights illuminate. Leo can feel M-Zero getting stronger. He has noticed the more time he spends connected to M-Zero, the stronger his mental bond with the Mech has become.

Eybriel, the deep voice suddenly calls from M-Zero.

"M-Zero?" Leo asks.

"Leo, how are you doing down there?" Iris asks.

"Good! Hiro was right. M-Zero is powering up," he responds before a shark-like creature suddenly swims in front of him.

"There's a Grey down here!" Leo communicates to his friends. He swats at the alien but it dodges and darts off before Hiro pulls M-Zero out of the frozen bay and back onto the shore. Hearts beat in the quiet as all eyes gaze at the breach in the ice. Suddenly, the Grey jumps out of the icy water and gracefully flips in the air before landing in the snow barefoot. With the body of a goddess, the attractive six-foot-tall Grey alien sports a grey spandex wetsuit with an ivory-colored utility harness strapped around her waist, beneath her butt, over her shoulders, and across breasts. On her ovoid head is a regally streamlined ivory helmet. Michael gawks in awe as Iris, ToraX, and M-Zero stand defensively.

"Do not be afraid," the Grey announces in a maidenly voice. "My name is Eybriel. I mean you no harm."

"Then what do you mean by being here?" Hiro asks through ToraX's whopping Sony speakers.

"I was following my father's voice," Eybriel says, pointing to M-Zero.

Hiro curiously looks at M-Zero as Leo opens its cockpit.

"M-Zero is your father?" Leo asks.

"No, my father is Eyseya, the king of Ede. He built this ivory transport. His soul still dwells within it."

"So the voice I've been talking to all this time is your dead dad's ghost?" Leo asks.

"Yes. My father and our kind can communicate telepathically. You must have also gained the ability through mental bonding," Eybriel says, shivering.

Removing his flight jacket, Michael approaches the Grey and puts his jacket around her. "It's nice to meet you, Eybriel," he greets her with a charming smile.

Eybriel touches his hand. "Thank you, Michael," she replies, smiling.

"How do you know my name?"

"My people can learn from a being through touch."

"And what have you learned about me?"

She smiles again. "That I can trust you."

"We should continue this inside," Hiro interrupts as he opens a hangar door to the factory.

With his hand on the back of Eybriel's waist,

Michael escorts her onto the helipad elevator inside as M-Zero picks up Iris and follows them.

"Michael, what animal is this?" Eybriel asks, pulling the wool-trimmed hood over her face.

"The jacket? It's made from a cow and a sheep."

"Did you eat the cow and sheep?"

"No." Michael laughs. "Why do you ask?"

"On Ede, all beings that live on land are carnivores and all beings that live at sea, such as my people, are vegetarians."

"Ede. Is that where you're from?" Michael asks.

"Yes," she replies. "It's a planet covered almost entirely in water."

"Here on Earth, some aquatic animals eat meat and some land animals don't," Michael explains. "I eat vegetables and meat."

"I know humans are omnivores. I've learned much of Earth and your kind," Eybriel says.

"How is that?" Michael asks.

"King of Earth taught me."

"Who is the king of Earth?" Michael asks, curiously amused.

"Your father, Cyrus," Eybriel says before Hiro closes the hangar door from inside.

ToraX hides Eybriel and Michael in its hands as it follows M-Zero to the factory's living quarters. Exiting the Mechs, Eybriel is hidden under the flight jacket and within the group as they escort her inside one of the unoccupied bedrooms. Yin stands guard in front of the closed room as Hiro, Leo, Iris, and Michael sit with Eybriel on the floor at the short and square table.

"Eybriel says she learned about Earth from our father," Michael announces.

"Our father died twenty-seven years ago. How could you know him?" Iris asks Eybriel.

"King is not dead. He lives on my home planet, Ede, subjugating my people. The Edens are being mentally controlled and King is responsible for their attacking Earth," Eybriel says to the room of skeptics.

"That doesn't make any sense," Iris objects. "Why would my father attack his own planet?"

"I don't know. He said it was for the greater good."

"For the greater good?" Iris touches the tattoo on the back of her shoulder.

At the back of her waist, Eybriel reaches into a large pouch on her harness. "I took this off your father," she says, pulling out a thick black notebook marked 'M-Zero' and handing it to Iris. "Perhaps this will better answer your questions."

Instantly recognizing the black book from her father's photo, Iris opens it to the first page which reads, 'The Log of Dr. Cyrus King.' Overwhelmed, her eye begins to water.

"Are you okay?" Michael asks his sister.

"I'll be fine," Iris responds. "I just need some time alone." She picks up her father's logbook and exits to the privacy of her own room.

"We should get M-Zero and ToraX back to Zone Eight," Hiro says to Leo.

"What about the Grey?" Leo asks.

"Michael, do you mind watching our guest?" Hiro asks.

"No problem," Michael responds.

Leo, Hiro, and Yin get back in their Mechs, leaving Michael and Eybriel alone.

"Do you believe me, Michael?" Eybriel asks.

"To be honest, I'm not sure what to believe yet," Michael tells her. "But if what you say is true, I am sorry for what has happened to your people. I never really knew my father. He disappeared when I was a kid."

"My father also disappeared over a hundred years ago," Eybriel replies.

"A hundred years ago? How old are you?" Michael asks.

"In Earth years, I am 117."

"You look incredible," Michael says.

"You like how I look?" she asks.

"Yes. I mean, that's incredible. You look as young as me."

Eybriel touches Michael's hand and smiles.

Meanwhile, Iris sits alone in her room and begins to read her father's log.

CHAPTER EIGHTEEN

The Log of Dr. Cyrus King

Day 1 of Mech Type Zero Project: I flew out to the Roswell Facility for the first time today and finally saw the Mech Type Zero robot that my wife, Michelle, discovered in the Pacific. It is truly astounding. The project team Michelle has assembled for me seem a capable group. [...] Side note: I rather like this new waterproof notebook Michelle got me. After my last logbook got ruined with blood splatters at the hospital, I will only use waterproof notebooks from now on. [...]

Day 13 of M-Zero Project: The bone-like alloy that composes M-Zero made breaching the Mech a challenge. However, through a special process of electrolysis, we finally gained access to the M-Zero's cockpit. We found an egg-shaped headpiece linked to a pilot's seat along with unidentified engravings. Based on the analysis of these findings, I believe that the M-Zero has extraterrestrial origins. [...] Michelle wants the team to engineer Mechs based on M-Zero. She is against bringing in additional people to the project but we will need more talent in order to meet her deadline. I think the impressive young prosthetics engineer from the hospital, Hiro Totaro, would be a most valuable addition. [...]

Day 91 MZP: Hiro has far exceeded our expectations. Not only has he turned out to be a fellow Hendrix fan but, today, he unveiled his human-piloted Mech, the Totaro Type 1 Trapper. Michelle says she can have a fleet of Hiro's Mech built within a year but she wants to change the name to M-1 Trapper, for consistency. [...]

Day 424 MZP: Today, we had a truly fortuitous event. The Axis launched a nuclear strike against the U.S. for the second time creating an opportunity for us to field test the M-1 Trappers under real conditions and they passed with flying colors. The Trappers beautifully diverted the Axis nuclear missiles. Our team has accomplished the goal we set out to achieve and we did it ahead of schedule. However, I find myself unsatisfied. There is still so much I wish to know about the M-Zero. Particularly, about its linked egg-shaped headpiece. [...]

Day 425 MZP: I hypothesize that the M-Zero may be controlled using the mind via its egg-shaped headpiece. I don't see any problem with designing a neuro-adapter for the headpiece to be used by the human brain. However, obtaining human test subjects for experimentation may prove difficult. Perhaps, instead of obtaining subjects, I can create my own.

[...]

Day 449 MZP: It has been a very productive month. I have built a neuro-adapter for M-Zero with various models of receptacle aperture units as well as created a large batch of clone cells from my own DNA. Once the cells have fully developed into humans, I will begin trials for installing the aperture units into the brains of the clones. [...]

Day 1818 MZP: I find myself deeply discouraged. I have already lost 36 clones to fatal experimentation and only have one left before I have to create a new batch of cells. I must remind myself that with each death I am one step closer to successfully mentally-combining the extraterrestrial Mech with a human subject. I must press forward for the greater good of mankind. I have installed an upgraded aperture unit into my last clone. There is something special about him. He's a survivor, a fighter. I am confident that tomorrow's test to insert Clone Subject #⊡Ǝ⅂ will prove successful.

"Subject 037?" Iris says, recollecting what Leo said the Secnav had told him. "Leo is a clone...of my father?" Suddenly nauseous, she runs to the restroom and vomits.

While Iris gets sick and all the others are sound asleep, Eybriel softly steps through the factory to Zone Eight. Making her way through Zone Eight, Eybriel marvels at Hiro's kooky creations until she finds M-Zero. The nimble Eden easily climbs the ivory Mech. Pulling herself atop its shoulder, she walks over and places her hand on M-Zero's head.

Father, she telepathizes, *it's me, Eybriel.*

My daughter, my heart, it is good to see you again, the deep and calming voice of King Eyseya telepathically responds.

It is good to meet you, Father. Eybriel smiles. *Are you alright cooped up back here?*

I am. It reminds me of my treehouse workshop back home, Eyseya responds.

How did you end up like this, with your soul dwelling within this ivory transport?

Before you were born, I swam out to Fall Island back home on Ede — Eyseya begins.

Why? Eybriel interrupts. *Was Fall Island not dangerous back then?*

It was but I have always been an inventor as well as an explorer and I wanted to know what it felt like to walk on dry land, Eyseya explains. *While exploring the ocean cliffs of the island, I discovered an interesting ivory ore that had naturally formed from Ede's regenerative waters. Observing the rock layers of the cliffs, I also discovered that the water levels marked against the rocks showed recent significant decline. After days of field research and study, I realized that Ede was heating up. Our sun is expanding and nearing Ede. When it reaches its limit, it will explode and kill everything on our home planet. I do not know how to save Ede but I tried to save the Edens.*

I decided to search the galaxy for a younger planet our people could inhabit. From the regenerative ivory ore, I built a transport that could endure years of space exploration and installed within it one of my earliest inventions, a teleporter capable of efficiently transporting the entire Eden population. It was this ivory transport that the humans have come to call M-Zero. Piloting through space for a lifetime, I eventually found this habitable planet of Earth. M-Zero was strong enough to endure space and time but my body was not. Without being able to constantly bathe in the regenerative, age-inhibiting waters of Ede, time took its toll and my physical body died.

However, I never believed I would find a habitable planet within my lifetime. Prior to my departure from Ede, I used the regenerative waters from Ede and a soluble form of the ivory ore to create a catabolizing chemical agent that would allow me to live on, at least in spirit. I stored the milk-like agent in M-Zero's tanks. When I felt my life nearing its natural end after 155 years, I aimed M-Zero at Earth and released the milky agent into the cockpit. As the cockpit flooded, my body's molecules were broken down and absorbed and my soul synthesized with M-Zero just before it crashed into Earth's waters. It was the only way for me to live on. I had to survive to ensure our people survive. And to see you and your mother again.

Mother is in danger as are all of our people. King, a human of Earth, threatens to destroy everything, Eybriel replies. *I need your help to protect everyone.*

I cannot do much without a physical mind to control this shell, Eyseya tells her. *King re-engineered my transport. M-Zero can only be piloted by the human, Leo.*

I have met Leo. His violent behavior is reminiscent of King's.

Leo has been misguided but is well-intentioned. As I

have gotten to know him, I have grown fond of him, Eyseya responds.

King also believes himself well-intentioned, Eybriel says. *He claims his acts of violence are to save the Edens. It seems most humans believe violence solves problems. Do they not know violence is the problem?*

The humans are unlike us. They struggle with always making righteous choices but it's not entirely their fault. They simply know not what they do.

Leo's friend Michael is the purest human I've seen. He is also the tallest. He almost seems of Ede. Eybriel smiles. *His heart reminds me of yours, Father.*

You have grown fond of Michael, Eyseya comments.

I have.

I am glad you are finding your way in this world alongside the humans. Perhaps with you, we can show them the way. I love you, my daughter.

"I love you too, Father."

CHAPTER NINETEEN

The Log of Dr. Cyrus King

Day 1820 MZP: The most remarkable thing has happened! Subject #037 successfully activated the M-Zero and my theory of the ivory Mech's extraterrestrial origins was correct. Yesterday, after #037 energized the M-Zero, it triggered a beautiful sapphire portal that transported me to this alien world. Short of breath, I awoke in a highly-sophisticated but long-abandoned workshop along with most of my team: Ed, Phil, Bob, Susan, Carol, and Aarav. Several stories of scaffolding and catwalks overgrown with vines crossed through the huge circular room. I saw a machine resembling a metallic jukebox (with its arched shape and blue neon lights) power down but before I got a chance to study it, we were attacked by fascinating, 10-foot-tall, black dingo-like creatures. They killed Bob and Susan. The rest of us ran outside into a tropical jungle which was engrossed with giant plants, larger than any I've ever seen on Earth. At that point, I

145

realized that the workshop was completely constructed within the trunk of a giant hollowed-out tree. Frank Lloyd Wright would be impressed. Unfortunately, I didn't have a chance to thoroughly admire because there were more dingoes waiting for us outside. Carol, Phil, and Ed were ripped to bloody pieces. Scared for our lives, Aarav and I ran along a river until we reached a waterfall at the edge of the cliff. As the dingoes closed in on us, I jumped into the river rapids. Aarav did not. I watched him get devoured as I plunged over the 100-foot waterfall and smacked the ocean head-first.

I estimate I was unconscious for about 24 hours before I was awakened by the amazing sight of tall and thin shark-like people. The blokes stand at least seven feet tall, the sheilas six feet tall, and all wear grey wetsuits. The noseless grey-skinned people are hairless with a small fin atop their sloped back and elongated egg-shaped heads. Their webbed hands each have three fingers and an opposable thumb and their bare digitigrade feet each have four webbed toes. With all of their features, the one that captured me most was their friendly, human-like eyes.

These people had pulled me from the ocean and given me medical care. Speaking English, they told me I was in Ede. One cautiously introduced himself as Meyko and informed me that he is a doctor. I initially doubted Meyko because he looks so young but was informed that he is actually older than me. I observed that the shark-people were apprehensive and asked Dr. Meyko why. The well-spoken alien explained that they were afraid because of my beard. On Ede, all land-dwelling creatures have hair and are savage carnivores while all aquatic creatures, like the Edens, are peaceful vegetarians. I must admit, it was an ego boost. No one's ever been intimidated by me before. I asked Dr. Meyko how his people came to speak English and he explained that they had learned it from me. Apparently, these marvelous beings can transfer knowledge through touch. I look forward to studying these Edens and their planet.

Day 3 on Ede: The small planet of Ede has a thinner atmosphere and lower abundance of oxygen than Earth. It will take some time to adjust to breathing here but I am managing. Ede has two moons and orbits a large, red sun. 99% of Ede is covered in ocean with only small islands scattered throughout the world. The Edens inform me that they found me just off the coast of the largest island which is located in the center of the northwest hemisphere. They call it Fall Island. [...] Along with the ability to transfer vast amounts of knowledge in an instant through touch, the Edens can telepathically communicate with each other over limitless distances. The stronger the biological bond between two beings, the stronger their telepathic connection. Strength of telepathic senses varies from Eden to Eden but none of them have a sense of smell or taste. [...]

Day 4 on Ede: About 100 million Edens inhabit this planet and live harmoniously in the massive and modern waterborne city of Ede. Located at the warm North Pole, this mobile circular floating kingdom has a 1,000-mile circumference. The clean and peaceful city is similar to an iceberg in that there is more of it below the water than there is above. The buildings are sleek, contoured, and in close proximity. The only structure that stands alone is the queen's palace in the very center of the city. All are welcomed to enjoy the lush, green park that grows around the open palace. The tallest structure in the city is the palace's control tower, which slopes skyward like the tail of an airplane. It rivals the high-rises of Dubai. Queen Teysuma is the ruler of this technologically-advanced kingdom but her husband, the king, was the primary contributor of those advances. 80-foot-tall metallic Mechs, simply referred to as 'transports' here, have long been a common staple within this culture. These transports are used for various day-to-day tasks. They somewhat resemble the M-Zero but are nearly twice as large. [...]

Day 5 on Ede: "Hello, King of Earth. I am Teysuma, Queen of Ede."

That is how the graceful Queen greeted me when I met with her and her daughter, Princess Eybriel, today. I like the sound of it. Like all Edens, the queen lives to serve others. Her beauty reminds me of my wife's. Teysuma and every generation of her beloved family have always been the most powerful telepaths. It is why every generation of her family has been chosen to rule. [...] The Edens' brains are more highly evolved than humans', yet the Edens are naïve in their innocence. [...]

Day 8 on Ede: I went swimming with Teysuma today. We have a mutual growing affection for one another. The amphibious Edens can live out of water or underwater. They have gills on the sides of their neck that are only visible when immersed in water, and they can swim at speeds up to 20 mph. They glide through the water with their legs together, swimming like a shark. The Edens are extremely agile and athletic beings. [...] The water here has age-inhibiting effects. The entire planet is like one huge fountain of youth causing all organisms to age about 4x slower than on Earth, by my estimates. [...]

Day 13 on Ede: I finally convinced Teysuma to take me back to the workshop on Fall Island where I first arrived. We took a transport Mech and had no issue getting through the deadly jungle. When we arrived to the treehouse workshop, there were streaks of blood from where the dingoes had dragged off the carcasses of my colleagues. Teysuma activated the shop's security defenses and explained that the workshop was built by her husband, King Eyseya, who had passed on. When I asked why Eyseya had constructed his workshop in such a dangerous place, Teysuma explained that he needed to excavate a rare ivory ore that is only found on Fall Island. Teysuma told me that the material is self-mending but also blocks the Edens' mental abilities.

I picked up a regally streamlined helmet and harness from a scaffold. The helmet's exterior and harness' buckles were of the same ivory ore. Teysuma said that it was Eyseya's safety equipment and explained how he used it to hang from the scaffolding as he built his ivory teleporter transport. She has allowed me to keep the equipment as a gift.

I told Teysuma that the ivory transport is known as the M-Zero and was discovered on Earth, but not Eyseya. When I asked for what reason the M-Zero was constructed, Teysuma said that Eyseya built it to save their people. Apparently, he departed in M-Zero nearly a century ago to seek out a new world because Ede orbits an oversized red sun that is in its final days. When the red sun dies, it will explode in a supernova, killing everything on Ede. Eyseya planned to use the M-Zero to find an inhabitable planet and teleport his people to it. I suppose he died just before he reached Earth.

Teysuma says that the metallic "jukebox" with the blue neon lights is the portal gateway; the other end to M-Zero's portal. When I asked Teysuma why not use the gateway to teleport her people to Earth, she said that the portal can only be opened from one side. M-Zero is the key to unlocking the portal. Eyseya apparently did this for safety purposes. I have no idea where I am in the universe, which means I cannot return to Earth until Leo activates the M-Zero again.

Day 14 on Ede: I asked Dr. Meyko to assist me in running some tests with King Eyseya's ivory helmet today and concluded that it is in fact resistant to the Edens' mental abilities. While I was wearing the regal helmet, Dr. Meyko tried to transfer knowledge but was completely unable to use his telepathic abilities on me. I prefer the privacy of my own thoughts and I kind of like the way the king's helmet looks on me. I'm considering wearing it indefinitely. [...]

Day 16 on Ede: Last night, I told Teysuma I loved her and then we slept together. Sexual intercourse with Edens is not much different than with humans. However, sex is about as exclusive as a bloody handshake here on Ede. The Edens have no sense of possessiveness or jealousy. Teysuma told me that Edens have enough mental control over their bodies to decide whether or not to allow pregnancy. She also revealed that the reason she and her bloodline are the most powerful telepaths is because they possess mental abilities that no other Eden does. One of them being the ability to control minds. She says she only used her ability once to calm an injured and panicked fish. [...]

Day 66 EDE: It is good I decided to wear the king's helmet indefinitely. I find myself restless with progressively darker thoughts that are better hidden in shadow. These Edens are the most impeccable beings I have ever encountered, far superior to humans in every way, and yet they face extinction. It is a crime against the universe to lose its most perfect species.

What depresses me furthermore is that even if Eyseya's plan was successful and he had survived long enough to teleport his people to Earth with the M-Zero, humans would never accept them. Humans can't even accept each other the way we constantly war. Our species is so fearful and intolerable of things that are different, surely we would have slaughtered the Edens the moment they set foot in mankind's domain. We're no better than the savage beasts on Fall Island.

Truly, the only way Edens could survive on Earth is if mankind was extinct. The time of the dinosaurs had to come to an end so that mankind could thrive as the next evolutionary superiority. Perhaps mankind's time needs to come to an end so the Edens can thrive. It is what's best for the greater good of the universe. But the Edens are so innocent they will never consider killing, even if it means saving themselves. They need a leader who knows what's best. A leader not afraid to act on the tough decision that must be made. [...]

Day 99 EDE: These naïve Edens will never commit genocide, not even to prevent their own extinction. But perhaps they can be forced into doing what is necessary. I have created a matching pair of telepathic neuro-units that, like Teysuma, allow for mind-control. One is the master aperture unit and the other the slave unit. The oblivious Dr. Meyko assisted me in surgically installing the master unit into the back of my own brain. My theory is that Teysuma's telepathic abilities are powerful enough to control the entire Eden population.

I plan to use an anesthesia on Teysuma when I get in bed with her tonight and implant the slave unit into her brain. If I can control Teysuma's mind, I can harness her natural abilities to control the minds of all the Edens. If I am successful in controlling the Edens, I will have them implant slave units into each other and build all the necessary tools for war.

It is only a matter of time before the M-Zero's portal is activated again. And when it is open, I will teleport the Edens to Earth just as Eyseya planned. The Edens will experience enhanced strength on Earth due to increased oxygen levels. This, matched up with their advanced technology and my leadership, will make the Edens an unstoppable force. I will eliminate mankind before they get the chance to eliminate the Edens and ensure the survival of the superior race.

CHAPTER TWENTY

On the third night after Eybriel's arrival to Tokyo, familiar sounds of clanging come from the gymnasium as Leo and Hiro swordfight with M-Zero and ToraX. Hiro attacks with his dual black katanas. Leo quickly dodges and manages to scratch ToraX's chest plate with his boomerang blade.

"Looks like the student has become the master," Leo boasts.

"Your skills have improved considerably," Hiro compliments before suddenly disarming the boomerang blade from Leo. "But your overconfidence makes you vulnerable. And your form is firm but not fluid. Bruce Lee taught that your form should be formless, flowing like water, and your strikes should crash like waves —"

"I got it, I got it," Leo interrupts, reclaiming his boomerang. "Let's go again. Best two out of three." Just then, Iris enters the gymnasium.

"It's all true. Everything Eybriel said is true," she announces. Leo secures the boomerang to M-Zero's back with a magnetic mount built by Hiro. Exiting their Mechs, Leo, Hiro, and Yin approach Iris.

"The Greys, I mean, the Edens are innocent," Iris continues. "They've been enslaved by my father and forced to attack us. He intends to use the ivory teleporter Mammoth to send all of the Edens to Earth and won't stop attacking until every human is dead."

"We know," Leo responds. "Eybriel used her telepathy to show us her memories of what Cyrus did."

"She did?"

"Yes." Hiro adds. "But Eybriel thought it would be better if you read your father's words for yourself."

Iris stands quiet for a moment. "We have to get back to the U.S. and shut down the teleporter Mammoth, now," she says.

"We'd need an army to destroy that thing. It's indestructible like M-Zero," Leo responds.

"I've been trying to persuade Chao to get the Axis to neutralize the Grey invasion for months," Hiro says. "Unfortunately, Chao's stubbornness in not wanting to aid Americans blinds him from reason."

"We don't need to destroy the Mammoth. We only need to shut down the teleporter inside of it," Iris says. "Michael is the best Mech pilot there is. He and I can fly inside the Mammoth and set a timed explosive on the teleporter. We only need enough Mechs to cover us while we breach it. Chao might not be willing to help us but perhaps the Russian President Anna Petrov will."

"Chao has all of our communications tapped here. If he discovers what we're planning, he will stop us," Hiro says.

"Then we'll meet with Anna face to face. With the advanced radar jammer you installed on the Totanov, we can get to Russia undetected and make direct contact with the president. Shutting down the Mammoth benefits her as much as us. Anna was sensible enough to help us once before, I am sure she will help us again."

"Sounds like a plan. We'll get the Totanov prepped," Hiro says before exiting the gymnasium with Yin.

In awkward silence, Iris avoids eye contact with Leo. "So where is Michael?" she asks. "He wasn't in his room."

"Haven't seen him since Eybriel got here."

"Speaking of which, I should go talk to her," Iris says, bumblingly dashing away from Leo.

Confused, Leo walks in the opposite direction to assist Hiro.

Iris returns to the room where Eybriel is being kept and knocks on the door. "Eybriel. It's Iris. May I come in?"

The door is opened by Michael.

"What are you doing here?" Iris asks, surprised.

"Watching Eybriel like Hiro asked," Michael responds.

"For three days?"

Before Michael can answer, Eybriel steps from behind him.

"Eybriel, I am so sorry for everything our father did," Iris tells her.

"Thank you but you do not have to apologize," Eybriel replies with a gentle smile. "Your brother has expressed wanting to redeem what King has done but it is not Michael's or your fault."

"You are too nice. And we are going to fix what our father did but first we have to cut off the attack to do it. We have to shut down the portal. If we can figure out how to free the Edens here on Earth, Leo and M-Zero should be able to get us to Ede so we can do the same for the rest of your people."

"The neuro-units enslaved them. Remove the slave units and free them," Eybriel says simply.

"You want us to perform brain surgery on fifty million hostile aliens?" Iris asks skeptically.

"We don't have the capabilities," Hiro says as he rejoins the group. "Only Dr. Cyrus knows how to perform such a procedure but we can still figure out a solution."

"We're flying to Russia now to convince the president to help us. I'd like for you to come with us," Iris says to Eybriel.

"I will do what I can to help."

"Leo and Yin are waiting for us on the Totanov," Hiro says.

Michael grabs a hooded bathrobe from the closet and cloaks Eybriel before walking with her, Iris, and Hiro across the factory and to the Totanov. Inside the ship's cargo bay, Leo helps the Japanese workers load

Stalker 332, ToraX, and M-Zero onboard.

"*Hermano*!" Leo says, smiling as he locks his hand with Michael's and embraces his friend. "Starting to see why they call you Archangel."

"How's that?" Michael asks.

"Like an angel, you're rarely seen," Leo jokes.

"That's my fault, I'm afraid," Eybriel says with a gentle smile. "I've been learning so much about human culture from Michael."

"Michael is an example of the best of human society," Hiro compliments. "I'm afraid the rest of the world may not be as honorable."

As the group converses, Iris tries to sneak pass Leo but he stops her.

"Are you alright?" he asks with genuine concern.

"I'm fine," she responds.

"It's gotta be tough finding all this out about your old man," Leo says.

Iris makes eye contact with Leo for the first time in days. Lingering within the moment, she finds herself suddenly overwhelmed with emotion. "I love you," she says sadly.

"I love you too, babe." Leo smiles. He leans in to kiss her but she backs away. Leo looks at Iris and her eye begins to water.

"I...I'm sorry. I...can't," she says, holding back tears as she turns away.

In awkward silence, the rest of the group tries their best to act like they did not see what just happened.

"Iris, I wanted to return this to you," Hiro says,

finally breaking the awkward silence as he hands back her purple cellphone. Iris turns the phone on and checks her messages. She starts playing a voicemail from the Secnav before putting it on speaker for everyone to hear.

"Iris, I can't understand how you and your brother could choose to help a criminal over your own mother. But you made your decision and forced me to make mine. If you return the prisoner, I am willing to forgive you and Michael for your foolishness. Until then, I am placing all of you on the NCIS Most Wanted. Also, Leo should know that I have Santana and will be using enhanced interrogation techniques on the old man until Leo is back in custody. Please understand that everything I do is for the greater good. Goodbye."

"Welcome to the club," Hiro says. "I've been on the NCIS Most Wanted for decades."

Staring at the phone, Leo snatches it from Iris. "What does she mean by enhanced interrogation techniques?"

"Torture," Iris answers sympathetically.

Silently swelling with rage, Leo's jaw clenches. He rushes out the Totanov and climbs into M-Zero while Japanese workers are still prepping it to load aboard.

"Leo! Hold up!" Michael calls as M-Zero marches off.

"Let him go," Iris tells her brother. "We have to get to Petrov. We can catch up with Leo when we get back."

As the cargo bay door closes, a Japanese worker notices Eybriel's digitigrade feet beneath the bathrobe. The worker looks up and catches a glimpse of Eybriel's noseless face. Seeing the boggle-eyed worker, Eybriel smiles and waves. Stunned and speechless, the worker waves back as the door shuts to the Totanov.

With ToraX and Stalker 332 onboard, the Totanov stealthily takes off under night's cover for Moscow, Russia. The ship quietly flies west through the dark sky. Aboard the ship's flight deck, Hiro and Michael sit in the pilots' seats as Iris and Eybriel sit in the back with Yin. Eybriel notices a bothered expression on Michael's face.

"What troubles you, Michael?" she asks.

"I was just thinking, it's official now," Michael responds. "My relationship with my mother is over."

"You should cherish time with your mother. You never know when it will run out," Eybriel says sadly.

"I'm sorry," Michael replies empathetically. "When was the last time you saw your mother?"

"The night King enslaved her," Eybriel starts. "I awoke in my bedroom when I sensed my mother struggling. I walked through the palace, entered her chambers, and saw King in bed with my mother just as he impaled her in the back of the head with a slave neuro-unit. She screamed in pain before turning to me. She said my name and pointed to the helmet and harness that King had taken off. Her eyes rolled back in her head and I suddenly got a headache. I could feel King using my mother's abilities, trying to control my mind. I snatched the helmet and as soon as I put it on, my headache stopped. Grabbing the harness, I ran out of my mother's chambers. As I fled the palace, I saw all of my people under King's control. With their eyes completely white, they chased me. I ran to the edge of the city and jumped into the ocean. I swam for miles before looking back, only to see that no one was chasing me anymore. King must have immediately put my people to work on his evil plan. I discovered King's plan only after finding his logbook tucked inside the harness' pouch.

"Over the years, I lived in exile and watched from afar as King docked the floating city of Ede onto Fall Island. He had the carnivores on the island caged or killed before excavating enough ivory ore to have the teleporter Mammoth constructed. Twenty-six years after King took over, I saw the blue portal on Fall Island activate from miles away. Amongst the commotion of my brainwashed people and their Mech transports, I snuck through the portal and arrived on Earth.

"Standing on the San Diego shore in the midst of the destruction, I heard my father's voice call to me as you all sped out over the waters with the ivory transport. I dived into the surprisingly salty waters. Sensing my father and following, I swam through storms and learned of Earth's carnivorous sea creatures as I narrowly escaped them. For six months, I swam across the ocean until my father led me to you all by the icy Tokyo Bay."

The group sits speechless, amazed by Eybriel's tale.

CHAPTER TWENTY-ONE

Late that night, the Totanov flies over a walled citadel in Moscow known as the Kremlin. With brick fortress walls and towers enclosing its colorful cathedrals and palatial buildings, the Kremlin is the center of operations for Russia's government and home to President Anna Petrov.

"You ready down there, Yin?" Hiro asks.

In rushing winds, the tiger droid hangs upside-down from the bottom of the Totanov with her magnetic paws as she scans the interior of the Kremlin. Using voice authentication, Yin locates the Russian President inside the Senate building.

"*Bansai!*" Yin yells to Hiro.

"Bombs away." Hiro laughs before diving the Totanov through dark clouds toward the Kremlin. A thousand feet above the rooftops, Yin releases from the aircraft just before it pulls up hard. Dive-bombing toward the ground, Yin cuts on her boosters, slowing her descent just enough to crack the cobblestone as she lands within the walls of the Kremlin. Without hesitation, she dashes for the Senate building. Russian guards wearing fur ushanka hats spot the charging tiger droid. They hit the alarm and open fire on Yin. The nimble tiger dodges the hail of bullets and smashes right through the front door of the Senate building. Politicians scream in fear as the half-ton tiger barrels down the hall. Yin races up a stairwell and scans for President Petrov's voice. She cuts a sharp turn at the top of the stairs and bursts into the Presidential Office.

"Yin?" Anna exclaims as the tiger slides to her desk. Yin pops open the video display atop her head. Looking at the display, Anna sees Hiro with Iris, Michael, and an alien.

"Miss President," Hiro says, "we need to talk."

After being invited into the Russian president's plush office, Iris and Hiro sit with Anna as she pets Yin.

"That is an amazing story," Anna responds after they fill her in on everything. "So you want Russia to back you up on a covert mission to take down the alien Mammoth. I assume Chao doesn't know of this?"

"No, he doesn't want to aid U.N. forces," Iris says.

"Nor do I but this is an issue that threatens the Axis as well," Anna states.

"So you will help us then?" Iris asks.

"*Da*, I will help you."

"Thank you, Miss President," Hiro says.

"But first I will meet the alien, Eybriel. She is with you now?"

"Yes, Eybriel is aboard the Totanov," Hiro tells her.

"Perfect. Let's go," Anna demands, standing from her seat.

"Wait," Iris interrupts. "We will need one hundred pilots and Mechs. And a powerful explosive."

Amused, Anna smiles. "Very well. I can spare one hundred pilots and Mechs. And you will have your big bomb."

"Good. Let's go then."

The guards wearing fur ushankas stand outside the office as Anna exits.

"Comrades, I'm leaving with these sputniks for a while. Have this door fixed before I get back," Anna orders the guards.

"Yes, Miss President." The guards salute Anna as she walks by with Iris, Hiro, and Yin.

Outside, the massive Totanov sits tucked in the city square just outside the Kremlin wall. Inside the ship's cargo bay, Eybriel watches Michael clean off his angel-winged helmet.

"Darling! You are gorgeous!" Anna exclaims as she approaches Eybriel.

"Thank you. You are gorgeous too," Eybriel responds genuinely as Anna circles her with admiring fascination. Michael defensively stands to his feet just before Iris enters the cargo bay.

"Relax. Anna's agreed to help us," Iris tells her brother as Hiro and Yin run up the side stairs to the flight deck.

"Your skin and your figure are perfect! I hate you," Anna jests in envy to Eybriel.

"You hate me?" Eybriel replies sadly.

"*Ostyn'*. It's just an expression, darling. It means I wish I was as gorgeous as you. Tell me, what's your secret? How do you keep your body so nice?"

"Well, I only eat vegetation and I swim," Eybriel responds.

Anna frowns. "Sounds dull and exhausting."

"Looks like you're all done meeting Eybriel," Iris says. "When are you going to assemble your troops?"

Anna smirks at Iris.

"What is it?" Iris asks, annoyed.

"You remind me of myself at your age, *devushka*. You're a spitfire," Anna replies.

Iris smiles.

"We will assemble them now," Anna says. "Hiro!"

Hiro walks down onto the side stairs. "Yes, Miss President?"

"We fly to Kubinka," Anna directs as she ascends the stairs.

"Kubinka, Miss President?" Hiro asks.

"It's the nearest base housing Russian Toras. Very close. Come, I will show you the way." Anna walks to the flight deck and all follow.

Hiro and Michael sit in the pilots' seats with Anna and Iris behind them. Eybriel sits in the back with Yin as the Totanov begins its vertical liftoff. Anna picks up the angel-winged helmet from beside Michael's seat.

"What is this symbol on your helmet, Michael?" Anna asks.

"It's my call sign. Archangel," Michael responds.

"Archangel Michael. This is a good sign." Anna smiles. "Let me show you something." Hovering over the Kremlin, Michael looks as Anna points out the window. "Look down there next to the garden. Do you see the cathedral with the single golden dome?" she asks.

"Yes, I see it."

"It is the Cathedral of the Archangel, Saint Michael. Archangel Michael was the protector of God's army in the war for heaven. He won the war by slaying the enemy leviathan. This cathedral was built in his honor and has been used to celebrate many Russian military victories. When we meet the alien Mammoth on the battlefield, I believe that you too will lead us to victory, Michael."

"Your faith is compelling. I'll do my best." Michael smiles. "Thank you, Anna."

"Don't mention it, darling."

CHAPTER TWENTY-TWO

Piloting from M-Zero's cockpit, Leo's jaw is clenched tighter than the purple cellphone in his fist. He makes a call and puts the ringing phone to his ear.

"So, my rogue daughter finally decides to call," Secnav Michelle King answers over the faint sound of battle in the background.

"This isn't Iris, you psycho *puta*," Leo responds.

The Secnav pauses. "037. Your lingual skills continue to unimpress."

"I'm not trying to impress you," Leo growls.

"Clearly," the Secnav snubs. "So, to what do I owe the pleasure of this call?"

"I want to do a prisoner swap," Leo says. "You release Santana, and I'll turn myself in."

"What's the catch?"

"No catch, just an even exchange. I'm the reason Santana got pinched. I'm giving myself up to set him free because it's the honorable thing to do. But I wouldn't expect you to understand anything about honor or loyalty," Leo snubs back.

"God. Country. Family," the Secnav states earnestly. "That is where my honor and loyalty lie and in that order. But I wouldn't expect you to understand anything about order. You're a criminal whose priority is putting your own personal interests first. My priority is doing what's best for the greater good."

"And you think trying to kill your own kids is the greater good? You really are psycho, *puta*."

The Secnav pauses again. "Perhaps I should kill Santana."

"How do I know he's not dead already?" Leo asks.

"Hear for yourself."

Seconds drag by before Leo hears a familiar voice.

"*Mijo*?" Santana says weakly.

"*Tío*! I'm here! Are you alright?"

"Are *you* alright?" Santana asks.

"I'm good, but are you hurt?" Leo asks.

There is no response.

"I'm coming to get you out of there, *Tío*!" Leo says.

"*Mijo*, I am an old man," Santana says. "Whether by the hand of the government or the hand of God, my days are numbered. Do not come here, *mijo*." His voice is suddenly cut short by the sound of a blunt hit and Santana crying out it pain.

"*Tío*!" Leo yells.

"There you have it," the Secnav says, returning to the phone. "He's alive, for now."

"*Puta!*" Leo yells. "If you hurt him again—"

"Next time I hurt him, I'll kill him unless you turn yourself in immediately," the Secnav threatens. "Now, type this in your phone so you don't forget it. Meet me tomorrow just before dawn at these coordinates: 33.3 degrees North, 104.5 degrees West. Come alone."

The phone hangs up and already over five thousand miles away from Japan, a boomerang-equipped M-Zero lands in the center of sunny Tijuana, Mexico. Leo throws the purple cellphone in a backpack. Opening the cockpit, a pungent odor sweeps in, hitting his nostrils so hard it makes him nauseous. Covering his nose with the collar of his shirt, Leo pulls the plug from the back of his head and walks to the edge of the cockpit. The homecoming is less than bittersweet as he is greeted by piles upon piles of hot, rotting corpses covering the streets of his city.

Leo climbs down from the ivory Mech and wades through the mass graveyard toward El Sanchez Sucio Bar, the cartel's hangout. Dead bodies barricade the door to the tavern. Leo looks for signs of an attack on the cartel building but it's hard to tell because the decrepit tavern always looked like it was just hit by a bomb. He pushes the bodies away from the door and enters. Inside the dark and dank bar, Leo's worst nightmare comes to life as he finds more corpses filling his home. Crouching down, he begins to turn over bodies and quickly realizes he does not recognize them. These corpses do not belong to cartel members. They are not his family.

With a short series of high-pitched whistles, Leo

does the cartel call. Suddenly, the dead begin to move. The floorboards beneath them rise as cartel cholos emerge from the bar's hidden basement. Sanchez the bartender, José the enforcer, Güey the mechanic, and a dozen others see Leo and excitedly rush to greet him.

"Leo! Welcome home, *vato*!" José says.

"Good to see you finally got a man's haircut, *hijo*!" Sanchez laughs, rubbing Leo's buzz cut head.

"We thought you were dead, *hermano*!" Güey says, relieved.

"It's good to see your ugly mugs too!" Leo jokes, momentarily forgetting the surrounding death. "So the Edens did all this?"

"The Edens?" José asks.

"The aliens are from Ede. They're called Edens," Leo explains.

"And how do you know that?" Sanchez asks.

"It's a long story. I'll catch you guys up but first tell me what all happened here."

"Like you said, Leo. The aliens did all this. They been wiping out everybody," Sanchez tells him. "After El Capo's house got hit, we were trying to find out exactly what happened to you guys but then the aliens attacked. Flaco took over and said it was more important for the cartel to focus on surviving instead of trying to find you guys. Flaco's had us hiding from the aliens during the day and scavenging for food and supplies at night. But we're running low now. We can't keep this up much longer. If Capo was here —"

"I am here," Flaco interrupts as he enters from the

back room wearing one of Santana's linen suit jackets over his shoulders like a cape.

"I was referring to your *padre*," Sanchez clarifies.

"My father is dead! I am El Capo now!" Flaco announces before suddenly freezing at the shocking sight of Leo. "Am I seeing a ghost or have you always been this white, gringo?"

"It's good to see you too, Flaco," Leo responds. "And Santana is not dead. We got pinched by the U.S. military but I escaped when the aliens attacked. I've been in Japan with Hiro, the Asian who first brought me to Tijuana when I was a *niño*. The head of the U.S. Navy, Secnav Michelle King, still has Santana locked up. She's agreed to exchange Santana for me."

"And why would the head of the U.S. Navy be more interested in you?" Flaco asks condescendingly.

"Follow me and I'll show you," Leo says as he starts to lead the cholos outside.

"Wait, you *idiotas*!" Flaco screams. "Did you forget about the aliens?"

"I was just outside. Nothing but corpses out there. Plus, it's midday so I'm pretty sure the Edens have already pushed far east of here."

"Pretty sure? Are you willing to bet your life on it, gringo?"

"Don't be such a scaredy cat, Flaco." Leo chuckles as he exits the bar. The cholos look back at Flaco before following Leo out of the dark tavern.

"This is why the Secnav wants me," Leo announces, pointing up.

The cholos squint as they try to adjust their eyes to the daylight. As their vision becomes clear, they are startled by the sight of the towering ivory Mech.

"What the fuck, mane! It's an alien Mech!" Güey exclaims as the cholos start to retreat.

"Chill out, *esés*! It's my Mech," Leo assures.

"Your Mech?" José asks.

"Yeah," Leo responds. "I just found out this thing in the back of my head was put in by the government when I was a baby. It's for piloting this Mech, the M-Zero. That's why the Secnav wants to exchange Santana for me."

"Damn, Leo. So what do you want to do?" Güey asks.

"I'm going to call the Secnav to set up the exchange. I need a few of you guys to back me up and make sure everything goes straight."

"José, Güey, and myself will go," Flaco announces as he cautiously steps outside, making sure there aren't any aliens around.

"You're volunteering to save El Capo, Flaco?" Sanchez asks skeptically.

Clenching his jaw and concealing his anger, Flaco responds, "Of course. Why wouldn't I?"

Sanchez prepares to respond but is interrupted by Leo. "It's settled. Sanchez can run things here while Flaco, José, Güey, and me load up a vehicle. We head out to the 104 after dusk."

"The 104?!" Flaco exclaims. "Where the aliens and military are fighting? You want us to go to the frontlines of war? Do I look like a soldier, *gringo loco*?"

"No, Flaco," Leo replies. "No one would ever mistake you for a soldier. But you are Tijuana Cartel and the son of El Capo. You need to start acting like it."

"Fine," Flaco agrees. "But the only vehicles we have are a couple cars and trucks. Our airport got wrecked in the invasion along with all of the planes and choppers. And it will be suicide to drive out in the open all the way to the 104."

Late that night, after dusk and the extraterrestrials have retreated back to the Pacific, Güey and Sanchez sit in the front of a matte gold Hummer with Flaco sitting in the back seat as the off-road vehicle flies through the air in the hands of M-Zero.

CHAPTER TWENTY-THREE

M-Zero flies under dark storm clouds and over miles of cool desert terrain with the boomerang blade mounted to its back and the matte gold Hummer full of armed cholos secured in its grip. Approaching the coordinates location given to him by the Secnav, Leo sees the ruins of an isolated military base in the distance. He touches down just outside the war-trodden base and exits M-Zero. Leo quickly realizes there is no place to escape the stench of death in America.

"You guys can hold here. I'm going to go ahead," Leo says, walking up to his friends in the SUV. "Santana must be in that base. As soon as you see him, pick him up and get out of here. The sun will be up soon and the Edens with it, so head for cover as soon as you get the Capo. If you don't see him within fifteen minutes, come in after us."

"So you're really just going to turn yourself in, Leo?" Güey asks.

"I have to do whatever it takes to rescue Santana.

And I need you guys to do the same. Got it?"

"We got it," José responds, sounding as somber as Güey looks. Flaco sits in the back loading the guns with ammunition.

"Let's do this, *hermanos*," Leo says before running back to M-Zero's cockpit. As the ivory Mech walks onto the corpse-littered base, it begins to rain. Following GPS on the purple cellphone, the coordinates lead Leo to a barren patch of sand in the middle of the base. Looking over the area and seeing nothing of interest, Leo exits the Mech wearing a backpack.

A mile away, José watches Leo through binoculars.

"What's he doing?" Güey asks.

"Just got out the Mech and now he's walking in circles. Looks like he's looking for something," José answers.

Leo notices a handle in the rain-spotted sand. He walks to it and finds a camouflaged door with a broken lock.

"What's he doing now?" Güey asks.

"He found something in the sand," José says. "It's a door. Leo's going underground. Start the timer. Fifteen minutes, we're going in after him."

Not a minute passes before the earth suddenly begins to rumble.

"Earthquake!" Flaco exclaims.

"No, look!" Güey yells, pointing forward as the endless sea of enemy forces emerge on the horizon.

Shielding their eyes from the sunrise, José and Flaco see the U.N. forces in the distance.

"We should get out of here before they throw us all in prison," Flaco urges.

"I don't think they are here for us," José responds before the distant sound of shrilling Mech engines comes from behind the Hummer. Stricken with fear, the cholos are silent as they listen to the familiar sound they have heard at every sunrise and sunset for the past six months.

"Aliens," Güey whispers in horror before springing out of the vehicle and into the rain.

"*Idiota*! Where is he going?" Flaco exclaims in a panicked whisper.

Frantically dashing to the back of the Hummer, Güey throws open the trunk where a folded, tan flatbed tarp covers their small arsenal of guns. He snatches the tarp and opens it before quickly tossing it over the Hummer. José exits and scrambles with Güey to conceal the Hummer beneath the camouflaging tarp as the alarming shrill of impending doom grows nearer.

"*Ándale*, Güey!" José yells before they both race back inside the vehicle, locking the doors behind them. The sweating cholos breathe heavily inside the hot Hummer, still with anticipation. The loud thudding of raindrops against the tarp is steadily drowned out as the piercing shrill grows louder from behind them. U.N. forces fire a barrage of bullets, rockets, and missiles in the Hummer's direction. Peeking through the windshield from beneath the tarp, the three cholos cover their ears as they see screaming alien Mechs tear through the sky overhead and charge straight for U.N. forces. The corroded alien Mechs pounce on U.N. forces like buzzards on prey, ripping man and machine to shreds.

As the rainstorm grows more violent, so does the battle. Roaring thunder is barely heard through the raging explosion of war as fire and steel viciously collide. The earth rumbles again. But this time the rumbling comes from behind.

Boom.

Boom!

BOOM!

What sounds like the nearing march of another sea of soldiers is in fact the footsteps of the ivory Mammoth. Slow and steady, the colossal mechanical monstrosity approaches, always escorted by squadrons of corroded Mechs. Caught in crossfire, ten minutes remain in the cholos' countdown.

Meanwhile, Leo descends a long and creaky metal stairway into pitch blackness. At the bottom of the stairs, he feels the wall for a light switch but has no luck. Shining the light from the cellphone, Leo looks around a dilapidated room the size of a hangar. The ceiling caved-in, tools are scattered everywhere, and tons of mechanical equipment is turned over. He shines the cellphone light onto his palm and sees it is covered in black soot. Suddenly, a dim light cuts on from a nearby hallway. Leo pulls a rifled shotgun out of his backpack before approaching it. He follows the light down the long, dark hall to a doorway with missing doors. Stepping through the doorway, Leo enters a poorly-lit room. Beneath the light, he sees a bloody and motionless Santana hunched over on the floor with his hands cuffed around a vertical pipe against a wall. As Leo runs toward the still body, he is struck by unusual feelings. A ball wells up inside Leo's throat and his eyes begin to water as fear and sorrow both hit him.

"*Tío*, get up! Get up, *Tío*!" Leo says before violently shaking the body by the shoulder. "Santana?! Santana!"

Santana gasps as his bruised eyes barely open. "*Mijo?*" he says weakly, looking at Leo.

"You're alive." Leo grins with relief, quickly wiping his tears.

"A little," Santana jokes before coughing in a violent fit.

Leo notices Santana's mangled leg. "What did that *puta* do to you?" he asks.

"Exactly what I said I would do until you turned yourself in," a familiar sadistic voice announces over intercom speakers. "Put the gun down, 037."

Looking up into the shadows, Leo spots the reflection off an actuating camera mounted to the ceiling. He drops the shotgun.

"Good," the intercom says. "Now, kick it away."

Leo kicks it.

"There are handcuffs hanging on a pipe on the wall. Cuff both your hands to the pipe," the intercom directs. Leo sees the handcuffs hanging several feet away from

Santana. Grabbing them, he cuffs himself to the pipe as instructed.

"Alright, I did what you asked!" Leo barks. "Now let Santana go!"

With pistol drawn, the Secnav emerges from the shadows. Dressed in a black peacoat and slacks, she walks to Santana and unlocks his cuffs.

"Follow the light outside, Mr. Guerrero," the Secnav directs.

CHAPTER TWENTY-FOUR

The ferocious battle rages on in the desert rainstorm. Thousands of Stalkers and desperate soldiers fight with great heart but fall like the raindrops against the extraterrestrial Mechs of the mindless Edens. Then, in the midst of hopelessness, hope soars in from the west as the Totanov charges through billowing storm clouds toward the 104. Behind the ship is a fleet of Russian Antonov cargo jets carrying one hundred Totaro Type 2 ToraVs and gung-ho Ruski pilots. The olive drab Russian-modified ToraV is fitted with more heavy armament than any other Mech. It has a cannon mounted on one shoulder and a missile launcher on the other, a rocket launcher mounted to each forearm, and holds two Uzi submachine guns with extended clips.

"The Mammoth is within range!" Hiro announces over radio as he sits with Eybriel and Yin in the Totanov's flight deck. "332, are you ready?"

In the open cargo bay below, Michael and Iris sit in Stalker 332's cockpit. Michael glances behind his shoulder at his sister who looks back at him with a reassuring nod and smile. "332, hot and ready!" Michael radios.

"Ruskis, ready?" Hiro asks.

"*Da*, we are always ready. Get on with it," a Russian pilot responds.

"Alright Ruskis, on my mark," Hiro announces. "Dropping in five. Four. Three. Two…"

One second later, one hundred ToraVs start dropping out of the Antonov cargo jets. Midair, the ToraV engines cut on and the Ruskis charge toward the corroded alien Mechs from behind.

"Michael! Iris!" Hiro calls.

"Go ahead, Hiro," Michael responds.

"I just want you guys to know that even though the circumstances of our meeting were not preferable, I am glad we met," Hiro says genuinely. "Over the months, I have come to think of you all as friends. And I pray for your safe return from this. I love you guys."

Michael smiles. "You're a good man, Hiro. I'm honored to call you friend."

"We love you, Hiro!" Iris yells excitedly.

"Alright, 332." Hiro smiles. "Prepare for drop. On my mark, in five. Four. Three. Two. One."

The Totanov pulls up hard. As it ascends with its nose pointed straight at the heavens, Stalker 332 drops from its cargo bay with a large explosive strapped to its chest. Freefalling face-first toward the bloody battlefield,

Michael is suddenly afflicted by thoughts of his parents and how he is the spawn of the treachery responsible for all of this bloodshed. What makes him different from the ones who caused so much pain, suffering, and death?

"Any time now, Michael," Iris says as Stalker 332 continues plummeting toward the ground.

Frozen within his thoughts, Michael does not hear his worried sister. From the Totanov's flight deck, Eybriel senses Michael's troubled mind.

Michael. Michael, Eybriel telepathically calls to him.

Eybriel? Michael responds in thought.

Michael, what worries you? she asks.

My family is responsible for this. We caused all of this, Michael responds.

Your parents caused this, Michael. Not you.

But the same evil seed within my parents' hearts must also reside in mine.

I have seen your heart, Michael, Eybriel replies. *And in it is only love and a need to protect from evil. I believe goodness is absent from your parents' hearts because it was all poured into you and your sister. Now go and show the world the man I know you to be, Michael…*

"Michael!" Iris screams as 332 nears the ground.

Snapping back to his senses, Michael kicks on 332's jet engines and rockets into formation behind the Ruski defensive line.

"Michael," Iris says, vexed, "what the…?"

"Hell! The Axis are attacking us too!" U.N. Lieutenant Canuck Devereux says from the eastern side of the 104.

"No," Lieutenant El Gato Rojas says, "it looks like they're flanking the aliens from behind. The Axis are helping us!"

The steel curtain of Russian ToraVs smashes a path through the corroded alien Mechs. Inspired by the sight, U.N. forces double their attack efforts with newfound strength. The Ruskis cover 332 on all sides as they guide Michael and Iris toward the ivory Mammoth.

"This takes me back to my college football days!" Michael laughs.

"Let's just focus on not making this our final day," Iris asserts after seeing a few Ruski pilots get killed. "We haven't won the game yet."

"Sorry about that, sis," Michael says. "I am focused on what I have to do now."

As Michael flies above the battleground, Leo stands chained below it. Regardless, Leo is relieved by the sight of Santana exiting the dark underground dungeon toward safety.

"So the soulless *puta* keeps her word," Leo says to the Secnav.

"Soulless?" The Secnav laughs. "You're one to talk."

"I've done a lot of bad stuff in my life but at least I never tortured a bunch of innocent kids. Only a soulless bitch would experiment on orphans."

"Is that what you think?" the Secnav sneers. "You are no orphan, 037. You are like the thirty-six others my husband created."

"Created?" Leo asks, confused.

"You are a clone, 037. You were created in this very facility from my husband's own DNA."

"You lie!"

"Your face even wrinkles like his when he used to get angry," the Secnav mocks. "How do you think I identified you so quickly? You are the spitting image of my late husband at your age but still nothing more than a soulless government experiment, created in a test tube."

"Late husband?" Leo laughs. "Your husband isn't dead, lady. He was teleported to the alien planet Ede by M-Zero. Cyrus is responsible for all of this. He's controlling the Edens and commanding them to kill every human. Including you. Looks like he doesn't love you as much as you thought."

Infuriated, the Secnav marches over to Leo and pistol-whips him in the face. Leo spits blood before laughing again.

"Don't take my word for it," he says. "Check my backpack and read your husband's words for yourself."

Resentfully curious, the Secnav jerks open the backpack still strapped to Leo's back and snatches out Dr. Cyrus King's log.

"I'm sure you recognize your husband's handwriting in that waterproof notebook you got him," Leo says.

"Shut up!" the Secnav screams, lividly reading and flipping the pages.

Too far away to hear the Secnav's scream, a wounded Santana drags himself upstairs toward daylight. He collapses in the sand a mile away from the hidden Hummer full of cholos.

"I see El Capo!" José announces from behind binoculars. "Let's go! *Ándale!*"

"We can ask El Capo what to do about Leo," Güey says, starting the engine. "I know he won't let us leave Leo behind."

"You won't have to," Flaco responds from the back seat before immediately shooting Güey and José in the back of their heads. Flaco carelessly pushes the dead bodies of the men he once called brothers out of the Hummer before climbing into the driver's seat and darting out from beneath the tarp's cover.

Battered and weakened, a shadow of the once mighty El Capo Santana Guerrero lies with his back on the ground. Rain and burning debris fall around Santana as he watches the battle amongst the clouds. It reminds him of a painting he saw as a boy of angels and demons at war in the heavens. The painting was inside a cathedral, which young Santana had walked into because he heard music but ran out of after stealing the offering money.

Turning his head, Santana sees a Hummer tire pull up in the sand. He smiles as Flaco exits the vehicle.

"Flaco, I'm glad to see you," Santana says, looking up at him. "Help me up, *mijo.*"

"*Mijo?*" Flaco says. "I think you're confusing me with Leo."

"What are you talking about, Flaco? You are both my *familia*. You and all of the cartel."

"No Papa, me and you are *familia*! But you don't act like it," Flaco says, disgusted. "I have been loyal and honest to you my whole life. But not you. No, you favor a gringo over your own son. And you lied about killing that Asian *chino* that brought him here! Leo said he's been with the *chino* all this time."

"I never actually said I killed Señor Hiro," Santana responds.

"That's because you are soft. Too soft to be Capo!" Flaco asserts.

"Watch your mouth, Flaco!" Santana responds angrily.

"Or what, old man? You're too weak to make threats. The cartel needs a Capo that is strong," Flaco says, pulling out a machete.

"You treacherous backstabber, you are the weak one!" Santana barks. "I fought my whole life to earn everything I have become but you plan to take my place, like this? Selling out your loyalty to inherit my title? You're a bigger whore than your mother, you disrespectful little vulture!"

"This vulture had respect for you once but you never respected me. You always treated Leo better than me!" Flaco yells with tears in his eyes.

"I treated you each differently because you two *are* different," Santana explains. "Leo is a fighter and I raised him to be a loyal enforcer. I didn't give you as much praise as him because a leader does not always get accolades for everything he does but I was always proud of you, Flaco. That's why I never sold that first Mech you stole on the black market. Some parents display plastic soccer trophies to recognize their *niños'* achievements. I kept a billion-dollar Trapper to brag on you. Everything I did was to teach you to be a strong leader, Flaco. To make you the next Capo!"

"And now I am a strong Capo," Flaco says, gripping the machete. Santana looks at his reflection in the blade of the machete, and karma stares back.

"No, Flaco. You're not," Santana responds solemnly. "You could never learn the most vital part of being a leader. You never learned how to earn the respect of your men. And no man respects a jealous backstabber. But go ahead, *hijo*, and do what you came here to do," Santana says accepting his inevitable fate.

Standing over his father, Flaco's need for pity fully evolves to a thirst for retribution. Raising the machete into the air, he lets out a terrifying shrill as he swings with all his might. Blood sprays Flaco's face as he chops his father's throat. Red bubbles gurgle out of Santana's neck as his son chops it again. Psychotic rage intensifying, Flaco violently and continuously hacks away until the decapitated head of the former Capo finally rolls across the whisking sand.

Overhead, Michael pilots 332 from within its thinning cocoon of ToraV Mechs. The Ruski ToraVs gradually get picked off by corroded Eden Mechs as Iris meticulously shoots short bursts of Gatling gunfire back on the alien pursuers. With precision aim, she disables the Eden Mechs without injuring the Edens within.

"Archangel, we are closing in on the Mammoth!" one of the Ruskis radios.

"Copy!" Michael responds as Iris retracts the Gatling gun back into 332's vertebrae. "Shedding cocoon on my mark! In five. Four. Three. Two…"

The Ruski ToraVs create an opening and, like a butterfly, 332 springs forward of the cocoon. The Ruskis defend 332's rear as Michael and Iris approach their target.

"In case we don't survive this," Iris says, looking back at her brother. "I want you to know I love you, Michael."

"I love you too, sis," Michael responds, ominously looking back at his sister. "That's why you will survive this."

"Michael?" Iris says, worried.

"Archangel to Totanov, Deadeye requires emergency pickup," Michael radios as he suddenly jettisons 332's canopy and ejects his sister from the cockpit.

"Michael!" Iris screams.

As she rockets into the air, Michael charges through an escorting squad of Eden Mechs before zooming into the narrow hangar entrance of the ivory Mammoth.

"Son of a bitch!" Iris curses before deploying the parachute to her ejector seat. As she drifts down from grey clouds, a bird's-eye view of the battlefield is revealed. Like a light in the darkness, Iris sees the ivory

M-Zero standing in the center of the grim battle.

"Leo?" Iris murmurs.

Just then, a corroded Eden Mech jets for her like a piranha to a dangling worm. Looking down at the charging alien Mech, Iris pulls a pistol strapped to her ankle and begins to hopelessly open fire. The ascending alien assailant reaches for Iris' heels before suddenly being gut-tackled by Stalker 334.

"Stalker 334 to Totanov. Come in, Totanov," El Gato radios while Canuck pilots from the seat in front of him.

"Go ahead, 334," Hiro responds.

"We intercepted Archangel's radio transmission. We are in progress now of Deadeye emergency pickup. Over," El Gato radios.

"Copy, 334. Thank you," Hiro radios, spotting Stalker 334 in combat with the Eden Mech. "We're ten klicks west, above your position. You're clear to board the Totanov once you have the package. Over."

Locked in the Stalker's grapple but still clawing for Iris, the alien Mech suddenly slashes one of the engines on 334's back. Canuck's engine stalls but refusing to release the alien, both Mechs begin to flat-spin and plunge from the sky. To keep the Eden from further damaging him, Canuck rips open the corroded Mech's cockpit and pulls out its pilot in 334's hand.

Seeing black smoke billowing from Stalker 334, Hiro pilots the Totanov into position. Sitting beside him, Eybriel looks out the window at the battle below.

"Eybriel, can you see the Mech transport marked

334?" Hiro asks.

"Yes," Eybriel says, spotting the entangled plummeting Mechs. "It's just below us."

Hiro opens the cargo bay door before turning to Yin. Rolling on the floor in the back of the flight deck, the tiger droid plays with a ball of steel safety wire.

"Yin," Hiro says, grabbing her attention. "Go fetch 334."

Yin immediately springs to her feet. "334! Aye aye, Hiro-san!" she says before dashing off.

The spry droid races to the opening of the cargo bay and without hesitation leaps from the back of the ship. Getting her bearings, Yin spots Stalker 334. Tucking her legs and paws in, she dives for the stalling Stalker. Like an orange torpedo, Yin quickly catches up to 334 before spreading her body to match its rate of descent. Extending her magnetic paws toward the Stalker, Yin attaches to 334 and walks to its damaged engine. She deploys various tools from her chassis and quickly repairs it.

Seeing both his engines back online, Canuck releases the corroded Mech before cutting his engines back on. Hovering, 334 watches as the corroded Mech drops to the desert and explodes.

CHAPTER TWENTY-FIVE

With a wild pack of corroded Mechs hot on his tail, Michael flies the open-cockpit Stalker 332 through tight passages within the ivory Mammoth. He notices that the Mammoth is not completely made of ivory like M-Zero. Only its exterior is plated with the regenerative ivory material. Maneuvering his open-cockpit Mech through the labyrinth reminds Michael of speeding through the narrow streets of Tijuana in the convertible Lamborghini with his best friend. The memory is calming before Michael is suddenly jerked in his seat. He looks back and sees a corroded Mech with its talons latched into 332's leg. The bogey uses its other razored hand to slash at 332. Still zooming forward, Michael manages to dodge the slashing attacks but in the process scrapes his Stalker against the interior structure of the Mammoth. Acting quickly, Michael aims his Mech assault rifle and shoots off 332's leg. Amputated leg and parasitic, corroded

Mech both crash into the other pursuing Mechs before exploding against the walls of the labyrinth. Michael strains to stabilize his one-legged Stalker as he maneuvers it through increasingly tighter passages within the belly of the beast.

"I see the core," Michael radios.

"Good," Hiro responds. "Set the timer to the explosive and get out of there."

Landing in the central core of the ivory Mammoth, Michael puts the explosive in position. Setting the timer, he is suddenly struck with despair.

"Hiro, the timer is inoperative. It must have gotten damaged when I scraped against the Mammoth's interior structure. I'm going to have to manually detonate."

The radio is silent as Hiro looks into Eybriel's sad eyes.

"Negative, Michael," Hiro radios back. "Just get out of there. We'll find another way."

"I don't see another way. And we may not get another opportunity. All of this suffering and death lies on my family name. I will redeem our name. For once, a King will actually act for the greater good."

As Michael cuts off his radio, a swarm of Edens enter the core.

"I'm only sorry that so many more will have to die," Michael says to himself, pointing his Mech rifle at the explosive.

I love you, Eybriel telepathizes to him.

"I love you too," Michael says before pulling the

trigger.

The Mammoth begins to slow down in its tracks as molten metal boils within its bowels.

"Go! Go! Go!" Yin exclaims, bracing herself to 334's back. Canuck grabs Iris' ejector seat in his Stalker's hand and zooms inside the open bay of the Totanov. Yin leaps off of 334's back and returns to the flight deck. Turning hard, the Totanov rockets off at supersonic speed as the ivory Mammoth erupts in a volcanic explosion.

Not too far away, Flaco notices the Totanov and every other vehicle speeding away before seeing the mammoth blast charging straight for him. Knowing there is no escape, Flaco looks at his father's severed head on the ground. El Capo Santana's dull eyes stare back at him.

"Your vengeance was swift, Papa." Flaco laughs maniacally, raising his arms as the explosion swallows him. The Roswell Facility below shakes violently.

Leo and the Secnav look up as the ceiling collapses on them.

Safe inside the soaring Totanov's cargo bay, Stalker 334 opens its hands, revealing Iris in one palm and the unconscious young Eden pilot in the other. With Yin piloting the ship, Hiro enters the cargo bay as Canuck and El Gato exit the Stalker's cockpit.

"The Mammoth, it detonated? Where is Michael?" Iris asks, anxiously unbuckling her seatbelt to the ejector seat. With all of her friends gathered around her, Iris sees the remorse in their faces. Her heart drops.

"Hiro?" Iris asks, trembling. "Where is Michael?"

"I'm sorry, Iris. There was a complication with the explosive's timer. Michael chose to detonate manually and destroyed the Mammoth. He sacrificed himself to protect all of mankind. Your brother's a hero."

Holding back tears, Iris tries to stand strong.

"I'm sorry, Iris. Michael's death is a loss to all of us," Canuck says. "You know I'm always here for you —" Before Canuck can finish his sentence, Iris hugs him and cries on his shoulder.

Just then, the seven-foot-tall Eden pilot gains consciousness and immediately charges at Iris and Canuck. With cat-like reflexes, El Gato grabs the wild, white-eyed alien. As El Gato struggles to restrain the strong Eden, Hiro quickly hits it over the head with a fire extinguisher, knocking it back unconscious. Just as El Gato pulls out a pistol to shoot the Eden, Eybriel steps into the cargo bay.

"Stop!" she cries. Surprised, El Gato points his gun at her. "Have enough friends not died today?" Eybriel asks as Hiro steps between her and El Gato.

"Please, Lieutenant, don't shoot. Eybriel is with us," Hiro calmly explains.

"What?" El Gato asks, confused.

"The female alien's not a threat, El Gato. Put the gun down," Iris orders, wiping her tears before removing the handcuffs from Canuck's and El Gato's harnesses. Lowering his weapon, El Gato looks at the equally confused Canuck. "There's a lot to explain," Iris says, handcuffing the unconscious Eden's hands and feet to the cargo bay wall. "These past six months have been crazy."

"Speaking of crazy…" El Gato remarks.

"Excuse me?" Iris questions.

"He's referring to the Secnav, your mother. She seems unstable," Canuck explains. "She's often M.I.A. and when she does show up, all she talks about is capturing that Mech, M-Zero."

"It's like she's oblivious there's a war going on and that we're losing it," El Gato adds.

"The troops are beginning to doubt her ability to lead," Canuck says.

"My mother should have never been leading in the first place," Iris scoffs. "She's behind all of this. She's the reason Michael and so many others died today," Iris says before walking to the edge of the open cargo bay. Concerned, Canuck attentively watches Iris as Hiro notices Eybriel staring at the handcuffed Eden.

"Do you know him?" Hiro asks.

"Yes," Eybriel replies. "He is my friend, Meyko. One of the gentlest souls I know and King has turned him into a savage."

"Perhaps not permanently," Hiro says, observing the slave neuro-unit implanted in the back of Meyko's skull. "I doubt I can remove Dr. King's slave unit from your friend's head but I can run some tests. With time, I'm sure I can find a way to safely deactivate it."

"Thank you, Hiro." Eybriel smiles.

Standing at the edge of the open cargo bay, Iris looks out over the battlefield. Even though it is the middle of the day, it appears the middle of the night. Grey clouds and thick dust from the Mammoth explosion engulf the sky and eclipse the sun. Iris sees pieces of ivory scattered across the sand as a completely decimated M-Zero lies on its chest halfway slumped over into a huge crater. A tear rolls down her cheek as her heart silently rips. In a single fleeting moment, she has just lost the only two people she ever truly loved. But even in the midst of Iris' deepest and most painful despair, the soldier in her refuses to allow herself to break down. She has to remain strong because the war is far from over. Iris closes the bay door as the Totanov flies out of sight.

On the ground, dust from the earth-moving explosion finally begins to settle. The decimated M-Zero lies with its arm and head slumped into the crater that used to be the Roswell Facility. Within the crater below, all but Leo's head, torso, and a tatted arm lies crushed beneath heavy cement rubble. His body is almost unrecognizable beneath the layers of grey dust covering it. His face lies motionless before suddenly coughing up dust. Blue eyes slowly open amongst the grey mound and peer up at M-Zero's open cockpit hanging above. Barely able to turn his head, Leo looks over and sees the Secnav's skull splattered beneath a cement boulder. He lets out a weak laugh before coughing up a pool of blood with chunks of his organs. Leo's vision fades and his pulse slows as life slips away. With a final gasp for air, Leo's heart stops beating in the same place it first started.

M-Zero gently glows a brilliant sapphire. The scattered pieces of ivory also glow as they begin to supernaturally move. With more pieces gathering and combining to each other and M-Zero, the Mech begins to mend itself. It steadily hovers from the ground, revealing the minimally-damaged boomerang blade hidden beneath it, before floating over the crater. The ivory Mech reaches out its hand for Leo's broken body. With Leo's left arm still handcuffed to a collapsed wall and legs crunched beneath rubble, M-Zero grabs the dead body and separates it from its trapped limbs. It places the legless, one-armed Leo inside its cockpit and closes it.

A milky fluid begins to flood the cockpit. As the fluid makes contact with every injured area of Leo's body, it solidifies, attaching him to the Mech itself. With Leo fully immersed, the cockpit overflows and a sheet of milk pours over the outside of M-Zero's windshield. After completely covering the windshield, the dripping milk begins to morph into shape. Inside the windshield, a thousand milky strands harden like muscle, permanently fusing Leo's remains to the M-Zero. One strand inserts the neuro-adapter into Leo's brain before solidifying around it.

As the strands illuminate in the same brilliant sapphire, the shape of two eyes form where the windshield once stood. A familiar voice calls. It is the deep yet calming voice of Eyseya, the king of Ede.

Eyseya commands with a single word, *Rise*.

Leo's heart suddenly pumps strong with new life. He opens his eyes and looks at his hands. But they are not the hands of flesh he knows. They are the ivory mechanical hands of M-Zero. Leo reaches for the back of his head to unhook himself from the Mech only to realize there is nothing to unhook. He touches his ivory Mech face with its newly-formed blue eyes.

Leo is no longer M-Zero's pilot. He is M-Zero.

His voice trembles. "What is this?"

We are one now, Leo, Eyseya answers. *You are the physical mind where mine died long ago, M-Zero our body, and I the soul for a clone that never had one. We are three symbiotic beings. Mind, body, and soul all as one.*

"You turned me into a goddamn monster!" Leo yells traumatically.

It was the only way to save your life, Leo.

"What life is this?"

A hypersonic blue light blazes off in the distant, dark sky unnoticed by the Totanov flying in the opposite direction.

PART IV: DEADFALL

CHAPTER TWENTY-SIX

Over two decades have passed since the Battle at the 104. Twenty-five million mind-controlled Edens continue their eastward campaign methodically killing off mankind. One-third of the human population has fallen already, leaving less than five billion survivors. After aiding U.N. forces in the Battle at the 104, Hiro Totaro was exiled from Asia by Paramount Leader Chao. Hiro lived aboard the Totanov along with Iris, Eybriel, Canuck, El Gato, and Yin. After figuring out how to deactivate the slave neuro-unit implanted in the back of Dr. Meyko's head and successfully freeing the Eden from his zombified state, Captain Hiro allowed the good doctor to join his crew. For the first decade following the Battle at the 104, the nomad crew of the Totanov traveled the world freeing hundreds of Edens while Chao stubbornly withheld Axis troops and watched North and South America get annihilated by the still enslaved Eden zombies.

As nations' governments fell, the crew of the Totanov rose as influential leaders. Leading U.N. forces, the Totanov crew helped a quarter of a billion people escape the Americas. In the second decade, British King Alistair Cooper led European U.N. forces in a valiant stand against the alien zombie horde but was forced to retreat with a quarter of a billion Europeans to the safety of the Commonwealth of Australia.

Aside from Asia, Australia remains the only continent not yet overrun by the white-eyed Eden zombies. As Europe fell, so did the elderly Paramount Leader Chao's health. On his deathbed, Chao called Hiro, his only friend, to his side. Realizing the inevitable alien invasion of his Asian empire, Chao expressed his regrets for not heeding Hiro's advice. Acknowledging Hiro's wisdom and ability to lead, the Axis leader appointed Hiro his successor.

Not long after Chao's death, the aliens ravaged Africa. An Egyptian and former Jihadi named Wes Nasser led a quarter of a billion survivors east. Accepting all refugees into Asia, the new Paramount Leader Hiro gave safe harbor to half a billion immigrants, including thousands of freed Edens. He then united the U.N., the Axis, and all surviving nations into one nation. Hiro formed the United Nation Council to govern humanity and the freed Edens, and joined all militaries into one United Nation Defense before renouncing his title as Paramount Leader.

The United Council consists of Hiro representing Asia, Iris representing North Americans, Eybriel representing the Edens, Felix "El Gato" Rojas representing Latin Americans, Wes Nasser representing Africans and the Middle East, and King Alistair Cooper representing Europeans and Australia. Although, the grumpy 74-year-old King Cooper is not the most cooperative of the council members.

CHAPTER TWENTY-SEVEN

On a typical autumn afternoon at the grave wasteland that is the western border of Asia, the United Defense of Earth desperately defends itself against the relentless Eden zombie horde. Charging ahead of the rest of the United troops, one Totaro Type 3 Tatsu Mech engages the extraterrestrial enemy. The olive drab Type 3 Tatsu has the stealthy frame and maneuverability of its predecessor, the Type 2 Tora, but its single-seat cockpit is located within the newly-featured pivoting head. The addition of a head was necessary due to the cockpit having to be removed from the torso in order to make room for the large hydro-powered jet engine. The Tatsus' jet engines are scavenged from fallen corroded Eden Mechs. In addition to its newly-integrated alien technology, the Tatsu also carries new non-lethal weapon technology. It wields the Totaro Electromagnetic Pulse Rifle. The EMP rifle fires a sapphire energy blast powerful enough to electrically disable a Mech.

Engaging two attacking Eden zombie Mechs, the lone Tatsu pilot easily dodges their slashing talons and with two quick shots from his EMP rifle paralyzes the zombie Mechs. Quick-deploying the rifle's retractable knife-edged bayonet, he peels open the two cockpits like a can-opener and looks down at the gnarling Eden zombies inside. The bayonet quick-retracts back inside the rifle before the Tatsu secures it to the magnetic mount on his back. He carefully picks up two Eden zombies within the safety of each pressurized fist. As the rest of the zombie horde begin their nightly retreat into the western dusk, the Tatsu takes off at hypersonic speed in the opposite direction.

Within an hour, the lone pilot approaches the United Nation's overly dense capital city of Hong Kong, China. Its gleaming skyscrapers contrast against the rest of the war-torn world. Decelerating to supersonic speed over the city, he looks down at crowds of people partying in the Day of the Dead parade that honors and celebrates the memories of deceased loved ones. The Tatsu gracefully sails from the sky into the sea.

Submerged chest-deep in the harbor, the Tatsu sets its fists on a dock at the Central District United Defense Base. The pilot hits one switch to refuel his hydro-engine and another switch to sedate his Eden passengers. As gas sedative is released into the Tatsu's fists, the pilot opens the cockpit. Lieutenant Ace Devereux's helmet bears an emblem of the letter 'A' with wings and he wears a green band for the United Nation Defense on the right sleeve of his modern flight suit.

"I am glad to see your safe return!" Dr. Meyko greets from the dock after exiting an odd-looking white ambulance van. The middle-aged-looking Eden doctor bears the same green band on his arm and the front of the van bears resemblance to the bow of a boat.

"What's up, Doc!" Ace responds, standing in the cockpit as he removes his helmet. The tall and brawny 20-year-old has mahogany skin and wispy hair on his chin. The top part of his dreadlocked hair ties back into a samurai topknot, the bottom part drapes to his shoulders.

"You have rescued more," Dr. Meyko says, sensing the Edens within the Tatsu's fists.

"Four zombies, already sedated," Ace responds.

"I hope they are. We do not want another incident like the last time."

"My bad, thought I hit the switch last time. Never heard them conscious and quiet before." Ace laughs. "But they're good to go now, Doc. You ready?"

Dr. Meyko hesitantly nods and Ace opens the Tatsu's hands. On its palms lie four sedated white-eyed zombies. Exiting the cockpit and running across the Tatsu's arm like a bridge, Ace helps Dr. Meyko carry the first zombie into the ambulance. After years of experience, the good doctor is able to quickly deactivate the slave unit in the back of each of the Edens' heads. As Dr. Meyko ties United Nation green bands around the freed Edens' arms, three soldiers wearing the same flight suit uniforms as Ace walk toward them from the base.

"You finheads can put on green bands but that don't make y'all one of us!" a drunk, young, red-haired soldier remarks as he approaches. His equally boozed-up buddies, an Asian soldier and an African soldier, snicker behind him.

"What the hell do you want, Jax?" Ace challenges the red-haired soldier.

"No worries," Dr. Meyko politely says as he assists the four Edens into the ambulance. "We will depart for the colony momentarily."

"You mean that finhead colony. Ain't that underwater?" Jax asks.

"The Eden Colony is, yes," Dr. Meyko answers as the soldier walks to the edge of the dock.

"Under this water?" Jax emphasizes as he unzips his pants and pisses in the water. "That's why they call it the Yellow Sea!" the soldier jokes as his buddies laugh.

"That's the South China Sea, genius," Ace interrupts. "Yellow Sea's two thousand klicks northeast of here."

"Ace, you're always siding with these finheads. We aren't like them!" Jax says, disgusted. "What is your problem?"

"Fucktards like you are my problem!" Ace asserts, pushing Jax in his face. Jax grabs Ace by the collar and balls his fist before Dr. Meyko suddenly seizes the redheaded soldier by his bare forearm. Jax tries to break free from Dr. Meyko's grip.

"What the hell are you doing, you crazy old

finhead? Let me go!" Jax panics.

Staring into the soldier's eyes while gripping his arm, Dr. Meyko transfers memories of the struggles of the enslaved Eden people. Jax's eyes widen as his mind is opened to all of the hardships endured by the Edens and caused by humans.

Just then, an open military jeep pulls up to the dock.

"Do we have a problem here?" Secretary of the United Defense Canuck Devereux barks after exiting the jeep. Now in his late forties, the tall, dark, and handsome Secdef is bald with a mustache and wears green military fatigues.

"No," the newly-enlightened and completely disoriented Jax replies, stepping away from Ace and Dr. Meyko.

"No, what?" Secdef Canuck barks.

"No, sir!" They all salute and fall into formation. The three intoxicated soldiers shake in their boots as the Secdef eyeballs them. Canuck stands in Jax's face, staring him down with disgust.

"Son, your breath reeks of alcohol," Canuck barks at the nervous soldier. "There better not be nothing else offensive coming out of your mouth. Understood?"

"Sir, yes sir!" Jax says, tightening his stance.

"Good. Now zip up your fly and get out of here. Dismissed!" Canuck orders as the three soldiers quickly march off.

"Hey, Dad," Ace greets Canuck.

"Hey, bud," Canuck responds, his demeanor

instantly calming as he embraces his son. "Are you two alright?"

"We are unharmed," Dr. Meyko responds.

"I know you can handle yourself, Meyko." Canuck laughs as he embraces his old Totanov crewmate.

Dr. Meyko smiles. "You know me. No worries, friend."

"Ace, your mother's waiting for us at the unveiling ceremony."

"Alright," Ace says before turning to Dr. Meyko. "Hey, sorry for that, Doc."

"Sorry for what, Ace?"

"For that ignorant ass pissing in colony waters."

"No worries, Ace. I do it all the time." The good doctor smiles before all three burst into laughter. After saying their goodbyes, Ace gets in the jeep with his father as the amphibious ambulance of Edens drives out to sea.

CHAPTER TWENTY-EIGHT

With the Day of the Dead holiday nightlife in full swing, Canuck and Ace drive the open jeep through the city's crowded Central District. The vibrant, lit streets are filled with reggaeton music, tremendous skeleton floats, women with faces beautifully painted like skulls, and costumed men walking on stilts as jubilant people toss colorful flowers. Ace discreetly removes his pilot gloves and puts on his no-fingered gloves as the jeep pulls up to Heroes Memorial Cemetery and parks behind a blockade of news vans. Peering over the vans, Ace sees two towering structures covered with sheets being erected in the center of the cemetery. Between the two structures, Councilors Hiro, Iris, Eybriel, and Wes Nasser stand gathered with a mob of press and cameras surrounding them. With bronze skin, dark wavy hair, and a neatly-trimmed beard, Councilor Nasser steps forward.

"Remembering the loss of so many brave soldiers and loved ones weighs heavy on my heart," he announces with an Arabic accent to the press. "However, being able to pay tribute to their memory brings joy to it. Today, on the Day of the Dead, we celebrate our heroes that have passed. As the newest member of the United Council, I am humbled and greatly honored to present, on behalf of the people of Africa and the Middle East, these two memorials."

The first sheet pulled reveals a heroically-posed 20-foot marble statue carved in Lieutenant Commander Michael "Archangel" King's likeness. Dressed in an attractively fitted pants suit at 48 years old, Iris is filled with sorrow as she looks with two eyes at the monument of her deceased brother. However, as the second monument of Secnav Michelle King is revealed, Iris is filled with nothing but resentment. The crowd cheers loud for the King memorial statues. Oblivious to the Secnav's immoral deeds, the public views both the Secnav and her son equally as heroes.

"Iris, I hope you are pleased with the statues," Wes Nasser says, catching Iris off guard. "I ensured their likeness was exact."

"They're very nice," Iris says as sincerely as she can. "Thank you."

"Thank you for voting me into the council," Wes responds. "I want you to know that I support the freed Edens and uniting us all. And I will do all I can to help end this war."

"Councilor Iris Devereux!" a reporter interrupts,

shoving a microphone in Iris' face. "How does it feel to be following in the footsteps of your heroic mother, Secnav Michelle King?"

"My mother? Yes, well um..." Iris stammers, conflicted.

"My mom and I are moved by the tribute," Ace interjects, wrapping his arm around Iris' shoulders. "My grandmother was strong. Like all the survivors of the United Nation, we stay strong to honor those who sacrificed themselves to protect us."

"Can we get a picture of you two with your family statues?" the reporter asks.

"Sure," Iris responds, posing with her son as cameras flash. "Thank you," she whispers to Ace.

Night rolls in as the news vans roll out. Eybriel stands staring up at Michael's statue. Wearing a chic green wetsuit, the 138-year-old Eden appears one-third her age. Like all Edens on Earth, she has aged as a human during her years away from home.

"How are you, Eybriel?" Ace asks. Eybriel hugs him and smiles.

"I am sad but hope brings me happiness," Eybriel says, touching Ace's face. Ace stands with his arm wrapped around Eybriel's shoulders as both continue to gaze up at Michael's statue.

In a shadowed corner on the far side of the cemetery, Iris stands at a small white tombstone with the name overgrown in ivy. Kissing her fingers, Iris touches them to the tombstone and weeps.

"Are you alright?" Hiro asks as he stands beside her. The old Mech engineer's smile is now framed by a salt-and-pepper beard and his face bears wrinkles, but Hiro remains as genuine and friendly as always. And he still wears the same cargo capri pants.

"They build an idol to a criminal while a true hero can't even get his grave cleaned." Iris bitterly chuckles, wiping her tears. "I can't continue to lie about my parents, Hiro. Ace doesn't even know the truth."

Councilor Hiro takes his time before speaking. "Heroes are symbols that give people hope and inspire us to unite," he says. "Your mother is such a symbol. Revealing the truth about her and your father would shatter that symbol. It would do the people more harm than good, and your parents have used people to do enough harm. Should we not now use them to do some good? Use them as symbols to unite the people and give them hope?" Before Iris can answer, she is interrupted.

"Look what the cat dragged in!" Canuck announces as he walks over with Councilor Felix "El Gato" Rojas. The same age as Iris and Canuck, the Mexican man has greying hair and wears a black cat pin in the lapel of his suit.

"Sorry I'm late. Holiday traffic," Felix explains. "Speaking of which, if anyone's hungry, there's this Mexican bar and grille I've been meaning to check out. It would be perfect for today's holiday."

"We're in!" Ace responds, walking over with Eybriel.

"It's kind of late to be going out," Iris says.

"Yeah, but you guys have fun. We'll see you tomorrow at the videoconference," Canuck adds.

"Alright, Grandma and Grandpa," the 74-year-old Hiro jokes. "I'll join you, Felix."

"What about you, Wes?" Felix asks.

"I'm afraid I have to retire as well. I actually am a grandpa. My family's waiting for me at home," Wes says.

"Come on, we'll give you a ride," Canuck offers.

"Thank you, my friend," Wes responds.

"Alright, it's just us then," Felix says to Hiro, Ace, and Eybriel.

Hiro smiles. "Lead the way, councilor."

Several blocks later, on the rougher side of town, a taxi drops off Ace and the three councilors near a riverfront at Santana's Bar & Grille. As they step inside, an old man in a wheelchair sits by the bar complaining to an even older bartender.

"Hola, Señor Hiro. Long time, no see," the husky Hispanic bartender greets.

"My apologies," Hiro responds to the familiar-looking man, "I cannot recall your name."

"Never gave it," the bartender says, "but the last time you stepped foot in my bar, you sliced it to pieces."

"The cartel hangout in Tijuana," Hiro says, recollecting. "You were behind the bar."

"And you were wrecking it. But you won't be wrecking nothing in here, *comprende*?" the former cartel member asserts.

"As long as there's nothing I need to defend myself against, nothing will get wrecked," Hiro assures.

"Rest easy, councilor. I'm legit now and too old for grudges."

"You and me both." Hiro smiles.

"The name's Sanchez," the bartender introduces. "Your crew actually helped me and the group of emigrants I was with escape the Americas back in the day. You are welcomed here."

"But the finhead isn't!" the old man in the wheelchair interrupts. "Can't you read? The sign says 'No Finheads Allowed'." The paraplegic points to a sign hanging above the bar. A silhouette of an Eden head is pictured with an 'X' painted over it. "We should not be cohabiting with the enemy!" he hollers.

"Stonewall, we've been through this. Everyone knows that the attacking Edens are being controlled by slave neuro-units," Felix tells him.

"And it's probably just another finhead controlling them!" Stonewall rants. "I lost my legs to those damn finheads!"

"Hiro has already offered to build you prosthetic legs. He built Deadeye's prosthetic eye," Felix responds.

"I don't need nothing from an Axis finhead-lover!" Stonewall scoffs.

"Who is this man?" Eybriel asks Ace.

"Jax Junior's dad, Mason 'Stonewall' Jackson," Ace answers. "He used to fly with Felix before his accident at the Battle at the 104."

"Alright, take it easy, Señor Mason," Sanchez says.

"Are you the manager?" Felix asks Sanchez.

"I'm the owner," Sanchez responds.

"Sanchez, *hermano*, you are a businessman interested in making money, *sí*?"

"Of course," Sanchez answers.

"The freed Edens make a lot of money working for the government but with so many anti-Eden businesses, they rarely get the chance to spend all that hard-earned cash," Felix pitches. "You have prime real estate near the riverfront with easy access to Eden customers. If you were to allow Edens to dine here, Councilors Hiro, Eybriel, and myself would be happy to give your establishment an official United Council endorsement. So as a businessman, which matters to you more, grey skin or greenbacks?"

"But my human customers may leave if I let Edens in," Sanchez counters.

"Polls show that most humans don't mind cohabiting alongside freed Edens. Racists like Stonewall are the minority. So why not be one of the first businesses to promote an already popular trend?" Felix persuades.

"You say all three of you will endorse Santana's Bar & Grille?" Sanchez asks, considering. Hiro and Eybriel nod and smile in agreement. "Then I say welcome, *amigos*! What can I get for you gentlemen and the lady?" Sanchez asks, taking down the 'No Finheads' sign.

"Tequila for the house, on me!" Felix announces. The patrons cheer as Stonewall picks up the sign and wheels it out in disgust.

"I'll just have water and a salad, please," Eybriel replies.

Hours later and after last call, Sanchez, Felix, Hiro, Eybriel, and Ace drink and play poker in the kitchen of the bar and grille.

"I fold," Felix says, placing his cards face-down. "Looks like the black cat is unlucky."

"Actually, black cats are considered very lucky in Asia. I think we're just bad at cards," Hiro jokes. "I fold too. How about you, Eybriel?"

"I fold as well," Eybriel replies, leaving only Ace and Sanchez in play.

"Eybriel, my dear, I am surprised you are losing at this game. I thought Edens could read minds," Sanchez says.

"We can telepathically communicate with other Edens and can communicate even better through a direct bloodline link, but we can only transfer knowledge through touch. Unfortunately, none of my abilities work on those who are still enslaved in a zombified state. And even if I could read your mind right now, as an Eden, I would not cheat."

"No offense but, Eden or not, you're a politician aren't you?" Sanchez jokes.

"None taken. Please do not be offended as I place my final bet on Ace to win." Eybriel smiles.

"Well, I hope you're ready to lose all that hard-earned Eden cash," Sanchez boasts before slamming four queens and a jack on the table. "Four of a kind, all face cards! Game over!" Sanchez announces jovially as he reaches for the pot.

"Hold on, my *grande compadre*." Ace smirks as he places his cards on the table. "Four kings and an ace. That, my *amigos*, is what I call a family flush." Ace laughs.

"Cocky *cabrón*." Sanchez laughs as Ace takes the pot. "You remind me of a young friend I had back in the day."

"Oh yeah? Who?" Ace asks, counting his winnings.

"Have you heard the legend of the Ghost Mech?"

"Yeah, old urban legend airmen tell about a dead pilot in a white Mech. They say the Mech appears and vanishes like a ghost and attacks like a demon."

"That pilot was my friend. His name was Leo," Sanchez says.

The councilors quietly look at one another.

"Leo what?" Ace asks, skeptical.

"Just Leo. He didn't have a last name," Sanchez responds.

"Now I know you're full of it!" Ace laughs.

"Actually, Leo didn't have a last name because he was an orphan," Hiro interjects.

"So you're telling me the white Ghost Mech is real?" Ace asks, still doubtful.

"It was more ivory than white," Eybriel says.

"Not you too!" Ace exclaims. "So how do you know it was ivory?"

"Because my father built it," she says.

"A human piloting a mentally-controlled Eden Mech? I didn't think that was even possible."

"Leo was special and so was the Mech," Hiro explains.

"Did you all know Leo?" Ace asks.

"I only saw him once," Felix says, "but he was friends with everyone else. Leo and Iris used to be together. She visited his tomb today."

"So Leo is my mom's dead ex-boyfriend? I've never heard her mention him but if that's his tomb, there's no question he's dead then," Ace deduces.

"It's an empty grave. Most of them are at Heroes Memorial Cemetery. All the dead aren't able to be retrieved from the battlefield," Felix explains.

"What is this, some kind of Day of the Dead joke or you all just been drinking too much?" Ace laughs skeptically as they all look at him with stone faces. "Come on, you guys are just messing with me because I took all your money. So, I'm going to call it a night." Ace downs his last beer before saluting with one finger and exiting Santana's.

In the dead of night, an intoxicated Ace returns home and sits on the balcony of his parents' high-rise condo in the Central District. The tower is gilded with the regenerative ivory plating scavenged from the fallen Mammoth. Looking down at the dark city, he suddenly sees two Ghost Mechs. Wait, one Ghost Mech. Having had one beer too many, Ace tries to focus through his double vision. Quietly leaning forward and squinting his eyes for a closer look, Ace nearly falls off the balcony. Catching his balance and holding in his laughter, Ace tiptoes inside his mother's study and grabs her old sniper rifle off the fireplace mantel. He quickly returns to the balcony and looks through the oversized sniper scope to get a closer look at the Ghost Mech, but all he sees is another white amphibious ambulance van.

"Ghost Mech." Ace laughs to himself with his eye in the scope. Suddenly, the Ghost Mech appears across his sights. Startled, Ace accidentally pulls the trigger and fires a round still left in the chamber. Holding his ringing ears, he drops the rifle and a device with a beeping red blinker light falls out of its stock. Ace picks up the device and quickly turns in the direction of the Ghost Mech but finds it has vanished. He notices the closer he moves toward the edge of the balcony, the faster the red blinker beeps.

"Tracker bullet." Ace smirks. Unzipping his uniform along the sides and inner legs, Ace quickly converts the flight suit into a wingsuit. Awakened by the gunshot and armed for intruders, Iris and Canuck charge the balcony.

"Ace?" Mr. and Mrs. Devereux say just as their son jumps off the balcony.

Spreading his arms and legs like a flying squirrel, Ace maneuvers himself toward the United base. Soaring past the base and out over the water, he splashes into the harbor and climbs into his fully-fueled Tatsu before blasting off in hot pursuit of the legendary Ghost Mech. Following the increasingly faster beeping of the tracker device, the Tatsu jets over the rooftops of Hong Kong. The fast beeping increases into one continuous tone and the Tatsu comes to an abrupt stop. Hovering in the vicinity, Ace scans the countless dark alleys of the dense city. He spots something white lurking in the black shadows and draws the Tatsu's EMP rifle as he descends into darkness. Landing in a narrow alley, Ace finds a white semi truck.

"Not again." Ace sighs, lowering his weapon. As he turns away, something moves beneath the tarp on the semi's flatbed trailer. Ace raises his rifle and approaches the grungy, tan tarp. Nearing it, the tan covering is suddenly snatched away by an ivory hand as the Ghost Mech reveals itself and takes off right in front of Ace. Irritated, Ace gives chase. Draped around the Ghost Mech's shoulders like a hooded cloak, the tan flatbed tarp flaps in the wind as it flies away from the Tatsu. Secured to the Ghost Mech with brown ratcheting tie-down straps, the cloak reads 'CAUTION: O' with the words 'OVERSIZE LOAD' cut off.

Ace fires several sapphire EMP blasts but the shifty Ghost Mech eludes them with supernatural speed. Pulling a thirty-foot, razor-edged boomerang from beneath its cloak, the Ghost Mech hurls it at the Tatsu cutting its engine. Smoke pours from the Tatsu as it crash-lands in the middle of the city. Bloody and bruised with a gash on his forehead, Ace crawls from the fiery wreckage and sees the Ghost Mech remounting the boomerang to its back beneath the cloak. Looking back over its shoulder with human-like blue eyes, the Ghost

220

Mech winks at Ace, then vanishes at hypersonic speed as a woozy Ace passes out in the middle of the street.

CHAPTER TWENTY-NINE

The morning sun shines down on the rooftop terrace of the Ivory Tower as Eybriel, Stonewall, Dr. Meyko, and Jax Junior sit together at a grand banquet table laughing. Ace runs out onto the terrace also laughing with Eden children and human children holding hands and playing together. One of the little Eden boys runs up to Jax and hugs him. Jax hugs the child back and lifts him up onto his shoulders. He looks at Ace and smiles before sunlight from the window shines in Ace's eyes.

With a smile on his face, Ace awakes to a nurse shining a light in his eyes.

"Ace, are you okay?" the pretty Asian nurse asks. The exotic beauty is as young as Ace, with sun-kissed skin and naturally blonde hair.

The day after the Day of the Dead, Ace finds himself in a hospital bed wearing a hospital gown. "I'm fine, Lynn," Ace responds to his childhood friend.

"You're lucky you got out of that crash with just a couple stitches." Nurse Lynn smiles as she sits on the bed and tends to the wound on Ace's forehead. "Dr. Meyko found you unconscious in the middle of the street. How did you crash?"

"It's a long story." Ace responds, checking his hair. It is still tied up in a samurai topknot. He checks his hands and feet and sees he is wearing his no-fingered gloves and hospital socks.

"No one else tended to you but Dr. Meyko and I," Lynn says.

"Are you sure?"

"Yes, bonehead!" The nurse giggles. "You know, I wasted most of my life trying to hide who my parents were. I was afraid of how people might judge me if they knew where I came from, or even worse, that I might be like my parents. Uncle Hiro taught me that where I came from makes me who I am but only I can choose where I'm going. And being afraid of people's opinions will only hold me back from reaching my full potential."

"What if I don't want to reach my full potential? Maybe I'm happy right here," Ace says, looking into Lynn's almond eyes.

"Maybe," Lynn replies with her heart fluttering. "Maybe you should stop being a bonehead!" She playfully pushes Ace's head.

"Ouch!" Ace shouts, reaching for his bandaged forehead.

"Oh my god! I'm so sorry!" Lynn panics as Ace begins to laugh, actually unhurt. "Jerk!" Lynn laughs.

"Is everything alright?" Dr. Meyko asks, entering the room.

"Yes, Doctor," Lynn answers, abruptly standing to her feet. "I was just checking on the patient."

"Well, I got *the patient's* tests back." Dr. Meyko smiles. "Besides a mild concussion and being a little dehydrated, Ace, you'll be okay. At least until your parents get a hold of you. I just got off the phone with them."

"What did they say?"

"They want to see you at the Ivory Tower as soon as I give you your hospital discharge."

"How mad are they, Doc?" Ace asks.

"You might be safer returning to the western border frontlines," Dr. Meyko jokes.

"Well, let's get this over with." Ace sighs, pulling off the gown.

Staring at his brawny physique, Lynn sees angel wings tattooed from Ace's spine to his elbows. "So you finally got inked," Lynn says, touching Ace's back. "Looks good."

"Thanks." Ace smiles before putting his flight suit back on. "My guardian angel's always got my back."

Back at the Ivory Tower, tensions run high as United Nation councilors videoconference with Councilor Alistair Cooper in a stately meeting room on the top floor.

"Asia never aided Europe in our time of need!" King Cooper declares over the wall-sized video display from his office in Australia.

"You are well aware, Councilor, that Asia was under old leadership then," Hiro responds.

"I am the king and you will address me as Your Majesty," Cooper decrees. "Now, European Forces aided the Westerners before the fall of the Americas but where was our bloody help in our darkest hour? The people of Europe have fought long and hard. When the enemy nears our front door, we will rejoin the battle but I will not sacrifice another European nor Australian life to protect Asia's border."

"Councilor Cooper—" Iris says.

"You discourteous slag!" Cooper insultingly interrupts. "I am King of the United Kingdom and you will address me as such!"

"Hey fucktard!" Iris snaps back. "You can't be a king if there's no United Kingdom. Britain is gone! All that's left now is one United Nation, Councilor! And if you don't unite with us, that'll be gone too! I'm sorry for what Chao did but Chao is long dead. And the rest of humanity will join him if we do not stop this nonsense and stand together!"

"It's not Britain, you cheeky slapper! It's Great Britain! And while her people still draw breath, I have a kingdom to protect. Good day!" Cooper dismisses as the wall-sized video display goes black.

"Did he really hang up on us?" Wes asks.

"Uncooperative Cooper strikes again," Felix remarks.

"What is a fucktard?" Eybriel asks.

"I got it from Ace," Iris answers as Canuck enters the meeting room with their son. "Speaking of the devil! What the hell were you doing last night?" Iris screams, frustrated.

"I take it the conference with Cooper didn't go well," Ace remarks.

"Can it, wise guy!"

"Wise guy? That's less offensive than fucktard," Ace responds.

"You heard me?" Iris asks, embarrassed.

"I think the whole tower heard you, honey," Canuck responds.

"Stop changing the subject," Iris replies, calming her demeanor. "Ace, sweetheart, what were you doing last night?"

"I was in pursuit of an Eden Mech."

"A zombie Mech made it this far east? Already?" Canuck asks.

"It wasn't a zombie Mech," Ace says to the room of puzzled councilors. "It was the Ghost Mech. It was Leo."

Caught off guard, Iris pauses for a moment. "Leo is dead. I saw his ivory Mech blown to pieces on the battlefield and no one's seen him since." Iris pauses. "Even if he was alive, why would he exile himself away from me and his friends for twenty-one years? Who even told you about him?"

Hiro, Felix, and Eybriel quietly pass guilty stares. "His name came up over a card game last night at the bar and grille," Felix confesses.

"He's not dead!" Ace asserts. "I saw him!"

"And how is it that nobody else saw this Ghost Mech last night, Ace?" Iris asks.

"Yesterday was a holiday. Everyone was passed-out drunk."

"You mean passed-out drunk like you were? Dr. Meyko said your blood alcohol level was high."

"Yeah, but you sober up quick when you see the Ghost Mech at your house!"

"I'm sure you were just seeing things, Ace. Even if you did sober up quick, that knock to your head could have made you delusional," Canuck says, touching the gash on Ace's forehead.

"That happened after the Ghost Mech made me crash-land!" Ace explains.

"No more excuses, young man!" Iris screams.

"But Mom!"

"But nothing! You recklessly endangered everyone by flying under the influence and you could have gotten yourself killed! As of right now, you're demoted to scavenge duty!"

Ace turns to Canuck but the Secdef stands by his wife. Ace looks to Eybriel and she subtly nods before Ace grimaces and walks out of the meeting room.

CHAPTER THIRTY

Weeks later, as Eden zombies threaten China's most western border, Yin the tiger droid pilots the old reliable Totanov to its eastern border. With passengers Iris, Felix, and Wes onboard, the large jet sails over a lake in Beijing toward Hiro's palatial home. The former Paramount Leader's oriental palace sits on a snug little island in the center of the lake. It is adorned in red, green, and gold and has a tiled roof rising with sweeping curvatures at every corner.

The amphibious Totanov lowers its pontoon landing gear before descending onto the water and docking on the island. Yin exits the ship and the three councilors follow her up the dock and along a winding stone path through the island's opulent landscaping. Curvy bonsai trees, bright lotus blossoms, and groves of bamboo cover the island. The stone path leads to a bridge going over a serene pond. It is filled with Koi fish of all colors and has a cascading waterfall at its far end.

The path eventually leads to the palace's open front gate. Walking through the large red gate doors, the four enter a stone courtyard with a big, golden statue of Paramount Leader Chao.

"My friends, welcome," Hiro greets, stepping out of the palace and walking down the wide steps of the veranda. His humble demeanor contrasts with his ostentatious surroundings. "Where are Alistair and Eybriel? I wanted the whole council to vote on my project proposal," Hiro says.

"Cooper wouldn't fly in. Big surprise. And Eybriel apologizes for her absence but says she trusts us. She will agree if the vote between us four is unanimous," Iris responds before pausing. "Hiro, why didn't you ever topple this thing?" she asks, pointing at the gaudy statue of Dictator Chao.

"I keep it so my goddaughter can remember her father and we can all remember the past," Hiro answers. "Philosopher George Santayana said that those who cannot remember the past are condemned to repeat it."

"I can understand that. I just told Ace everything about his grandparents," Iris states, staring up at Chao heroically posed like the Secnav, "but I still don't think we should memorialize villains."

"Chao stood for what he believed in just as we stand for what we believe in. Besides, would it have not been harder to unite the nations had Chao not united Asia already?" Hiro asks genuinely with a smile.

Iris cannot help but to smile back. "I never

understood how someone as good as you could be friends with someone as bad as Chao."

"We can only unite once we've learned to accept the differences of others. It is our differences that make us strong as a nation," Hiro says. "Chao grew up poor in a single-parent home, like I did, but he was raised in the impoverished slums of China. When Chao was a boy, his father used to always tell him that he was destined for greatness. His father worked seventy hours a week in American-owned factories and still could barely afford a decent living for the two of them.

"Chao was only 12 years old when his father fell ill. With his father unable to work, he dropped out of school and worked in an American factory to keep food on the table. Not being able to afford proper medical care, his father died shortly after. Chao felt great sadness but even greater anger. And his anger only grew as he worked at that American factory day in and day out. He couldn't afford to save his father and he blamed America. He could never understand how the United States, the wealthiest nation in the world, could pay Chinese factory workers mere cents an hour. Chao carried his hatred for America into his adulthood, eventually founding the Axis Workers Party.

"The Axis started off as a small group of radicals with the goal of securing higher wages for factory workers but quickly gained support from most of China's citizens. With overwhelming support, the Axis overthrew the Chinese government and Chao became its Paramount Leader." Hiro pauses as he looks up at

Chao's statue. "Chao's journey started with good intentions. On his deathbed, he admitted to me that he fell astray along the way. When he asked me to godfather his daughter, he asked that I promise to guide her that she won't fall astray as he did. After Lynn's mother, Anna, died in the fall of Moscow, she came to live with me. I've been keeping my promise to my old friend ever since."

Hiro's goddaughter, Nurse Chao Lynn Petrov, with her sun-kissed skin and naturally blonde hair, steps out onto the palace veranda. "Hello, Iris! Hello, Felix and Wes!" she greets with a pleasant smile.

"Good to see you again!" Iris replies as Felix and Wes wave.

"I can't believe two people that could create a child so good could be all bad to begin with," Hiro says, looking from Lynn to Iris.

"Alright, point taken. I guess Chao's actions weren't completely unjustifiable," Iris admits. "Hiro, you're like a wise monk."

Hiro laughs. "No, I'm just really old."

"Uncle Hiro, aren't you going to invite our guests inside?" Lynn interjects.

"Yeah, we want to see this new project you've been talking about," Felix adds.

"Of course. You actually inspired my idea, Felix." Hiro smiles again. "Come inside and I'll show you."

Entering the palace and descending a spiral stairway into Hiro's basement workshop, Jimi Hendrix music blares from Sony speakers as the councilors behold a baker's dozen of tall, black cat droids. They are similar to Yin but larger and have heads that resemble EMP rifles.

"These are my black panther droids. I call them Yangs," Hiro presents.

"They are the size of Arabian horses," Wes admires.

"That's because the Yangs have heavily-armored chassis," Hiro responds as he pets Yin's head. "Where Yin's main function is to repair, the Yang's main function is to defend. However, they're not as versatile as Yin and their A.I. not as advanced. It took many years to develop her winning personality."

"*Watashi wa sūpāsutāda!*" Yin cheers.

"Yes, you are a superstar," Hiro responds before continuing. "You can see the Yangs have EMP cannons integrated into their heads. As a pack, they should be able to take down a Mech. These are just prototypes but I would like to mass-produce the panther droids at the Tokyo Mech Factory. I know materials are scarce and we would have to cut back on Mech repairs, but with the millions of zombified Edens fast-approaching China's borders, I believe producing the Yangs are a more efficient way to quickly increase the quantity of our defensive measures. With that said, I would like to put my proposal to a vote."

"All in favor?" Iris asks.

"Ay!" all respond.

"That was easy," Hiro says.

"Have we ever said no to any of your ideas, Captain?" Iris smiles.

"Yes," Hiro responds. "Quite a few, actually."

"But never when it came to you wanting to engineer something," Iris tells him.

"Yeah, so do me a favor and build some more quick," Felix adds. "Thirteen black cats in one room is making even me a little uneasy."

"*Bibiri!*" Yin teases as Hiro laughs.

"What did she say?" Felix asks.

"Pardon Yin's sassiness, but she said you are a scaredy cat," Hiro says.

"What?!" Felix asks over the loud music.

"Perhaps you should turn the music down, Uncle!" Lynn suggests.

"There's only one way to appreciate Jimi Hendrix and that's at full volume." Hiro responds.

"Who is Jimi Hendrix?" Lynn asks.

Hiro immediately turns down the music. "Jimi Hendrix is a legendary guitarist, music innovator, and cultural icon from the 1960s," he explains. "During his years as an Army paratrooper, he played with a band called The King Casuals. He later made albums such as *Axis: Bold as Love* and *War Heroes* and created songs like 'Astro Man' and 'Angel'. He traveled the world uniting people of all cultures with his music. Jimi Hendrix said that when the power of love overcomes the love of power, the world will know peace. Iris' father actually introduced me to Hendrix's music. He gave me a CD back when I was your age."

"Oh, okay," Lynn replies. "So what's a CD?"

Hiro smiles warmly at his goddaughter. "Ancient,

233

like me."

That night, over four thousand miles away, near the ancient pyramids, Ace works the graveyard shift on scavenge duty. With his feet kicked up on the cockpit console of an old Antonov cargo jet, Ace snores while freed Eden workers scavenge parts from the wreckage of corroded Eden Mechs out in the desert sand.

"Ace," an Eden worker calls as Ace jolts awake from the pilot's seat. "We are ready for you outside," the worker says.

"Be right out," Ace responds, wiping drool from his mouth. He walks to the cargo bay of the Antonov and climbs into a yellow construction Trapper.

Ace marches the repurposed construction Mech out into the desert where a group of workers await him by a fallen Eden Mech and its scavenged engine. As Ace lifts the enormous engine from its former owner, he notices slice marks on the fallen Mech. The cuts are too broad to have been done with a Tatsu bayonet and too clean to be done by Eden talons. Remembering the Ghost Mech's thirty-foot, razor-edged boomerang, Ace's flight suit suddenly starts beeping. He reaches into his pocket and pulls out the blinking tracker device. Without warning, Ace drops the engine and takes to the sky. Following the accelerating beeping north, he eventually finds himself over the southern seaboard of the Mediterranean. Landing on the beach as the beeping becomes a continuous tone, Ace peers into the distance. Far out in the middle of the water, the engrossed Ghost Mech ferociously fights off a horde of zombie Mech stragglers left over from the day's raid. Their feet form wakes as they skate along the surface of the sea in the moonlight.

One by one, the cloaked Ghost Mech drops the zombies. Its boomerang drips with red Eden blood as it mercilessly jabs it into the zombie cockpits. Angered, Ace springs into action to stop the butchery of enslaved Edens. Spotting the yellow Trapper, the Ghost Mech flees for the second time. Zooming across the water at supersonic speed, Ace chases the Mech out of range of the zombies. The ivory Mech's engines flare blinding blue flames as it prepares to go hypersonic.

Leo! Ace telepathically calls out.

The Ghost Mech looks back before suddenly reducing its thrust. Flying to a giant, secluded rock jutting from the middle of the sea, it lands and waits. Finally catching up, the Trapper lands on the rock as waves crash against it and cautiously approaches the boomerang-wielding Ghost Mech.

Ace opens his cockpit and exits the Trapper. Noticing the winged 'A' emblem on Ace's helmet, the Ghost Mech mounts its weapon beneath its cloak. Standing on the shoulder of his Trapper, Ace removes his helmet.

"Are you Leo?" he asks.

We are many things, the Ghost Mech telepathically responds. *You are Iris' son, Ace. But how is it you can telepathically communicate?*

"How is it you know who I am?" Ace asks.

You did not answer my question.

235

"And you didn't answer mine."

Hmm, the Ghost Mech ponders before answering, *We are the mind of Leo, the soul of Eyseya, and the body of M-Zero all permanently conjoined as one. We know you because we have been watching Iris, and those around her, for many years.*

"You sure you're an Eden Mech because you sound a little M-2 Stalkerish," Ace wisecracks. M-Zero pauses before suddenly chuckling.

"Leo," Ace says, "all of your friends, Hiro, Sanchez, and my mother think you're dead. If you've been watching us for years, why hide from us?"

Most of our friends are dead, M-Zero responds after pausing briefly in reflection. *We are trapped inside this Mech. When we exit it, we will fall dead too.*

"But you still could have revealed yourself. Everyone speaks of you as if you're a myth. They call you the Ghost Mech."

The Ghost Mech? So people do think I'm a monster, Leo responds somberly. *I never expected people to accept me. Iris never would if she found out what I am. Why would they, when I brought the Edens and devastation?*

"Don't blame the Edens, or yourself," Ace tells him. "My mother just told me about my grandparents. She told me that my grandfather experimented on you and my grandmother forced you to open the portal."

We have stayed away all these years so that no one could ever again force me into opening the portal. But it's pointless now, M-Zero responds.

"What do you mean?" Ace asks.

Recently, the hostile Edens' numbers have increased nearly twofold— M-Zero begins to explain.

"Doubled?" Ace interrupts. "Where are they coming from?"

I'm not sure, but I believe there is a second portal hidden somewhere. I have been searching the world for the source of the enemy's surge in numbers.

"The Edens aren't the enemy—they're victims," Ace defends.

You favor the Edens, M-Zero responds.

"I am Eden," Ace reveals. "Iris and Canuck raised me but they're not my biological parents—Michael King and Eybriel are. Eybriel didn't want me to grow up facing anti-Eden prejudice. She had Iris and Canuck adopt me when I was a baby and I've been passing for full-human ever since. Dr. Meyko, Hiro's goddaughter Lynn, and all of the councilors except Wes and King Cooper are the only ones who know I'm half-Eden. They accept me and guard my secret just like they'll accept you and guard yours."

M-Zero opens its hand to Ace and Ace stands on its palm.

Yes. You are our grandson, M-Zero telepathizes, sensing Ace's lineage before placing him back on his Trapper, *but there is no need for anyone to see me as the ghost abomination they already think I am.*

"No one thinks that. They think you're a legend!" Ace exclaims. "I know what it's like not wanting anyone to see your abnormalities. But someone told me that fearing people's opinions will only hold you back from reaching your full potential. And everyone needs you at your full potential to stop the zombie attacks. We have to get to the source. We have to get to Cyrus and you're the only one who can get us there. I know the M-Zero can teleport to Ede."

No one needs me, Leo responds. *The world would be better off had I never existed.* He disappears in a blinding flash of sapphire flames as M-Zero rockets off across the sky.

Ace sighs, looking up at the impossibly fast ivory Mech. He puts on the helmet marked with his father's emblem before returning back toward the scavenge duty post.

CHAPTER THIRTY-ONE

The following morning, Ace flies the Antonov back to the capital city of Hong Kong. With a cargo of scavenged Eden engines, he lands the jet at the Central District United Defense Base. Driving down the taxiway, Ace spots the Totanov parked inside the main aircraft hangar. Standing outside the closing hangar doors, Lynn laughs as Yin the tiger droid runs in circles. Ace parks the Antonov near them before exiting. With a controller in her hand, Lynn plays with an RC car that looks like a mouse as Yin tries to pounce on it. Spotting Ace, Lynn smiles and waves.

"Hey Ace, how are you?" she asks as he walks up.

"Tired of scavenge duty and ready to get back to the battlefield," Ace responds, hugging her. "What are you doing here?"

"I flew in with Uncle Hiro and some of the councilors. They're meeting inside the main hangar to figure out how to defend against the enslaved Edens closing in on the city."

"I already got it figured out," Ace says.

"Is that right?" Lynn laughs. "Well do tell, Councilor Ace."

"Do you remember when I was telling you how the Ghost Mech is actually M-Zero and how it has the ability to teleport to Ede?"

"Yeah...?" Lynn answers.

"I ran into the Ghost Mech again last night and talked to him. The council needs to convince him to teleport troops to Ede so we can stop the guy who enslaved the Edens in the first place, Cyrus King."

"Maybe you're not such a bonehead after all," Lynn jokes. "You should talk to the councilors after they get out of their meeting."

"I just got off duty," Ace says. "I'm tired and they always take forever."

"I'll wait with you and you can relax with me." Lynn smiles. "It'll give us time to catch up."

Inside the main hangar, Secdef Canuck and all of the United Councilors, minus Uncooperative Cooper, gather in the war room.

"At the zombies' recent and unusual increased pace of attack," Canuck says, "we estimate a week before they reach us here in Hong Kong. That should give us just enough time to evacuate all civilians eastward before the United Defense has to make its final stand. Without Cooper's support, our troops will be spread too thin if we try to hold the entire longitudinal frontline. We'll have to focus our troops around the capital city."

Hours pass. While the meeting drags on, Lynn and Ace sit outside watching the sunrise as Yin lies down repairing a broken RC mouse car between her paws. Still tired from scavenge duty, Ace's eyelids grow heavy. Just as he begins to doze off, he senses something new yet familiar.

"What is it?" Lynn asks.

The tracker device in Ace's pocket beeps. Suddenly, the cloaked Ghost Mech drops and lands so hard it cracks the tarmac right in front of them. Lynn screams.

"It's okay," Ace says, wide awake.

"Leo-san!" Yin cheers as she runs up on M-Zero's arm. As he pets the tiger perched on his shoulder, alarms sound and the main hangar doors quickly slide open. Armed with rifles, Iris, Canuck, Felix, and Wes charge out the hangar with Hiro piloting the ToraX behind them.

"Leo?" Iris says, immediately dropping her weapon at the sight of the ivory Mech. Lightheaded, she passes out and Canuck catches her. Canuck looks up at M-Zero as dozens of soldiers run out with guns targeted on it.

"Hold your fire!" Canuck orders his soldiers.

"Who is Leo?" Lynn asks.

"A haunting memory we've been trying to forget," Canuck answers.

"Sun's up," Ace says to M-Zero. "Thought you'd be off killing enslaved Edens about now."

"What?" Eybriel asks, shocked.

They never showed. Only human soldiers are present on the battlefield, M-Zero telepathically responds.

"He says the zombies aren't at the frontlines," Ace translates. "Soldiers are just standing around waiting."

"And they'll keep standing guard until I order otherwise," Canuck tells M-Zero as Eybriel makes her way through the crowd of soldiers toward it.

Father, I thought you were dead! Eybriel telepathizes. *I sensed your arrival but how is it I have not sensed you for over twenty years? And what is this about killing Edens?* she asks.

My daughter, my heart, the deep and calming voice of Eyseya telepathically says. *Where you are my heart, Leo is my mind and he is in control. After the Battle at the 104, he and I had to become as one. You could not sense us because he wished not to be found. We hid ourselves both physically and mentally from the world. We are sorry for any sadness we have caused.* M-Zero pulls his cloak's hood from his head.

"Are you communicating with it?" Felix asks Eybriel. "What's it saying?"

"He says he is sorry for any sadness he caused," Eybriel translates.

"We are simply glad for your return, old friend," Hiro says. "We should continue this reunion inside."

M-Zero nods and enters the hangar as all follow.

"So, what made you finally choose to come back?" Ace asks Leo.

You did, Ace, he responds. *You made me remember the source of everyone's problems. Me, I mean, Cyrus. It's my obligation to stop Cyrus once and for all.*

"So you'll teleport me to Ede?" Ace asks.

We will, M-Zero agrees.

"Wait, what? Why do you have to go?" Iris objects.

I'm the only telepath that's related to Cyrus, Ace telepathically responds to Iris. *I can sense him quick, track him down, and put him down.*

"What about Leo?" Iris asks.

"He can't teleport himself back from Ede. He has to stay here to keep the portal open on Earth," Ace responds.

"It is too dangerous," Eybriel interrupts. "King has control of my mother, Teysuma. He will make you face her before you can get to him and Teysuma is more powerful than you know."

"The princess is right," Dr. Meyko announces, entering the hangar. "Under Cyrus' control, Queen Teysuma is more dangerous than an army of enslaved Edens," he says before turning to M-Zero. "It is good to see you again, my king."

M-Zero acknowledges the good doctor with a nod.

"It is more dangerous to not confront Cyrus! Facing Teysuma's a risk I'll have to take." Ace interrupts.

"Then I will go," Eybriel volunteers. "My mother taught me some of her powers but not all. I am the best chance of surviving her to stop King."

"And I'll go with you," Ace says. "We should send an entire fighter squadron."

"Ace, you would be more vulnerable to Teysuma's power than other humans and Teysuma has shown that numbers are futile against her," Eybriel replies. "Stealth is a better route than force. I will go alone. You can make arrangements for the freed Edens in my absence."

"I just finished operating on another Eden. I am taking him back to the colony now, if you would like a ride," Dr. Meyko offers to Eybriel and Ace.

After all adjourn, Ace and Eybriel follow Dr. Meyko aboard his amphibious ambulance and travel out into the ocean. Sitting in the back of the ambulance while it cruises over waves, Ace stares at the unconscious Eden patient as Eybriel tenderly touches the patient's head.

"Doc, do you remember what it was like being a zombie?" Ace asks.

"No," Dr. Meyko answers. "It is like a bad dream. When you wake up from it, you know you were dreaming but you cannot quite remember it."

Hours pass before they finally stop at a dock anchored in the center of the South China Sea. Ace removes his flight suit revealing a black wetsuit underneath. Resembling a superhero, he removes his gloves and boots exposing his webbed fingers and toes before diving into the ocean with Eybriel as Dr. Meyko carries his patient. Swimming down into the watery depths along the illuminated chains that anchor the dock, the gills on the sides of Ace's neck become visible as he breathes out bubbles underwater like his Eden peers.

Descending deeper into the murky sea, an underwater city glows in the darkness. The lively colony is built from the scavenged hulls of fallen Eden Mechs and is inhabited by millions of freed Edens. With its sleek and contoured buildings in close proximity, the sparkling neoteric city resembles the floating kingdom of Ede back on the extraterrestrials' home planet.

As Dr. Meyko takes the patient to the colony's medical facility, Ace follows Eybriel to her home overlooking the city. Ace enters his mother's elegant, subaquatic penthouse. She opens an ornate box with the regally streamlined ivory helmet inside.

"What's that for?" Ace asks.

"It will protect my mind from my mother's power," Eybriel replies. "Our family's bloodline is special. We have mental abilities superior to all other Edens. My mother did not teach me all of her abilities before King enslaved her but I can transfer all she did teach me to you."

Touching her son's hand, Eybriel transfers all of her knowledge of her own powers to Ace. His eyes grow wider than his smile as he instantly learns how to utilize his newfound abilities. He telekinetically raises the ivory helmet from the ornate box and spins it.

"Why wait so long to show me this?" Ace asks, setting the helmet back down in the box.

"Power and violence are not a good combination. You have grown up in war, Ace. You are brash and prone to violence like humans but I teach you this now in case I do not return from Ede."

"Sometimes you have to fight violence with violence. We have to cut off the head of the snake, Cyrus

King," Ace insists.

"Ace, killing is not our way."

"Tell that to the zombies. Either way, people will be killed."

Standing near a window, Eybriel looks out over the bustling city. "We do not know what effect killing Cyrus King will have on our people still enslaved by him," she says. "It is a risk."

"But we risk more being killed if we don't cut Cyrus down now!"

"I sense you are frustrated and tired," Eybriel says. "It would be better to speak further after you have slept."

That evening, back at Central District Base, M-Zero sleeps in the corner of the main aircraft hangar when suddenly his sleep is disturbed by the sound of someone creeping in the darkness. M-Zero reaches for the boomerang at his back to find it has been removed. Stealthily springing to his feet, the Mech's blue eyes peer intensely into the darkness to spot the intruder.

Iris, M-Zero telepathizes as she steps out from behind a corner, *where is my boomerang?*

"Is that all you care about?" Iris asks, infuriated, as M-Zero quietly sits on the hangar floor with one knee propping his arm and the other knee near the ground. "Hiro took it back to his workshop for restoration," Iris says, climbing up on M-Zero's lower knee. "You and Michael are just the same. How could you abandon me and leave me to believe you had died?"

I did die, Leo answers, *but then Eyseya brought me back, as this monstrosity.*

"Is this why you didn't come back to me? Because of what you've become?"

No. I didn't come back to you because of what I came from, Leo responds. *Iris, I am a clone of your father.*

"I know," she says.

You do?

"I found out from my father's log that Eybriel brought."

Then you see why I didn't come back. Your father, Cyrus, was a monster and I am the same, Leo tells her telepathically.

"But you're not the same. You and I and Michael were born from monsters but where we come from does not decide who we are or where we're going. Cyrus went to Ede and enslaved the innocent. You are going to set them free. You are not a monster, Leo. You're a hero."

I never wanted to be a hero, he says. *I only wanted to be with you.*

Iris looks into Leo's big blue eyes and opens her mouth to speak.

But that's impossible now, Leo interrupts her thoughts before she can express them.

"Yes. Impossible," Iris reluctantly agrees, holding back tears. She leans toward M-Zero and he leans toward her. With her hands caressing his cold ivory face, Iris kisses him.

By the way, you were hotter with the eye-patch, Leo

jokes.

Iris laughs through her pain before forcing herself to turn and walk away from him for the last time.

CHAPTER THIRTY-TWO

The Eden Colony drowns in destruction as it falls under attack to savage Eden zombies. Smoke pours from its once glistening buildings as corroded Mechs slash them apart. Eybriel cries for help as a zombie pounces on her in her bedroom.

"Mother!" Ace yells, awaking from the nightmare. Still hearing his mother's screams, Ace immediately realizes the nightmare is reality. He rushes into Eybriel's room and finds her incapacitated on the bed with a zombie on top of her. The white-eyed zombie lunges at Ace and Ace quickly locks his brawny arms around its neck. Struggling to keep his grip around the wild beast's throat, Ace looks at Eybriel lying motionless and becomes enraged. He uses his newfound power to telekinetically hurl the zombie out of the penthouse window.

"Eybriel! Eybriel!" Ace calls, running to his

mother's bedside. Her eyes closed, Ace taps the side of her face.

"Mother! Please, get up!"

Eybriel's white eyes snap open as she suddenly lashes at Ace. He falls back on the floor as she snarls. Just before the zombie princess jumps out of the broken window, Ace notices the slave neuro-unit crudely implanted in the back of her skull.

Just then, Dr. Meyko busts into the penthouse. "Ace, are you injured?" he asks.

"The zombies got Eybriel. She's one of them now," Ace says, examining Doc's eyes before walking to the window to witness the city being destroyed and its people mercilessly impaled in the skulls with slave units. "Enslaved by the enslaved," Ace mutters. "How did this happen?"

"They ambushed us," Dr. Meyko responds. "They came from the south after sunset."

"The south? After sunset? They've never attacked like this before."

"I know. I tried to radio the United Defense but was unable to get a response. We have to go for help."

"I have to find Eybriel," Ace asserts.

"I'll find the princess. It would be more effective if you contact the other humans for help," Dr. Meyko advises.

Ace stands in thought for a moment.

"Find her, Doc," he says before snatching the ivory helmet from its ornate box.

"I will," Dr. Meyko responds as Ace reluctantly

races up toward the moonlight shining on the sea's surface and climbs into Doc's amphibious ambulance.

"This is Lieutenant Ace Devereux to United Defense! The Eden Colony is under attack!" Ace repeatedly yells over the boat's radio to no avail as he speeds back to shore.

Racing through the night, Ace makes it to the Hong Kong coast in record time only to find the capital in flames as millions of Eden zombies and Mechs tear through the city. The entire United Defense engages in urban warfare as countless soldiers, Stalkers, Tatsus, Toras, and even old Trappers desperately battle throughout the city warzone.

"Dammit. This is why we couldn't get radio contact," Ace says, speeding to the Central District harbor. As Ace docks at the base, he spots Secdef Canuck climbing into the front seat of Stalker 334 parked in front of the main hangar.

"Dad!" Ace calls, grabbing Canuck's attention before grabbing the ivory helmet. Wearing his flight suit, Ace jumps out of the boat and runs up the dock. "Zombies ambushed here too?" he asks his dad.

"Troops were exhausted from standing guard at the frontlines all day. As soon as they got off duty and returned to the city, zombies attacked from the north." Secdef Canuck takes a deep breath before confessing, "It was my decision to have the men guard the frontlines all day and it's my fault they weren't prepared."

"You couldn't have known this would happen, Dad. No one could. The Eden Colony got ambushed too.

They're re-enslaving the freed Edens. They got Eybriel. I raced here when I couldn't make radio contact."

Ace suddenly spots M-Zero battling zombies in the center of the city.

"We have to stop this," Canuck says.

"Where's Mom?" Ace asks.

"Getting geared for battle inside the hangar."

"Me too," Ace responds, running into the hangar. Alarms sound throughout the base as soldiers rush to their stations.

"Mom!" Ace calls, spotting Iris also running through the crowd.

"Ace, you're safe!" Iris runs to her son and hugs him, relieved.

"I just saw Dad outside," Ace says.

"I know, he's waiting on me," Iris tells him. "Where have you been?"

"I just came from the Eden Colony. It's under attack too. They got Eybriel."

"What happened to Eybriel?" Felix asks, running up before noticing the ivory helmet in Ace's hand. "Cool helmet."

"Eybriel gave it to me before they made her a zombie," Ace says sadly. "She taught me my family's power and now I'm the only one who can face Teysuma. I'm going to M-Zero so I can teleport to Cyrus and end this thing once and for all."

Iris pauses. "Alright," she says reluctantly. "Alright. Good luck, sweetheart."

Ace nods before rushing off for an empty Tatsu.

"I love you, sweetheart!" Iris yells.

"Love you too, Mom!" Ace yells back.

"Let's go," Felix says to Iris. The two old Navy pilots run into the locker room to gear up. Felix stands behind Iris as she pulls off her shirt.

"I never took you for the tattoo type," Felix says, reading the letters inked on Iris' shoulder. "F.T.G.G. *Felix the Gato Guapo*." Felix chuckles, zipping up his flight suit. His chuckle comes to an abrupt stop as does the zipper when he tries to pull it up over his round gut.

"It stands for Full Throttle Gatling Guns, *El Guapo*." Iris laughs, patting Felix on the gut before she rushes out the locker room. Running outside, she waves to her husband. As Canuck waves back from the cockpit of Stalker 334, an Eden zombie pounces on Iris.

"Iris!" Canuck yells as his wife is knocked to the ground.

With her arms and legs pinned, Iris looks up at the snarling zombie's teeth as it drools on her face. The zombie lunges to bite her just as Iris' prosthetic eyeball snaps open and shoots a dart into its neck.

The enslaved Eden lurches back. Its eyes get heavy as the tranquilizer dart takes quick effect and the Eden passes out on top of Iris. Snapping her prosthetic eyeball shut, Iris pushes the heavy, unconscious Eden off of her. As she stands to her feet and dusts herself off, United soldiers rush to the councilor's aid.

"Carefully secure this Eden in the infirmary," Iris orders the soldiers.

Finally zipping his flight suit over his gut, Felix jogs past the soldiers carrying the Eden. Stepping outside just as Mr. and Mrs. Devereux take off, he spots an empty M-2 Stalker parked beside them but with no co-pilot.

"Hey, Wes!" Felix calls as Councilor Nasser runs by dressed in a black military uniform with tactical body armor and a shemagh scarf around his neck.

"Can you fly a Mech?" Felix calls out.

"I am afraid not, my friend! My brothers and I fight in shadow, not in the sky," Wes answers before dashing off to join his Jihadi brethren. The rarely seen Jihadi warriors all wear matching uniforms. Feeling excluded, Felix frowns as he watches them band together.

"Need a front-seater, sir?" a young redheaded pilot asks. He carries a helmet with a jack of clubs emblem painted on the side.

"Jax Junior!" Felix greets. "You know how to fly one of these old things?"

"Yes sir, my pa taught me," Jax answers.

"Then let's move out, *hijo!*" the excited veteran says as he and Jax run to the empty M-2 Stalker. "*Ay dios mio.*" Felix suddenly sighs, less excited as he superstitiously reads the number '666' painted on the Stalker.

"No worries, sir. I'm part Irish. We make our own luck," Jax says as he and Felix climb into the cockpit and take off.

Donning the ivory helmet and following his senses, buildings crumble around Ace as he pilots a Type 3

Tatsu toward M-Zero. Ace wields the EMP rifle with surgeon-like precision, shooting down zombie Mechs as they attack from every direction.

"We have to teleport!" Ace telepathizes out loud, finally reaching M-Zero.

Where is Eybriel? M-Zero asks.

"Zombies got her. If we teleport to Cyrus now, we can save her before it's too late. We can save everyone!"

We need our boomerang blade to defend the open portal, M-Zero responds.

"There's no time!" Ace says impatiently. "I'm strong enough now to fight off anything that comes my way! I just need you to get me to Cyrus, now!"

As M-Zero senses Ace's newfound power, corroded Mechs encircle. Like a noose, they tighten around Ace and M-Zero.

"Leo-san!" Yin cheers, suddenly flying overhead in the Totanov as Hiro jumps out the back of the jet piloting ToraX and wielding a finely-polished boomerang blade. Hiro throws the boomerang and M-Zero catches it just in time to mow down the pouncing zombies. Ace's Tatsu, ToraX, and M-Zero stand with their backs together, fending off zombies in the center of the chaos.

"Where's Lynn?" Ace radios to Hiro.

"She's safe at home in Beijing. Sorry I'm late. I had to pick up something and finish restoring the boomerang blade," Hiro announces over ToraX's Sony speakers before turning to M-Zero. "You have not taken care of it, by the way. The blade's only titanium, not as resilient as yourself, but now it's sharper than it has ever been."

M-Zero nods in agreement as the boomerang blade slices through corroded Mechs like a hot knife through butter.

"Hiro, what did you have to pick up?" Ace asks while rapidly firing his rifle.

Hiro points to the descending Totanov. As Yin lowers the jet to the ground, a large pack of black panther droids charge out its cargo bay and attack a zombie Mech. Quickly scaling it with their magnetic paws and blasting it with their EMP cannon heads, the panther droids instantly reduce the zombie Mech to scrap metal.

"You guys got it here," Ace says to Hiro before turning to M-Zero. "You got your boomerang. We need to go, now."

M-Zero nods as it mounts the flawless titanium boomerang to its back. Focusing its energy, the Mech gradually illuminates in sapphire blue. Its chest opens up and the blue portal bursts from within like a giant premiere spotlight. Somewhat hesitant, Ace takes a deep breath before zooming into the portal.

CHAPTER THIRTY-THREE

Streaming through the whirling wormhole to the edge of the universe, Ace's Tatsu Mech drops backwards from the blazing sapphire portal and plunges into dark and dense fog. Landing on Fall Island, Ace looks up at the broad and illuminous portal. The towering wall of glowing light magnificently shines like a blue aurora. Lining the base of the portal, a row of what look like metallic jukeboxes amplify it.

The Tatsu turns around to find itself standing in a humid and dreary, leveled forest where Eyseya's treehouse workshop once stood. Ede is no longer the beautiful blue world Eybriel described to Ace as a boy. The planet is scorched by the sun and its life wrung out. Sweat pours from Ace's dreads in the sweltering heat as he sees shadows lurking in the gloom. A horde of corroded Mechs and white-eyed Edens creep from the fog. Jerking their necks, the zombies spot Ace and shrill as they stampede straight at him. Gripping his EMP rifle, Ace braces to fight but is suddenly stunned as he realizes many of the attacking zombies are Eden women and children and many of the children are mixed with human.

Disheartened and disturbed, Ace stands frozen before the ground suddenly trembles and cracks. The zombies tumble as Ede quakes and Ace takes off. Flying up through what seems endless fog, the Tatsu ascends the clouds before escaping it. Alerts sound inside the cockpit as the overheating Mech floats in the scalding hot atmosphere under the two moons of Ede. Ace peers into the distance. In a clearing in the clouds, the top of a palatial tower peeks through the fog. It is the control tower jutting from the center of the massive, mobile city of Ede. The city now sits docked against Fall Island and the island now stands much larger than it did when Eyseya first stepped foot upon it. Its once sandy shores are towering cliffs above the sea after generations of the sun boiling away and evaporating almost all of Ede's ocean surface.

Ace senses Cyrus near the control tower and immediately jets off. Rocketing down toward the tower like a kamikaze, the Tatsu suddenly jerks violently.

"What the—" Before Ace can get out the words, his Tatsu is snatched from the air and slammed into the ground.

A moment later, another edequake shakes Ace awake from unconsciousness. With the first gash on his forehead now barely a scar, Ace's head throbs beneath the ivory helmet as he sees his EMP rifle lying beside him. Reaching for it, the EMP rifle suddenly flies back miles into the dense fog. Curiously in awe, Ace stands his Tatsu to its feet and finds a single elderly Eden zombie posed menacingly before him. Draped in a grey sarong, the zombie has extensive metalware implanted throughout the back of her skull. Sensing her unparalleled power, Ace meets his grandmother.

The Tatsu rockets toward Teysuma to grasp her in its hands. Ascending into the air, Teysuma attempts to telekinetically toss the Tatsu as she did its rifle but is caught off guard when she is met with resistance. Telekinetically blocking her attack, Ace smirks from within his Mech. Teysuma tears the deeply-rooted forest stumps from the ground and hurls them at Ace's Tatsu. The veins on the side of his head pulse as he exerts all his mental might to stand against the effortless superiority of the matriarch.

Meanwhile, back on Earth, Armageddon falls hard and fast upon Hong Kong as corroded Mechs decimate the capital city. Its gleaming skyscrapers shatter against its blood-stained streets as crowds of terrified people trample each other trying to flee the inescapable legions of savage zombies. Stars in the night sky are eclipsed by smoke billowing from the mass wreckage of countless burning Mechs as humanity's extinction nears imminence.

Marching between the buildings on Main Street, a platoon of zombies closely follows behind the protection of an eighty-foot, corroded Mech. As panicked people scurry like mice, the Jihadi warriors strike like ninjas. A Jihadi swiftly darts across the corroded feet of the gigantic Mech before vanishing into the shadow of a nearby alley. Before the zombies can give chase, the Mech's feet explode. The footless Mech teeters forward before a second Jihadi fires a rocket-powered grenade at its chest, knocking it back. The Mech teeters backwards and the Eden platoon retreats rearward. Standing behind them, Councilor Wes Nasser watches as the zombies charge at him only to explode on the line of mines he stealthily laid in their path. With nowhere to run under the Mech's shadow, the gigantic teetering Mech falls back, crushing the rest of the zombie platoon.

Wes smirks beneath his shemagh as a pack of panther droids suddenly stampede right behind him. Turning around as the black cat droids cross his path, Wes mounts one of the panthers. Veering off from the rest of the pack, he rides the panther straight at an approaching zombie Mech and runs up its leg. Trying to shake the clinging panther off, the corroded Mech takes off for the sky. Airborne and still mounted to the clinging panther, Wes passes Mr. and Mrs. Devereux's Stalker 334 unnoticed as they tear through the night sky.

Stalker 334 rains bullets on zombie Mech hordes as a nearby Hiro slices them down with ToraX's dual black katanas. With skilled mastery of their weapons, Iris' gun and Hiro's blade disable the enemy Mechs without harming the Edens. ToraX flies over as a zombie Mech suddenly strikes 334's engine.

"I'm hit!" Canuck radios from the front seat.

"Yin!" Hiro calls as the tiger droid finishes a repair on ToraX's back.

"*Yin! Yin! Watashi wa yotsu dake ashi ga aruyo!*" Yin gripes.

"I know you only have four paws but the Devereuxs need your help too," Hiro explains.

"Okay!" Yin says, leaping from ToraX's back and diving onto the Devereuxs' flaming Stalker. As the tiger droid quickly repairs the descending Mech, Iris stops firing as she notices someone in her Gatling gun sights.

"Is that Dr. Meyko?" she asks.

In that same moment, Wes stays saddled to his panther as it clings to the zombie Mech flying over the rooftops. The councilor pulls out a mine explosive and plants it on the Mech before pulling his panther off and landing on a rooftop. The mine detonates as Wes rides back down to the fighting on the ground. The detonated zombie Mech suddenly collides into the Ivory Tower jettisoning a one-ton piece of ivory plating. The jettisoned ivory plate heads straight for the oblivious Dr. Meyko as he docks an ambulance at the United base harbor.

"Meyko!" Iris panics, too far away to save him in time.

Seeing the ivory plate's shadow on him, Dr. Meyko quickly looks up and closes his eyes just before the ivory hits.

Opening his eyes, Dr. Meyko looks down at the one-ton ivory plate as he soars in the hands of a Stalker

Mech. Looking up at the Stalker's cockpit, Dr. Meyko sees Jax giving him a thumbs-up.

"Wooh! Nice catch, Jax Junior!" Felix cheers from the back of the cockpit before waving back at the waving Dr. Meyko.

"I think he's trying to tell us something," Jax says, noticing Meyko's mouth moving. Unable to hear outside the cockpit, Jax and Felix watch as Dr. Meyko wildly waves his arms.

"There's a second wave coming!" Dr. Meyko yells to deaf ears as he points to the south.

Turning southward and looking out on the sea's horizon, Jax and Felix's hearts drop as millions of enslaved and re-enslaved Eden zombies storm toward the shore. The terrifying shrill of infinite zombies abolishes all hope. As disheartened United Defense soldiers turn to gaze upon their eminent annihilation, the cavalry arrives. Led by King Alistair Cooper, the Royal Mech Fleet charges from the east one million strong. With British flags emblazoned on their arms, the blue M-2 Stalkers flank the zombies and hold them at bay. The rest of the United Defense cheer before returning to the fight with reinvigorated strength against the zombies from the north.

"The British won't make a difference!" Stonewall announces from his wheelchair in the middle of a panicked crowd. He holds the 'No Finheads' sign with the added statement '...Or Else The End Is Nigh!' as he watches the naval battle ensue on the dark sea. "The world is already over as long as we're trying to separate good finheads from bad finheads! Now, you see they're all bad and the only good finhead is a dead one! Kill'em all!" the old war vet rants as Eybriel suddenly comes crawling from the dark sea, snarling.

"I remember you, filthy finhead!" Stonewall barks as the zombie princess charges. Pouncing on his wheelchair, Eybriel rips out Stonewall's throat as he pulls a shotgun from behind his sign and shoots her in the head. The same red blood that gurgles from Stonewall's neck drips from Eybriel's freed skull as the two die on top of each other.

Billions of miles away on Ede and standing in telekinetic deadlock against Teysuma, Ace's dented Tatsu continues to get pummeled with giant tree stumps when he suddenly senses his mother Eybriel's death. Distracted, Ace mentally drops his guard and Teysuma telekinetically rips a hole in the Tatsu's head before tearing Ace from its cockpit. Ace drops to the ground as metal shards land around him and his Tatsu collapses behind him. As Ace lies motionless, Teysuma picks up one of the spiked shards and jumps at Ace with it. Before she can kill him, Teysuma is electrically blasted out the air. Ace looks back to see the cloaked M-Zero holding his EMP rifle as the portal wall closes behind it.

"No going back now," Ace says.

Same result had you been killed, M-Zero responds.

"Thanks," Ace says before getting up and walking to his fried grandmother. The back of Teysuma's head sparks as her slave neuro-unit deactivates, and all other slave units with it.

On Earth, fifty million once-enslaved Edens drop their weapons as they are set free. The confused Edens look around as if they just woke up from a long sleep. Edens to the north land their Mechs before exiting into the city and Edens to the south simply wade in the water. As apprehensive humans stand defensively watching the Edens curiously roam about, Stalker 666 lands in the center of the city, sliding open its cockpit.

"They did it!" Felix announces to the trodden masses. "Ace and the Ghost Mech freed the Edens! The war is over!"

All of humanity instantly cries out in jubilant celebration as the brave men and women of the United Defense lower their weapons. Their hollers of joy shake the earth and fill the sky.

On Ede, there is less celebration as Ace holds his dying grandmother in his arms and removes his helmet.

"You look like your grandfather." Teysuma smiles, looking up at her grandson. Ace smiles back as she touches his arm.

Teysuma turns to see M-Zero.

I am truly sorry, my love, Eyseya says to his wife.

"I am sorry for all that you and the people of Earth have suffered at my hands," Teysuma says softly. "I am sorry that I was not strong enough to stop it from happening."

"It's not your fault," Ace says sympathetically.

"You are strong enough." Teysuma smiles again as she transfers all of her knowledge into Ace. Instantly enlightened and empowered, Ace's eyes grow wide and his hair turns white as his mind broadens with wisdom. He looks down to find Teysuma has already passed away.

"I love you, Grandmother." Ace smiles with a matured demeanor. He gently lays Teysuma down as he stands to his feet a changed man.

The M-Zero drops the EMP rifle and draws its boomerang blade before pointing it to the control tower at the center of the city of Ede.

"Cyrus," Ace says.

M-Zero nods and takes off just before another tremor cracks the ground on which Ace's Tatsu lies. The ground collapses into a gaping chasm as Ace reaches out to telekinetically catch his Mech. Holding the hovering Tatsu with one hand, he looks to his deceased grandmother lying on the ground. He stretches his other hand to her, telekinetically lifting Teysuma, before gently setting her inside the Tatsu's cockpit. Lowering the Mech coffin into the chasm, he buries his grandmother. Ace picks up the ivory helmet before telekinetically ascending into the sky and taking off behind M-Zero.

CHAPTER THIRTY-FOUR

Ace and M-Zero fly toward the palace control tower in the center of the city of Ede. Dead vines scale the tower from the once lush, green park that surrounded it. All that surrounds it now are a million newly-freed and confused Edens gathered at its base. Nearing the multi-story top level of the tower, Ace shatters its large, panoramic windows with his mind as he and M-Zero enter. A bald and bearded Caucasian man wearing circular spectacles awaits.

"Nice boomerang, mate," the man says to M-Zero in an Australian accent before turning toward Ace. At 86 years old, Dr. Cyrus King looks nearer 50 due to his long exposure to Ede's regenerative waters. "I sensed a powerful bond to you through Teysuma before your ivory knight defeated my queen," Cyrus King says to Ace. "So you think you have me in check, mate?"

"Yeah, and now you're about to get the royal

flush," Ace responds. Cyrus and M-Zero both look at young Ace with puzzled expressions. "Sorry, not really a chess guy," Ace says.

"I mentally recognized Eyseya and Subject 037, but who are you and what are you doing with my helmet?" Cyrus asks, looking at the ivory helmet in Ace's grip.

"We all know this helmet belongs to Eyseya. He and Teysuma are my grandparents and my late father was Michael, your son."

"I always knew some bloke would come and try to stop me. Who more worthy than my own descendent?" Cyrus says, pleased. "You should know that the Edens are a pure and superior people but your grandmother, Teysuma, was the purest and most superior of them all. Because of her admirable righteousness, she never tested the extent of her incredible power. Early on, I discovered that Teysuma's abilities would allow her to easily control the minds of her people on Ede, but the distance from Ede to Earth would lessen her effectiveness. My slave neuro-units suppressed the Edens' will, making them even more susceptible to the effects of Teysuma's power. All of the slave units followed the set programming of her customized slave unit, which I had upgraded throughout the years. I only manually controlled her on special occasions such as today. When every human was dead, the neuro-units would have automatically deactivated. Sacrificing mankind should have meant the Edens' salvation, not sacrificing my innocent queen. The sinful greed of humans will not allow them to sacrifice for the greater good."

Ace shakes his head. "Did you even hear me say your son is dead? And you're responsible. He sacrificed his life trying to stop the Edens you forced into killing mankind."

"Michael and all of mankind are the bloody problem," Cyrus says. "We are sinful creatures deserving of extinction and we have been since the fall of Adam. The Edens, on the other hand, are without sin and deserve to survive on Earth without the endangering presence of human wickedness."

"What about your Eden children?" Ace asks. "I saw them on the island."

"They are abominations, tainted with my human blood. Once all other humans had fallen, I planned to live out my days here with them."

"Man, my mom was right. You really are looney tunes. And what do you mean, the end?" Ace asks as yet another edequake rocks the planet.

"Call me what you want, son. It doesn't matter. The sun is very near death, and Ede with it."

"And so are you," Ace responds, readying to crush Cyrus with his overwhelming telekinetic power.

Stop, Leo interrupts, looking at Ace. *I have waited decades to face the man who created me. This is my fight.*

Ace looks at M-Zero and reluctantly powers down. "Alright," Ace agrees before he and M-Zero look forward to find Cyrus gone and a door at the back of the tower ajar.

"Head him off around back," Ace says to M-Zero.

The ivory Mech exits back through the shattered

windows as Ace runs after Cyrus. Busting through the doorway, Ace stands on a balcony helipad at the back of the tower just as Cyrus closes himself in the cockpit of a second ivory Mech and takes off. Cyrus' Mech is nearly identical to M-Zero but has human-like hands and legs as well as antennas poised upon its head like points on a crown. Cyrus' doppelgänger Mech jerks in the air as Ace telekinetically grapples it. Cyrus lunges at Ace before getting tackled downward by M-Zero. Entangled in battle, the two ivory Mechs plunge toward the ground where bewildered Edens gaze upon their unfamiliar world.

Ace jumps from the hundred-story tower balcony and softly lands on the ground before telekinetically shoving the crowd of Edens back. Pushing his people from harm's way, Ace clears the area just as M-Zero mercilessly smashes the doppelgänger into the ground. Standing over Cyrus, M-Zero holds the blade of its boomerang to the doppelgänger's face. Cyrus puts his Mech's hands up in surrender. As M-Zero lowers its blade, the ten fingers on the doppelgänger's hands suddenly extend into ten long claws piercing through M-Zero's blue eyes. M-Zero lurches back in pain as the doppelgänger breaks its razored tusk-like claws off in M-Zero's face. With the claws jutting from its eye sockets, the blinded M-Zero swings its blade at Cyrus as the doctor amusedly dodges.

Ace steps forward to intervene. Sensing him, M-Zero signals Ace to stand back. Focusing through the pain, M-Zero calmly poses and taunts the doppelgänger to attack. Annoyed, Cyrus' claws grow back as he charges. Like the matadors of Mexico, M-Zero sheds its cloak, throwing it over Cyrus' head before sweep-kicking the blinded doppelgänger's legs. The crowned Mech falls face-first into the ground as M-Zero quickly lobs off its legs and tosses them out of reach before they can mend.

Finally pulling the cloak off its head, Cyrus' legless Mech crawls away. Its boosters flare but M-Zero stomps them to pieces before lobbing off the doppelgänger's arms and tossing them away as well. M-Zero flips the immobile Mech on its back and raises his boomerang blade into the air to deliver the final blow before another edequake violently shakes the entire planet.

"It won't be long now," Cyrus says, looking to the sky. "Ede's sun will explode any moment."

With its boomerang blade still in the air, the M-Zero strikes down. Inside the sliced-open cockpit, Cyrus shakes in his boots, too scared to cry out as he looks down to find his toes amputated. M-Zero reaches in and snatches Cyrus from the cockpit, yanking the doppelgänger's adapter from the back of Cyrus' head. With Cyrus tightly grasped in one hand, M-Zero uses its other hand to grab the claws jammed in its own eyes. It removes the claws along with its entire face and milk gushes from the Mech's open head. With its cockpit exposed for the first time in over twenty years, M-Zero holds Cyrus to its own faceless head. Still fused inside the cockpit by a thousand hardened ivory strands, Leo stares into identical blue eyes as he and Cyrus sit face-to-face. Leo's legless, one-armed body is pale, hairless, and scarred but at 51 years old, he and the slow-aged Dr. Cyrus from which he was cloned look like twins.

Closing his eyes, Leo mentally breaks the ivory strands that bind him. He moves his muscles for the first time in decades and slowly raises his tatted arm to pull the adapter rod from the back of his head. His heart and lungs straining without the life support of the ivory Mech, Leo stubbornly uses his one arm to drag his legless body to the edge of the open cockpit. Trying to climb down, he falls from M-Zero's head but Ace telekinetically catches him, setting him down easily. Leo sits on the ground as Ace kneels next to him, propping him up.

"Good to meet you, Leo," Ace says. "You look like crap. But still."

"But still look better than you." Leo laughs as he coughs. Struggling to breathe, the one-armed Leo points to the similarly disabled doppelgänger.

"Cyrus' Mech?" Ace asks.

Leo nods and points to himself. "Cockpit." He coughs and points to the doppelgänger again.

Curious, Ace stands to his feet and telekinetically carries Leo to the head of the doppelgänger. After being set down in its cockpit, Leo plugs the doppelgänger's adapter into his own head. As he focuses, the Mech's chest emits a broad, blue beam that opens an immense portal just like M-Zero.

"Get everyone to safety," Leo says.

"You know where this portal leads?" Ace asks.

"Not really. But any place is better than here right now."

Ace telepathically calls all of his people from across the planet. Moments later, droves of Edens flood into the city like Noah's ark.

"Through the portal quickly, everyone," Ace directs as a million frightened Eden telepaths simultaneously communicate. With extraordinary efficiency, they instantly organize and run through the portal lined in perfect rows.

While Ace directs his people through the portal, Leo powers it from the doppelgänger's open cockpit. Struggling to breathe as he fights to stay alive, Leo looks up at Ede's rapidly expanding sun. Solar flares dance wildly around the beautiful, burning star before shooting off into the far reaches of space like fireworks. The ferocious yet dazzling display calms Leo into a serene trance as Ede's shifting tectonic plates finally take their toll, forming canyons of boiling hot lava throughout the planet. Soon, Fall Island crumbles and begins sinking into molten abyss.

The sun starts to set but Ede continues to heat up as Fall Island lies nearly submerged in the fast evaporating ocean. Leo stays strong and focused as he holds the portal wide open for the speedily evacuating Edens.

"Let's go home, Leo!" Ace yells, running up to the doppelgänger's cockpit.

"I'm almost there," Leo responds gravely, looking

up into the fading sunlight.

"What? Come on, there's no time." Ace pulls on Leo.

"My time was up the moment I opened M-Zero's cockpit. Once the symbiotic bond between M-Zero, Eyseya, and myself has been broken, it cannot be remade. And without it, all three of us will fall dead. I will keep the portal open until the last of the Edens escape."

"So, you're not returning to Earth?" Ace asks despairingly.

"There's nothing left for me to return to." Leo pauses for a moment. "Please, tell your mother I love her."

Ace locks hands with Leo and Leo smiles with a reassuring nod. Agreeing to honor Leo's last request, Ace respectfully nods back before leaving him and following the Edens into the portal.

Still trapped within the grasp of M-Zero's lock-tight grip, Cyrus smiles as he watches the last of the Edens escape through the portal. Scorching seas of lava consume the last of Ede's ocean, instantly evaporating it into blinding hot steam that swallows the planet.

As the giant red sun grows nearer, Leo looks up at its solar flares as they slice through the dense steam. Cyrus cries out and laughs in pain as the intense heat sears off his and Leo's skin.

"This is what we deserve, you know!" Cyrus tells Leo. "All humans deserve to burn! We are the cruelest creatures in the universe and I am my own best example for exactly why mankind is no longer needed! All I did was for the greater good of the universe! You can see that, can't you, mate? You must. You and I share the same mind!"

"I share my mind with someone else and we both agree with the kid," Leo says, turning to Cyrus. "You are one looney tunes fucktard."

Cyrus laughs psychotically as his beard hairs burn like candle wicks. Suddenly, the whole planet jerks violently as massive geysers of lava erupt through Ede's collapsing terrain. The ground breaks beneath the ivory Mech's feet and it begins sinking into lava. Trapped in the Mech's grip, Cyrus panics as he slowly descends into the lava pit. He screams out in agonizing pain as the fiery pit consumes him. Leo watches as Dr. Cyrus King and the M-Zero forever fade into the inferno.

"Ashes to ashes," Leo says.

The body goes to ashes but the spirit does not die. It just moves from one state to the next, Eyseya speaks to Leo.

"Your spirit," Leo says, gritting his teeth in pain as his flesh melts.

Leo, you and I are of one spirit, Eyseya responds.

His organs shutting down, Leo gasps for air as he watches fiery waves wash over the planet. "So, what's the next state?" Leo asks with his final breath.

Love, joy, peace, kindness, and goodness forever, Eyseya answers. Their spirit ascends just before Ede is swallowed whole by the brilliant blaze of its colossal crimson sun.

CHAPTER THIRTY-FIVE

A week later, Hiro flies the Totanov over icy Antarctica with Iris, Canuck, Lynn, and Dr. Meyko onboard.

"I don't see anything," Hiro says, shielding his eyes from the sun as he looks over the desolate sheet of snowy terrain. "Are you sure they're here?"

"Yes, this is where he communicated they would be," Iris responds.

"There! I see something!" Lynn exclaims, pointing out a cockpit side window. In the distance, a giant metal halo the size of an Olympic ice rink lays half-buried in the snow with a million fur seals gathered around it. As big as bulls, the normally aggressive fur seals are unusually tranquil as the Totanov banks toward them.

Telepathically calming the massive herd of seals, Ace untucks himself from the warmth of one of the furry beasts at the center of the halo. With dreadlocks as white as the pristine snow draping from beneath his ivory helmet, Ace waves to the approaching Totanov as a million escaped Edens suddenly emerge from the rest of the fur seals. The Totanov lands at the halo and opens its door.

"Ace!" Lynn yells excitedly as she runs out of the ship to him. She jumps on Ace and kisses him as he holds her up. "Cool bone-dome, bonehead," Lynn says, knocking on the ivory helmet. Ace laughs as his mother walks up to him.

"Son," Iris says with a big smile, hugging her son. "Are you alright?"

"I'm good, Mom. But Leo didn't make it. He stayed behind to keep the portal open so we could escape before the planet Ede was destroyed by a supernova. Apparently, Cyrus had the Edens construct this halo portal door while they were still enslaved. This is where the zombies that attacked the Eden Colony came from. But the portal is inoperative now. The Mech that controlled it was destroyed on Ede with Leo inside. Before he sacrificed himself, he told me to tell you he loves you."

"Thank you for telling me," Iris responds somberly, holding back tears.

"United Defense ships are right behind us," Canuck announces as he walks up with Hiro and Dr. Meyko. "Good to see you, son," Canuck says, hugging Ace.

"You too, Dad."

"The ships will be here shortly to escort the Edens to the China Sea," Canuck tells him.

"My condolences for your grandmother and

mother. I was too late finding Eybriel," Dr. Meyko tells Ace regretfully. "When I found her, it appeared she had gotten into a fight with a human and the outcome was fatal for both. All Edens felt your family's passing. As I have been leading the reconstruction of the Eden Colony this week, all have been mourning their loss."

"As have I," Ace says somberly as the massive fleet of United Defense ships anchor on the icy shore. "Everyone, board the ships! The humans will take us to the rest of our people," Ace announces as the Edens follow his lead.

"You are truly a natural leader," Dr. Meyko compliments Ace. "You know, with your family's passing, we all look to you to take your place."

With a concerning stare, Ace turns away and glares off into the distance.

That night, as the last of the Edens efficiently board the United Defense ships, Ace sits on the bed in a private cabin while Lynn brushes her teeth in the cabin's bathroom.

"What did Dr. Meyko mean when he said everyone's looking to you to take your place?" Lynn asks, spitting toothpaste in the sink.

"My grandmother, Teysuma, was Queen of the Edens. She passed away along with my grandfather, King Eyseya, on Ede. My biological mother, Princess Eybriel, also passed away, making me the last heir in the royal bloodline."

"So, you're a prince?" Lynn asks, looking at Ace's

reflection in the bathroom mirror as he stares back seriously. "No, you're a king!" Lynn says in awe.

"Yes but being King of the Edens means revealing myself to the world."

"You want things between Edens and humans to change for the better, don't you? People will never accept change unless someone shows them the way. As the king and being mixed with both races, who better to show them than you?" Lynn asks. "Besides, what are you afraid of with your new powers and new due? Like the white hair, by the way. It makes you look mature."

"I hate it." Ace frowns, grabbing one of his white dreads and staring at it. "Makes me look old."

Putting away her toothbrush, Lynn turns from the sink. Wearing no bra beneath her T-shirt with panties, Lynn poses in the doorway.

"Maybe, it's time to try something new," she says.

Ace grins. "We can try anything you want."

Eight days later, as the last of the fleet ships dock in the Honk Kong harbor, the United Council gathers at Heroes Memorial Cemetery. Standing before a mixed crowd of humans and Edens, Councilors Iris, Hiro, Felix, Wes, and King Cooper stand between two towering marble statues. One is of Eybriel and the other of Leo. Looking up at his statue, Iris steps to the front of the stage to address the crowd.

"We find ourselves mourning the deaths of too many lost but celebrating what they died for. After more than half a century of war, we can finally say that those who sacrificed their lives did not die in vain. The war is over and we are still here!" Iris announces to the cheering crowd whose celebratory roars are heard for miles. "We honor all who fell protecting their fellow man but today we honor two specific heroes.

"First, I would like to honor a man named Leo. Many of you may have known Leo as the pilot of the mythical Ghost Mech. But he was no myth. He was a friend close to our hearts. Leo sacrificed his life setting the enslaved Edens free from their zombie state and saved us all.

"Second, I honor our fallen council member and close friend, Eybriel, who peacefully worked to unite us all. She had one of the kindest spirits I've ever known. A spirit we must strive to emulate if we are to keep ongoing peace. With that said, I would like to introduce our newest councilor. Many of you already know him as famed pilot of our brave United Defense. He and Leo fought side-by-side to end this war. Please welcome my son, Lieutenant Ace Devereux."

The crowd stands and applauds as Ace walks to the center of the stage wearing his flight suit and angel-winged helmet with the visor open.

"I am honored to succeed to the council in lieu of Eybriel after her tragic death. Many of you may be wondering why I was elected to Eybriel's position representing the Edens. The explanation is simple." Ace hesitates and looks to Lynn in the crowd as she smiles with a reassuring nod. "Ace is short for Eyseya, my grandfather and the last king of Ede. My full name is

Michael Eyseya Devereux. The truth is, Councilor Iris and Secdef Canuck Devereux are my aunt and uncle. Lieutenant Commander Michael King, who fell at the Battle at the 104, was my biological father. My biological mother was Councilor Eybriel."

Ace removes his helmet, revealing a bald head with a folded fin that had been hidden beneath his dreadlocks. The confused crowd gasps as the unfolding fin erects in the center of Ace's head.

"I am part human and part Eden. My parents, Michael and Eybriel, loved each other but died in a war caused by the fact that the rest of us don't know how to love each other. For too long we have been at war over money and race. We have divided ourselves and killed one another over things that hold no value compared to the value of life. Too many lives have been lost over our dividing ourselves.

"I had a dream not too long ago of human children and Eden children joining hands and laughing and playing together. There was no war, no hatred, no sadness or mourning of death. Only peace, love, joy, and prosperity of life. Fifty years of war and death is too painful. Fifty years of being divided is too long. Let's not endure one year more. Let us choose to join hands today. Now is the time for all humans and Edens to unite! Now, is the time for peace!"

The masses cheer wildly as humans and Edens embrace as brothers and sisters, ushering in an era of world peace like never seen before.

"Well said," King Cooper compliments Ace.

As all of the fellow councilors smile and applaud, Dr. Meyko walks on stage. The good doctor smiles as he proudly sets a crown on Ace's head. The crown of polished African elephant ivory is carved in the shape of an olive wreath and encrusted with blue sapphire jewels from the island of Sri Lanka. Dr. Meyko turns to the masses and makes an announcement.

"Presenting, the uniter, a king of Earth and Ede descent, his majesty King Ace, sovereign of the Edens!"

Jax Junior smiles and applauds along with the crowd as a black-hooded man with a pointed grey beard steps behind him.

"My condolences for your father's death, Jax," the hooded old man says in an Arabic accent. "He was a brave man."

"You knew my pa?"

"Yes," the old man says, "I saw him die."

"Pa always said a real soldier dies on the battlefield," Jax responds. "It's how he would have wanted to go."

"But did you know that your father's killer was the mother of the man you applaud for now?" the old man asks. "I watched Councilor Eybriel rip out your father's throat."

"What? Who are you?"

"I am Jin al-Azra, former Axis leader of the Jihadi. Your father and I once butted heads but we were knowledgeable enough to finally agree that the true threat is the Edens. These finheads have been killing us off for generations and when they are finally vulnerable to receive their due punishment, we instead welcome them to live on our planet and steal our resources. The United Councilors are weak. They have no interest in getting justice for the families of the victims, no interest in getting justice for your father's murder."

Jax clenches his fists as he listens to al-Azra's words.

EPILOGUE

One year after the end of the war, Councilors Hiro and Ace stand before gathered human and Eden masses in Moscow, Russia.

"Are you ready?" Hiro asks.

"I'm ready," Ace answers, facing the crowd packed inside the Cathedral of the Archangel. Holding a basket in her mouth and tilting it, Yin spreads flower petals down the aisle as Ace's beautiful bride walks behind her. All eyes are focused on Lynn in her ivory wedding dress as she walks down the aisle, but her eyes see only Ace. The beaming bride smiles through her veil at her handsome husband-to-be. Wearing a grey tuxedo with the ivory crown around his finned head, Ace smiles back at his best friend. Lynn's human and Eden bridesmaids get teary-eyed with joy in their blue dresses as do proud parents, Canuck and Iris, sitting in the front row. Doc Meyko stands beside Ace as his best man and

Councilors Felix, Wes, and Cooper as groomsmen.

As the officiant, former captain Hiro commences the wedding ceremony but before he can speak, an explosion sets off at the side wall of the cathedral. With lightning reflexes, Ace telekinetically forces back the explosion and flying rubble before a single person is harmed. Containing the explosion with his power, Ace smothers the fire. He looks through the blown-out wall of the cathedral and sees a man dressed in black fleeing, his face wrapped with a shemagh. Ace notices red hair peeking from beneath the shemagh.

"It's the Jihadi!" a guest of the wedding announces. "The Jihadi are attacking again!"

"Ace," Wes says, "the Jihadi are no longer at war and honor our time of peace. All my brothers know I am attending this wedding and would never attack a fellow Jihadi. I promise you the Jihadi did not do this."

"I know," Ace says, "someone else is responsible. Stay here and make sure everyone is alright."

Ace runs outside through the blown-out wall of the cathedral and spots the alleged Jihadi dashing through the trees within the Kremlin's garden. He gives chase but loses the man in black in a thicket of trees. Searching the thicket, Ace finds a grey-haired groundskeeper planting an apple tree.

"Did you see a guy dressed in black run by?" Ace asks.

"No, but I heard an explosion. Is everyone alright?" the groundskeeper asks.

"I think the guy I'm looking for planted a bomb at

the cathedral, but yes, everyone's alright," Ace responds as he begins to run off.

"Surely Chao and Anna's daughter is upset her wedding got ruined," the groundskeeper comments.

Ace stops. "How do you know about that?" he asks suspiciously.

"Apple?" the groundskeeper offers, picking a fruit from the tree.

"Who are you?" Ace demands.

"Chao, Anna, and myself were the three Axis leaders. Some know me as Jin al-Azra but I am whoever I need to be to get close to whomever I want," the groundskeeper answers, stroking his pointed beard. "I got close to Chao back when he first lost his father. Michelle and I grew closer when she lost her husband. I helped her husband justify the decisions he made throughout his life and was there when Dr. King got killed. I was there in the beginning of the Edens," al-Azra says, taking a bite of the apple. "It was not until the second time, I was able to have my way. I also got close enough to butt heads with Archangel Michael."

"My father?" Ace asks.

"Him too," al-Azra responds. "When your father locked himself inside a room for six months contemplating suicide after his mother betrayed him, I was with him in the darkness."

"You're either really senile or really evil," Ace ponders.

"You think you're so holy? A seed of evil lies within us all, my friend." Al-Azra laughs. "You remind me of this Mexican Catholic bitch named Miss Guerrero who I knew some ninety years ago. She thought she was holier than thou too before I got done planting a seed in her, if you know what I mean." Al-Azra smirks.

"Ninety years?" Ace asks. "How old are you?"

"Time is irrelevant," the man answers. "Enjoy your time of peace while it lasts. It's only a matter of time before man once again gives itself to the evil seed within. There will always be another war but I draw pleasure from even the simplest of things. A man frustrated by his job unleashing his anger on others. Women tearing each other down. After you marry Lynn, the two of you will fight and I'll laugh as you curse about the things you hate about one another. Like a seed, that hatred and anger will be planted into the children you two will one day have. And the cycle of evil will continue throughout the world."

"There may be an evil seed within everyone," Ace says, "but there are also seeds of love, joy, peace, patience, kindness, faithfulness, gentleness, self-control, and overall goodness. As long as there is at least one person who chooses goodness, it will always ultimately trump evil."

Out of nowhere, a grenade launches at Ace. He telekinetically catches it and once again contains the explosion with his power. After neutralizing the decoy attack, Ace finds al-Azra gone. With roaring jet engines, Stalker 666 ascends from outside the Kremlin wall. Looking up, Ace sees al-Azra sitting in the cockpit behind Jax Junior before the Stalker zooms off at supersonic speed.

"Who was that?" Lynn yells, running to Ace along with his family and friends.

"Nobody we can't handle."

"You know who did this then?" Wes asks. "Tell me the name of the imposter who threatens our peace. With your powers, we can easily strike him down!"

"True. But when we use violence in the name of peace, peace is gone already. As smart as Cyrus was, that was one thing he could never understand."

"Then use your mind-control to make people peaceful," Felix suggests.

"Forcing control on others is slavery. Besides, Edens are telepathically linked, making them vulnerable to telepathic control but humans are not. Even if they were, most humans are far too stubborn to be telepathically controlled," Ace says. "I think Earth has seen enough violence and slavery. We must face prejudice with dignity, fight hatred with love, and free our enemies from their ignorance with education."

ABOUT THE AUTHOR

Joe Ponder was born in 1988 on an Air Force base in Georgia. His mother was a psychologist before becoming a Christian minister and his father a retired United States Air Force Major. Joe comes from a family of aviators. His grandfather was a Navy jet pilot and his uncle an Army helicopter pilot. Growing up a military brat, Joe traveled the world. After high school, he moved out on his own and got work as an aircraft mechanic. While living in Kentucky, Joe frequented a lounge called the Cat's Den, a gathering spot for local artists. There, he regularly wrote and performed poetry. Still turning wrenches as a mechanic, Joe decided to further his career and attended Middle Tennessee State University, where he met his future wife, Sam. Their son CJ was born in 2010. Joe's son and book, *Kings of Earth*, celebrate diversity. CJ is mixed with African, Pauite Native American, and Creole from his father's side and Laotian, Thai, and Chinese from his mother's side. After graduating with his aerospace bachelor's degree, Joe took an aviation maintenance management position in Texas where he lives with his family today.

Made in the USA
San Bernardino, CA
21 December 2016